PRIORS

a novel by
Francis Verlaine

Francis Verlaine

DOUBLE NICKELS
— PRESS —

Cover design by Khanh Ngo.

Manufactured in the United States of America

Edited by Maria D'Marco, Pandora Armstrong and Katherine Dye

Special thanks to the cities of Saint Louis, San Francisco and Los Angeles for providing the author both shelter and inspiration.

Double Nickels Press, San Francisco, CA.

francisverlaine.com

More Praise for
PRIORS

"Finally a novel that shows the real San Francisco, my hometown: a hardboiled city that the world seems to think is stuck in the Summer of Love. It captures the gritty, fast-paced nastiness of the city by the bay, while exposing the love that is deep in its heart, albeit with a thick-ass skin. Francis wrote the screenplay for a film I acted in several years back, and "Priors" proves the author still possesses those darkly humorous chops." – Dewey Weber, writer, musician and actor, *The Doom Generation*, *Ulee's Gold*, *Melrose Place*, and *Showgirls*.

"A rare novel, set partially in St. Louis, full of toasted ravioli, unforgettable characters, a ton of heart, humor, and a wild ending in Mexico, Missouri. A MUST read. Two giant thumbs up!" – Tony Patrico, Radio Co-Host, KPNT 105.7 FM, St. Louis, Missouri.

"A smart, well-crafted debut that jumps time and space between the Midwest in the late-70s and contemporary San Francisco, Francis Verlaine's "Priors" combines the heft of a literary novel with the page-turning drama of a hardboiled detective story." – Randall Roberts, arts and culture writer, Los Angeles Times

For Vincent,
and for Brie and Genevieve

Acknowledgements

I am forever in the debt of the following talented, patient, humoring, wonderful people: Brianna Foehr, Nate Lane, Katherine Dye, Michael Guerra, Maria D'Marco, Ron Rodenmeyer, Pandora Armstrong, Bob Schmitz, Scott Kritz, Rachel Friesen, Jean Martin, Steve Finch, Khahn Ngo, Ed Sinchai, Carol Threlkheld, Doug Carney, and to Neil Rodenmeyer, a nudnik of the highest order, but without whom this book never could have been written.

Soft-boiled Origins

I was a sad, sad bricklayer—an honest-to-goodness malcontent. But this is no mason's tale.

It was a career not chosen but born of circumstance, of opportunity–or an awful lack thereof. My uncle owned *Iocca Brick and Masonry*, a company outfitted entirely with our blood relatives. *"Who ya gonna trust?"* It was right there in italics on every company truck.

I began working summers at the brickyard when I was thirteen and went fulltime right out of high school. By then I had earned the faith implied in our motto and was trained to lay bricks on a crew. Throughout my twenties I was healthy enough to remain the low man on the totem pole, which in masonry terms means your knees still function so you work from them. I was a "first runs" guy, strictly lower wall. I hadn't asked for this life of labor - had no interest in it if I'm being honest- just did it, six days a week until the snow came each winter, then days off, days spent lost in books, days I loved, days I hoped for, days where I felt like anything but what I inarguably was. I was living a life of quiet desperation and I was looking for an acceptable place to scream.

White flight was carrying people from our once bustling and vibrant downtown to the surrounding sleepy suburbs of Missouri and nearby Illinois, the kinds of places that were never settings in Raymond Chandler and Dashiell Hammett's books. I had availed myself, so they say, of the hardboiled classics, and any love I may have held for St. Louis—the place of my birth, the only place I had ever set eyes on really—was extinguished with each description of livelier cities: megalopolises filled with provocative lives and moral ambiguity.

It's been said that necessity is the mother of invention. I'd make the argument that misery has given birth to some fine progress in this world. I couldn't be who I wanted to be in my town, certainly not in my cozy, little part of it anyway. I had let them make a mold of me, these well-meaning dagos. Natural-born mason. It's what they saw when they saw me. Never any talk of higher education or higher purpose for young Joe. This was it, my path, the one I paved myself, brick by brick by infernal goddamn brick.

So at age thirty, with no wife or kids to stop me, I made a decision to leave St. Louis and pursue a roughshod plan I had spent a dozen years hatching from calloused knees, yet had scarcely prepared myself for: I would become a private investigator.

With my company truck returned, I bought a reliable car that felt the part and made my rounds through the city's Italian Hill, saying tearful goodbyes to everyone in my neighborhood, and to everything I had ever known.

I dropped into my brand-new Chrysler and headed west to the city by the bay. Me, the man that sorrow had reinvented. I was activated, exuberant, and ready to travel the brick-less road.

CHAPTER ONE

Objects of My Affection

San Francisco, CA, 2011

Thirty Years Later

I entered my office from the reception area and softly shut the door behind me. The light in the place came in from four recently-cleaned glass walls, and I now saw things squeegee-clear. The piss-poor quality of my props and possessions was on tragic display. Al had raised the blinds on the windows that looked out onto reception, so that he could wipe the panes from both sides. He had noted a cleaning deposit in the lease I had signed with the owners back in '81 and was hoping well beyond hope I'd see that $150 again.

We were packing up and moving out, and I was opting to become one of those sad sacks who worked out of his home to save the double rent. There was yet another tech boom happening in my adopted metropolis, and the place I had modeled after every PI's office I had ever seen recreated by Hollywood set dressers had now become unaffordable, and so the set had to be struck.

Boxes were everywhere, each one labeled with months and years. Three decades of my day-to-day comings and goings, packed up neatly by Al, my current and would-be last secretary, the items placed in adult diaper boxes for reasons I had neglected to ask. Al had sold the file cabinets themselves on Craigslist the week before. I didn't know what Craigslist was. Al had succeeded in his effort to liquidate every item of worth, as most of it wouldn't fit when I relocated my firm to my cramped one-bedroom apartment in the Richmond district. I imagined my home soon full of *Depends* boxes and dropped my head to my desk with a cartoon thud.

The agency was quiet that day, just as it had been for every passing business hour over the several months prior. Al blamed the Yelpers. He said they complained that we weren't technologically savvy, not advanced enough in the modern science of detective work. He said their critiques had put the final nail in our agency's coffin, with just a few simple and hurtful words. What the fuck were the Yelpers? Some secret society bluebloods with handshakes and agendas that dated back to the days of Jesus fucking Christ? What did I do to offend them? A man couldn't simply rely on skills acquired over decades on the job, some pure goddamn know-how? I didn't *sign on* or *sign in* or whatever it was they expected of me. And so an already slow period ground to a pathetic halt.

"He's here, Joe," Al said as he opened the door that separated our reception area and my private office.

"This is an obnoxious waste of my time, Al," I said.

"Give him a chance. Please."

A man wearing short sleeves with an oxford collar and no tie came through the front door and inspected the place like he was paid to do it. He walked around with all of the audacity and impunity of a municipal bus negotiating traffic. His shirt was crisp and peach colored—I probably should have mentioned that first—and it was tucked into his pleated pants. It looked like he couldn't decide when he got out of bed that morning if this was a golfing day or a day of work so he'd dressed for both. Al once told me they called this "business casual" and he said there's this thing where companies allow their employees to dress however they are comfortable on Fridays. It's that kind of nonsense that spells the decline of the damn republic.

"Hey, you," I said. "Stop snooping around and get in here."

"Joe," said Al.

"He's right, Al," said our guest as he walked in. "That was rude of me. Joe, I'm Corey," he said with his hand extended.

"Corey?" I asked, as if that couldn't possibly be right.

"Yes," said Corey proudly.

"Is that a grown man's name? Corey?" I asked Al.

"Joe!" said Al with the proper amount of mortification that comes with knowing me well.

"You told me he was colorful, Al."

"Colorful?" I said to Al.

"I'm going to let you two talk in private," Al curtly announced as he left my office.

"Good," I said to Corey. "Now I can be blunt."

"Now?" said Corey with a stupid chuckle at the end.

"You're here to tell me that my business is dying, that it's not just me, that people need us less and less, that all PI firms are scaling way back."

"Clearly I don't need to tell you any of this," he said as he took a seat in front of me.

I leaned on my desk like a newspaperman in a film. "Agreed," I said.

"As a professional courtesy, I'll skip the pitch. I can see you're uncomfortable with the conversation. I know it's just you humoring your employee."

"Al's more than an employee, pal. He's a friend."

"Of course," he said in a condescending way that made me want to throw my dusty hole-punch at him.

"Julie," he said, "Al's wife," he continued as if I didn't know who the fuck Julie was, "she's done excellent legal consultation for our company. This was Julie's idea. You know that, of course."

"When you tell me something I don't know you get a lollipop, Corey." I looked down at an empty glass jar on my desk. I was fresh out of lollipops.

"I'm here to offer you an interview. Whenever you're ready. We'll get you up to speed. We have excellent retraining and our health plan is—"

"I'm not a Cairn fucking terrier. I don't need retraining. Now, if you don't mind, I'd like to go back to packing up my things and relocating my thirty-year-old business. How old are *you*, Corey?"

He smiled at me. "The offer stands, Joe. Whenever you're ready," he said as he stood. "I'll show myself out."

"You're damn skippy you will."

Corey said goodbye to Al loudly, and then leaned in to speak about me, as if I couldn't see the jackass. He looked my way and then turned back to Al. A few vaguely insulting words later they both looked back at me and I made a hand gesture that you'd need a vowel on the end of your name to fully understand. Corey flashed a patronizing grin at me and then stopped to look at a picture on the wall near the exit. It was a photo of James Garner on the set of *The Rockford Files*. He was leaning on his car, studying the day's script, but glancing up at the photographer with a wry look on his face. My older clients always got a kick out of it. Ramona, my second secretary, had given it to me. She forged his signature too. That was Ramona's idea of humor, and I always appreciated her particular brand.

Corey left and Al began composing an email to the building manager, confirming that the keys would be turned over Sunday morning, as I watched a Chrysler K car pull into the spot out front.

Muriel rang the bell and Al buzzed her in. They exchanged pleasantries and Al apologized for being unaware of Muriel's office visit. He also asked that she forgive us for the state of things around there.

I opened the door to my office and greeted Muriel warmly, as I had for many years, asking her to please come in. I knew her well enough to gather that she was there to voice some displeasure.

"Sorry for all of this, Muriel," I said, motioning toward the boxes that lined the walls. "Please, come into the office and have a seat."

"Are you relocating?" she asked as she primly sat.

I walked around my desk and took a seat in the chair across from her.

"Didn't you get a letter?"

"We just got back from the Cape," she said. "I've had no time to sort through the mail. It's all junk these days. No one writes letters, Joe. They email now."

"Well, there'll be a letter from us in that pile-a-junk. Explaining how we're leaving this place, giving you the new address and phone number."

"Joe, I just… I'm not one to complain, you know that, but I just, well, we felt it had to be said."

I looked at the K car parked on the street as she stammered through whatever it was that was threatening to relieve her of her polite society ways.

"Since when do you drive an old Chrysler, Muriel? What's that? An '81?"

"What? Joe, I'm trying to tell you that we've found Phillip."

I got up, walked to my office door and studied the car through the large pane of glass that was partially obscured by a backwards spelling of my name and title: Joe Iocca, Private Investigator.

"Joe, are you listening to me?" she said as she craned her leathery neck. "We found him."

"Who?"

"Phillip. Who do you think? We found Phillip."

"Why, that's wonderful news."

"Yes, of course it is. It's nearing five years."

"I know, Muriel. I know." I worked hard to focus on her and put the curb feelers on the K car out of my head, as I returned to my seat.

"Certainly you know, Joe. We've paid you many times to know."

"Is that why you're so upset? Why, you know how hard I've tried. You understood how my business works. Every time you and Len came to this office we had an open and forthcoming dialogue about what I could and couldn't promise. I always told you, if your boy didn't want to be found there might be no finding him, especially if you didn't want to involve the police directly. He could be anywhere. Anywhere." I watched her face purse up as she adjusted the large-brimmed hat that protected her chest from further sunspots. "How exactly did you find him, Muriel? Did you hire another agency without consulting me first?"

"Facebook."

I looked at her as if she had suddenly shifted to a long-dead tongue.

"Facebook," she said again firmly. "He was right there. His cousin asked how Phillip was and we confided in her that he hadn't so much as called for five years, much to our embarrassment, of course. She took out her computer, typed in his name and there he was. Not hiding. Just there. On Facebook. For all to see and find."

Weeks had now passed since we shuttered the office doors and I finally took Al up on his long-standing invitation to join him at his place for dinner. He had cooked a fine Italian meal, impressive for the kind of pale and fair Jew that he was, the type that no one would ever mistake for a Guido, as if only my people were the ones chosen to properly boil a little macaroni. When after-dinner coffee was ready Al carried a tray of espresso and some biscotti into the dining room and found me admiring the view of the bay. We took our seats at the dinner table and I saw what appeared to be tan sugar cubes in an antique crystal bowl on a doily.

I almost asked if these brown squares were indeed sugar, but instead just added two cubes to my coffee, hoped, and stirred.

"My nana had this exact same bowl. What are the odds of that?" I said. "We used to eat candy out of it, me and my cousins. She gave it to me a few years before I moved here—she knew how much I loved those Werther's candies—and somehow I just lost it along the way. Isn't that something? How you can just—"

I sat there, slightly hunched, and the buttons of my Cardigan sweater threatened to pop off at my belly. I felt like I had aged more in those last few months than in the seven years Al had known me. I was suddenly ashamed of my appearance in a way I had never before been with Al: my oafish stomach, my salty hair, the bags under my eyes as pronounced a feature as my dago nose.

"Julie's at her wine club tonight," said Al. "I may have said that. She did say to tell you hello."

"Is that a good idea?" I asked.

"Hmm?"

"Is she supposed to be drinking I mean?"

"Oh, yeah. She can have a little wine. It's mostly social, this thing. They say it's fine for a pregnant woman to have a sip now and then, though."

"Well, I bet my Ma dropped her carafe of Sangiovese when her water broke with me," I said.

"Yeah, that was just how it was with that generation, right? They didn't know any better. It's funny how things change, isn't it, Joe?"

I gave Al a boss look, remembering as I did that I was no longer Al's boss. He had taken a position at an insurance company, and that dope Corey was now his employer. I stood up and went back to the view of the San Francisco Bay.

"So is this the part of the evening where we talk about how things change, Al?"

Al stood up and joined me at the window, putting his hand on my shoulder in a comforting way, as a woman might more typically do.

"You may not want to hear it but these investigators seem happy, Joe. They work normal hours; they get steady pay. Just go out into the field and figure out what happened."

"It's not the same," I said.

"I know. But it's where things are heading. It's pretty much just insurance, employment background checks, and corporate investigation work now. I've done my homework for you. Those can be good gigs for guys nearing retirement age. There's less running around."

"Less excitement."

"True. It's not the job you've known all these years but it's one that you're equipped for, one that wouldn't take much in the way of training or transition. And they offer health care benefits. They'd be lucky to have you, Joe."

The conversation was dispatching my spirit, which had suffered enough hits in recent months. I conveyed my obstinacy with another look and Al tried a little less.

On the drive home I ruminated on Al's reasons for approaching me as he had. I wished I had handled my end of the talk a little differently, maybe been a little more considerate of Al's feelings, giving him the false hope that might have seen him worry less.

I had fallen asleep mid-*Mannix*. When Al let me know there was a cable station deep down the dial dedicated to the great television shows of the 1970s, I had him sign me up that very day. For months now I had been knee-deep in thick-haired gumshoe lore. I went along for the ride, like every other viewer, trying to solve the episode's mystery with the investigator. Aside from the advantage of being a PI myself, there was the added cheat of my strong memory. I had seen most of these crimes brought to justice when they had originally aired.

The quick ring of the doorbell made me lurch in my La-Z-Boy. It was less a bell and more a buzzer to be certain; it came off like electroshock therapy and was just as unpleasant: short shots right to the brain. I muted Detective Mannix. In the silence I was suddenly overcome by sheer and unexplainable panic.

The entrance to my apartment was windowless. Someone was standing out there on the landing, having ascended the polished concrete stairs; a stucco wall stood between us. There was another jolt of turn-of-the-century technology. It was brief again but the resonance was now far more ominous in the dead-quiet of my compact accommodations. I'd heard that buzzer a thousand times if I had heard it once. Why couldn't I move?

If it rings again I'll gather myself and answer the damn door. That's what I told myself, right through the third buzz and into the fourth and well past the fifth, adjusting the count each time. It could simply have been a client who got my hours wrong. The digital clock on the cable box read 7:17, and proof of dusk came in from the large-paned window behind my chair. We were in the P.M., and my new office hours only ran until 5:00 in the P.M. With the final ring I came to realize they had been rhythmic, like contractions coming in at steady intervals, not getting any closer together, the baby not ready to see the light of the world.

As I walked toward my foyer I thought to stomp my feet. I lowered my voice and bellowed, "This better be good," in a vain effort to quell my anxiety with some textbook manliness. What do women do, I wondered, to attempt to steel themselves in situations such as these?

Pulling open the heavy door, I expected to be greeted by the dying light of the day. It was instead entirely obscured by a box that stood roughly 90 inches tall and was 30 inches wide and deep. The stairs descended to my left and from that side a hand appeared, sliding slowly along the box. Whoever rang that buzzer had been standing behind the package and was now reaching out. He had been extending his long, thin fingers to press the doorbell on my metal gate, with no inches of his reach to spare. Using only the single hand on the box, he effortlessly pushed it deeper until it hit the wall to my right. With no more than 10 inches of landing to stand on, the young reed of a man shimmied from around the back and now stood facing me, his body hugging the box but his neck turned toward me.

"What the fuck is this?" I said.

He'd been about to begin speaking precisely when I had asked my question. He did a slight double take that included the smallest of laughs and a judgment of me for my choice of initial greeting.

"Special delivery for Mr. Joe Iocca, Private Investigator," he said as he slid down the box, still hugging it, until his hands reached the marble landing. He then made his way back up and with his left hand moved a small machine across the box and toward his right. When the device was in the middle of his body he turned to look as it came to life with lights and noises.

"I didn't order this. What is this?"

He turned back and looked me in the eye. He took a deep breath and gathered himself to speak, like a timid grade school kid about to address the entire student body from a podium in a gymnasium.

"Special delivery for Mr. Joe Iocca, Private Investigator, PI, if you will, detective for hire, dick for short, care of the Northern California Association of Integrated Technologies for the Betterment of Humankind, with a home-base in St. Louis, Missouri, for your convenience, maximizing the services of AFTERCARE!, fully bonded, LLC, providing goods guaranteed to survive in any conditions, even the most grave of conditions, sincerely, CEO, COO and President for life, of the Northern California Association of Integrated Technologies for the Betterment of Humankind, specializing in sturdy encasements, air tight and waterproof, equipped with sonarific apps, lab tested to ward off critters and creatures, the slimy variety and burrowers alike, entirely worm-proof to coin a phrase, firewalled, wifi –ready and, might we add, spacious and not at all frightening."

I closed the door.

"San Francisco," I muttered as I returned to my program.

At the next commercial break I got up and looked through the peephole in my door. Dusk was turning into darkness. The boy and the box were gone.

CHAPTER TWO

Saint Lewis

Ferguson, MO, 1977

The town was Ferguson, in the north of St. Louis County, Missouri. In 1977 it was at best a starter-home township for the young and perhaps upwardly mobile. For the rest it wasn't a postal code so much as an admission of defeat.

The neighborhood kids walked home together after school. There were some that dawdled. Lewis figured these boys had some place down by the main road where they went to smoke or buy more time away from the watchful eyes of their mothers. The parents seemed to pay a passing attention to the kids when they were in their sight, same as they did in Lewis's old neighborhood in East St. Louis, same as parents did everywhere he supposed.

Lewis could feel Marco eyeing him as Lewis lumbered toward his home on Barto Street. Lewis was alone, as he had been for the weeks since his arrival to the neighborhood. He was a portly young man with a deliberate pace and was already several minutes behind the pack.

"Hey kid," Marco said to Lewis as he passed. "Yeah. You."

Lewis slowed his gait. Marco said it was hot, "a good day to just sit your ass down and chill out, man."

Lewis hesitated but took him up on the offer.

There were two well-worn folding chairs on Marco's lawn: the white, blue and yellow colors having faded, the plastic strips frayed at the ends where they wrapped under the round metal framing. A pitcher of lemonade and two Styrofoam cups were arrayed between them.

"You like it here? You're new, right?" asked Marco.

"It's alright I guess," Lewis said as he struggled to get comfortable in the camper's chair.

"Which one's your house?" Marco asked.

"White one down the road," said Lewis as Marco tilted his head back in acknowledgment. "My daddy know some man from the airport where he work. Man said he was finnin' to rent it out so he can move over to St. Charles."

"Weebie," stated Marco with certainty.

"Yeah, that's him. I only seen him one time. You know him?"

"I've seen him around. Wouldn't say I know him. I don't think anyone really knows him around here. He's got a reputation as a fuck-you kind of guy."

"What that mean?" Lewis asked through a giggle.

Marco reached for the refreshment. He poured a cup for each of them and explained.

"Well, you're the only black family living on this block. First ones ever. Downright historical it is. Anyway, this Weebie, he always struck me as the type that didn't give a shit what anyone thought. Little stuff, like letting his yard go, or the kind of women he brought home, or hanging out on his front porch drinking on Halloween. No candy, just out there getting waaaay fucked up, mumbling shit, scaring the kids. Never actually talking to people here, though. So if you were to ask me which of these honkeys might be so enlightened as to rent their home to a black family, well, it wouldn't have surprised me to learn it was Weebie. Kinda saying fuck you to everyone. Waking their racist asses up. Fucking with the status quo. Yeah, I dig it, man. Well done, Weebie," he said as he raised his cup toward the end of the street. "Well done."

Lewis squinted into the sun.

"The moral of that story is," said Marco, "to hell with what everybody thinks, man."

Lewis rocked his body, which was a nervous habit that went hand-in-hand with a stutter, except that Lewis hadn't stuttered once speaking to Marco.

It was several days of conversations on the lawn before Marco had invited Lewis into his home. Lewis was happy to have made a friend, even if his new companion was ten years older than Lewis and talked a little strange. Lewis had been respectful of Marco's privacy, never asking what he did for money, largely because Lewis was a teenage boy and as such didn't give much thought to what anyone did for money.

"Kids at school be smoking weed all out in the open," Lewis said as they sat together in Marco's living room.

"Really?" answered Marco. He took a long drag from a joint. "You mean your old high school?"

"This one. White kids," he said.

"That is some highly interesting shit, Lewis. Highly interesting. I wonder how they're scoring."

Lewis shrugged. Lewis was a big shrugger.

"And you never?" Marco asked, offering Lewis the joint.

"Nah, Marco. My daddy'd whoop me good."

When they first met, Marco had made it clear to Lewis that he was not to come around on Saturdays or Sundays. Lewis didn't ask why. Now that Lewis knew that Marco dealt drugs, Marco said it would be fine for Lewis to hang around there on the weekends if he liked, but he'd want to stay pretty quiet when people dropped by because, "Those fuckers can talk if you let 'em."

Marco had a simple system. The same three visitors came by on Saturdays and another two arrived each Sunday. He sold most of what he grew in his backyard greenhouse to these regular callers. A sixth man came by as much as he liked and dropped off LSD, pills, cocaine and hash. The sixth man always came after dark and never stayed long. Lewis hardly saw him and they never spoke; this man wasn't a talker. Marco sold the drugs to the five that came by on the weekends, who in turn sold them wherever it was that they did. Marco didn't ask. Under no circumstances were any of the five men to stop by other than Saturdays or Sundays.

There was a grocery store a half a mile away. They didn't normally deliver but Marco had worked it out so that they brought him what he needed for the week every Monday morning. The clerk liked speed, the owner preferred hashish. The operation had been working well for nearing two years. Marco hadn't left the premises in that time.

Lewis still enjoyed the front yard, particularly when the other kids in the neighborhood would see him there. He was proud to have a friend. Marco said they both could benefit from a little exercise, so they took to tossing a football or Frisbee around each sunny day.

Marco had his back to the street on the edge of his maladroitly-maintained lawn and Lewis had gone long, nearly to the porch. Marco was about to throw the ball when Lewis dropped his hands to his side.

A man had materialized behind Marco, seemingly from nowhere.

"Eh, ha ha, eh, ha ha, eh, heh, heh, heh."

It was a long cackle of a laugh from the man on the street: a laugh that would come to make Lewis's insides turn. Marco dropped his head to his chest in seeming defeat but never turned to look.

"What the shit is all this?" asked the man.

The house had become the most comfortable place Lewis had ever known until that first day in the living room with Denny, Marco's stepfather.

"So where's your mama and daddy, boy? They know you spending time with this jive turkey?" asked Denny.

"His father works," answered Marco. "Two jobs. A third sometimes."

"Well, I'll be damned," said Denny. "See, that's why stereotyping folks will get you nowhere in this world no more. Ah, heh, heh–"

"Fuck yourself, Denny," said Marco.

"Watch yourself, boy," said Denny.

Lewis didn't say a word before he left. He had stayed a little while because he was worried for Marco, as the air had taken a turn. But this man was short and skinny and old, probably not as old as he looked to Lewis, but old for sure.

He was a deficient man, little Denny. He appeared as though someone had drawn him and done so poorly—a stick figure frame that implied false height. His gums dwarfed his piss-colored teeth and as such one hoped never to see him smile. It was only water—applied to his head by hand several times a day—that kept his near shoulder-length hair slicked back, thin strands of gray and white, made slightly thicker by all other forms of neglect.

Marco's stepfather had robbed a convenience store in nearby Hazelwood over two years prior. The robbery alone wouldn't have sent Denny running but he had been speeding for days and he tended towards unnecessary violence when he was flying like that. The butt-end of an unloaded rifle to the head, all because some dopey counter kid was moving too slowly for Denny's taste.

Marco had been told that "the courts" had given Denny the home on Barto Street and with it the responsibility for raising the boy after Marco's mother had permanently mitigated her rage with at least a half-dozen too many valiums. This story Denny fed him about the workings of the family legal system was an absolute non-truth. No paperwork had been filed, no phone calls made. Marco's grandparents had left their daughter the house in Ferguson several years prior, free and clear, and it remained in her dead name, therefore rightfully being Marco's to inherit. For Denny, the then-teenage Marco had been little more than a nuisance that came with free lodging.

Lewis parked himself on the doorstep and quietly listened as Marco and Denny yelled at each other.

"Why you keeping company with fat coons?" Denny asked.

"What's it to you who I spend my time with?" answered Marco.

"It's my goddamn house," Denny growled.

"My house too," said Marco.

"The fuck it is," screamed Denny. "You're grown. You got no claim. I got papers, boy. I should put your ass on the street this goddamn day."

Marco arose from the couch and walked toward Denny. Lewis could hear his voice clearer now as Marco calmly spoke.

"Threaten me with that again, and I'll see you buried in the backyard, little man."

Lewis made his way through another school day, avoiding eye contact and speaking only occasional words like "excuse me" to his fellow classmates. Everyone seemed to have settled on a policy of ignorance. He heard no words spoken to or about him aside from those of the faculty. He wasn't the only black kid in his new school, but he was part of a minority, and even that group minimized him further by issuing him no invitation to socialize. It seemed to him that his size ostracized him as much as the color of his skin. Years later he would consider the notion that it was his shy demeanor and nervous stutter that made most take him for simpleminded. Kids seemed to think "retarded" was contagious.

It was Salisbury steak day at the cafeteria. This was a gastronomically reprehensible meal but Lewis lacked the frame of reference to say as much. He washed it down with two small cartons of chocolate milk, slowly picked at the mashed potatoes and completely dismissed the limp green beans that floated in their section of his tray, buoyed by whatever thick-as-snot liquid they had stewed in. He ate alone at a large table, as much of the student body opted to take their lunch breaks in the outdoors. A bell rang and he knew he'd be late for his next class given its lack of proximity to the lunchroom. Late bothered Lewis. While the policy of ignorance typically stood as rule where words were concerned, it didn't exclude judgmental looks from the girls and open laughter from the boys. He imagined them speculating to each other that he was so damn stupid that he got lost going to the place he went to every day, or that he was so damn fat that he couldn't walk fast enough to get there like everyone else. He preferred not to walk into a class already in session for these reasons.

The layout of the school was confusing and he hadn't taken the time to explore the grounds. A staff member gave him a tour of his class routes on his first day and he hadn't deviated from that path since. He did, however, understand that if he were to take the back door out of the cafeteria he would likely make better time walking behind the buildings that stood adjacent. He grabbed his biology book and made his way out the back.

The hill was steeper than he'd imagined. A hot summer had bullied a perfectly fine spring and wouldn't submit to fall just yet, with the whole of the Midwest enveloped in a static calefaction. Sweat began to percolate in his tight, round Afro and quickly migrated south.

This area of the high school felt unlike the rest of the campus to him, unoccupied and with an industrial complexion. It was where they ran the cooling system into the buildings, where the plumbing came through with enormous pipes and red gate valves, where stairs took extreme angles in short runs and led to rooms that were mysteries to most.

As he turned a slow corner he heard a soft moan come from the far side of a wooden shed that held trashcans and push brooms. He stopped and attempted to quiet his own wheezing, having huffed his way up the hill. A girl made another wonderful little noise and before he could consider it, Lewis's feet softly shuffled forward a few more yards and his neck craned, an innate response from a boy who had yet to have a sexual experience of his own. At the edge of the shed he made out Angel—sandy blond, light blue eyes, short but leggy, a winsome, flirty "burnout" girl that likely put most of the men of the high school's staff on edge.

With her back to the wall and her boyfriend's best friend writhing across her body, Angel saw Lewis out there in the open, yet her expression didn't change, leaving him to wonder at that moment if he were alive at all. The boy worked Angel's neck with his lips and tongue while his fingers explored as much of her privates as her buttoned jeans allowed for. She grabbed the boy's member through his pants and he moaned higher than she had, inspiring a laugh from her as she continued to stare at Lewis. The boy took his right hand and dove down her back to grab her ass. Angel looked at Lewis and gave him an exaggerated wink. Lewis turned and ran back down the hill.

Marco was on the couch. Lewis stood outside of the screen door and surveyed what he could of the rest of the house.

"Your step daddy here now?" asked Lewis quietly.

"Nah. Come on in," said Marco. "Dickwad took off. Don't call him my step daddy. Please."

Lewis plopped down on a beanbag chair. It was the only other piece of furniture in the living room aside from the couch and the wooden TV console. Denny sold every item of value during his leaner times, which were often dogged in their tenure.

"Why he gotta be such a…such a…"

"Dickwad. There's your word. Born too stupid and cruel to be anything else I suppose," Marco said.

"You still want me coming by here now, Marco?"

"Screw him, man. You're welcome here same as always. You don't have to worry about that asshole."

Lewis nodded toward the pillow and sheet gathered at the end of the couch.

"Now you sleeping out here, Marco?" said Lewis.

Marco got up and walked into the kitchen.

"Iced tea?" said Marco.

"Okay. But you got that other room in the back, ain't you? Why you gotta sleep here?"

"How do you know it isn't Denny that's sleeping on the couch, huh?" said Marco as he came back into the living room. "Why do you assume that it's me sleeping on the fucking couch now that he's come back?"

"I…I'm s-s-s-sorry, Marco."

"Fuck. I'm sorry, Lewis. He's got me all wound up," he said as he shook his body, making his arms flail like gym socks on a clothesline. "Up his, man. Tell me about school."

Lewis reflexively smiled and shook his head as he eyeballed the floor.

"What?" asked Marco.

"I seen this girl today," he said, still grinning and moving his head back and forth.

"Oh, yeah?"

"I think she older. She look it."

"Pretty?" Marco asked with game show gusto.

"Oh yeah. Real pretty."

"You're blushing. Can black folks blush? I think we have our answer."

"Come on now, Marco," Lewis said as he waved at him playfully and turned his head away.

"You don't get to fall in love with some beauty queen down at school and not get the business from me pal," said Marco, laughing through his words.

"I ain't said nothin' bout no falling in love."

"Ain't got to. It's all over your face. And what's gonna happen to me when you go off and get married and I'm stuck here all alone?"

The screen door opened, putting the laughter on ice.

"Well, well," said Denny as he entered. "Saint fucking Lewis. Here he is again. Ain't we the lucky ones? Only honkeys on the block got their own house Negro."

Marco started to lift himself off the couch. Lewis stood up from the beanbag chair even quicker somehow.

"I ba... ba... best be gettin' home now, Marco."

"Ya....ya...ya... yeah, boy. You best be g...g...g.. getting on," mimicked Denny.

Before Marco could stop him Lewis worked his way around Denny and out the open door. Denny mocked his waddle and made one more shitty remark before closing the door hard behind him. Lewis heard the slap of Denny's face being met with Marco's right hand. Lewis turned back quickly, looking all around him in a nervous fit, searching for help that wasn't there and wasn't required. Inside, Marco was winning a decision that was never really in doubt, easing up and opening his hand after the first blow took a tooth, as he'd later tell it.

CHAPTER THREE

The Once-Over Twice

The front door of my shitty little apartment was wide open but the security gate was closed. It got cold in San Francisco, particularly during the summer, just as Mark Twain had said it did. I don't know why exactly that my residence felt more like a place of business if a client were to walk up to an open door and a closed gate, but I took the bracing winds with that half-considered logic in play.

"Well 'ello in there, mate. Is you my Dick then?"

I came out from behind my piddling desk and peered into the sun that poured in behind my three o'clock appointment.

"Yeah, then," he said. "You're the one. Ain't you, old boy?"

"Please, come in," I said as I opened the gate. "Mister?"

"Nah, ain't no Mister at all, mate. I'm Sanguine, then. Sanguine Youth is what I'm called."

"Wait," I said.

"Not *Wait*. Sanguine. Say it wif me, geezer. Sanguine."

Sanguine froze a look at me and then began to snicker.

"I'm taking the piss, mate," he said.

"You're not called Sanguine Youth?" I asked.

"Oh, bugger. You 'ave 'eard of me then. Bloody 'ell. Recognized by the likes of you. See now, I used that fake name wif you on the phone yesterday finkin' you might well know who I was, maybe call the press, right? Take advantage? Then I see ya and you're an old fucker—no offense, don't know why I thought you was younger— anyhow, I see you slumped over that pathetic li'tle desk there and I fink to myself, no way this bloke knows who I am, right? Bloody 'ell. You got confidentiality or wha'evah, right mate? If I'm wrong I don't want 'im finding out, now do I? Scary, short-armed fucker that he is."

I needed to sit down. I made my way back to my roundly criticized desk while Sanguine watched and shook his head in a clear mix of disapproval and pity. I stared at Sanguine and he squinted back at me. I closed an eye and leaned in closer. Sanguine took the seat in front of the desk and his eyes began to dart back and forth between me and the things that hung on the wall behind me that I imagine looked important and possibly official to him. I could see that he was growing uncomfortable with the leering and the now prolonged silence in the room.

"Ain't you gonna ask me nuffin', mate? Why I'm 'ere and what 'ave you?"

"Did your father recommend me to you, son?" I asked.

"Me dad? That geezer? Why would you fink that then?"

"Well, I know him. Or I knew him. Years ago. He came to me and, well, obviously I can't talk to you about that. I'm sorry. You look so much like him. It startled me at first."

"I look like a fat, baldy mailman to you, do I?" he said incredulously.

"This was nearly thirty years ago now. He was young, like you. He's a mailman now is he? Back then he was, well, he was like you. Exactly like you," I stated, gesturing toward him with both palms facing up.

"Why you keep saying that? 'Like you'? What you mean like me? In what way exactly do you mean, mate?" he asked, clearly taking offense to any comparison.

"He was a punk," I said. "You say punk rocker, don't you? Just like you. Same kind of ripped clothes and spiky hair. The bracelets, the safety pins. Same as I remember him anyway. It's uncanny really. And you took his stage name as well?"

"What the 'ell you babblin' on about, geezer? Me dad never had no spiky hair or rags like these. Never looked like me at all. And he never had no stage name neither. What's he need that for? Carrying the fuckin' mail all his sorry lit'le life? And why would he hire you anyway then? He's the one cheated on me mum with that fatty."

I looked closer at Sanguine but I just couldn't understand it. This was the man I had met in 1981. This was the man who came to my office downtown and hired me to find evidence that his manager was stealing from him. This was that man—somehow unchanged.

Sanguine Youth was the first person to ever hire me as a private investigator—my first professional client. Back then I hadn't been in the city long and, to tell you the truth, I didn't even have my license yet. I'd rented the place on Geary and immediately hung a shingle: the enthusiasm of my youth. I say youth now about being thirty. Funny.

He hadn't called to make an appointment as he did this time around; he just barreled in one day.

"Do I call you Mr. Youth?" I said that morning in late 1981.

I recall asking him that. He was at least five years younger than me then but he seemed older in a way, or I just felt younger, immature. Maybe because I was a fraud then and he was supposed to be somebody real, somebody that people had heard of in his world.

If there'd been a "punk scene" in St. Louis I hadn't seen it. I came here thinking hippies and homosexuals and whatnot and the whatnots turned out to be in the majority, or at least that's how it seemed to me. There were transvestites, your druggie dirtballs, what they called the New Wavers, artists, pushers, surfers, pimps and more ethnics than I had ever dreamed of. Why, I was meeting people from places I'd never even heard of. It was exhilarating and it made me feel swiftly cultured.

I remember Sanguine seemed convinced that his manager was ripping him off, so much so that I figured this ought to be easy enough to prove, and I could always say that I nailed my first case. I had read every book on investigation work in the library back home and a half a dozen more I picked up when I got here. I'd even taken to studying the television shows of the day that starred private investigators and I'd picked up quite a few tricks of the trade from them, believe it or not. I heard they had Dicks consulting with the writers.

I set off thinking I would take a close look at this manager's life and see what kind of books he was keeping. Thing is I was so green that almost everything I could think to look at I had to ask Sanguine to provide for me. He made a few smartass comments about him doing my job for me and I tried to pretend like it was your standard protocol and that it didn't hurt my feelings when it did.

With my office now fully established in my home, I tried to put Sanguine's bizarre visit out of my head. I had politely told the impostor to take a hike and he obliged, but not without dropping a few very British insults on his way out the door.

I began a new routine. I started my day with a coffee from a café near my place, as Al had always taken care of the coffee. There I'd sit and read the paper, feeling less and less pressure to return home by any certain hour. No one would be waiting for me there. No one was calling to make an appointment. My business had flat-out flat-lined.

I hadn't seen this coming and I really wasn't financially prepared. I was never much for saving money and I figured the work wasn't going anywhere. I could bank on that. My profession had always provided a steady income, completely recession proof. People need dirt. That will never change. I couldn't imagine the day would come when technological advances alone would replace a man of my expertise.

My rent was low, having lived there under the rent control laws of San Francisco for so many years. The car had been bought a while back, used and outright. I'd heard it said that no automobile was more invisible than a Toyota that is five to seven years old. But the city was no cheap place to live, even for a man who lived as cheaply as I did.

I had little else to do with my time and this Sanguine thing was eating at me. After a few days I began to wonder if I'd fallen asleep at my desk that morning and had dreamed the entire exchange. When I returned from the café I found the number Sanguine had provided. It was written in red permanent marker across the face of a tarot card known as The Fool, and it was the sole item in the top drawer of my desk. If it had been a dream, how did this get here, I wondered aloud to myself, card in hand. I called the number and he answered on the first ring. After stumbling through an invite, I got him to agree to come back in. Whoever he was, he was running a game on me. It was now time to figure out his angle. I tried to find Sanguine's file but I hadn't handled that part of the business too well in the beginning, not until I hired Heather, the first of my three secretaries. I was playing the whole thing close to the vest with this person who claimed to be the once-upon-a-time mildly-famous Sanguine Youth. I asked him to bring some accounting records and he gave me some grief about doing my job for me but assured me he would.

I staked out at a modern bus stop kiosk, sitting next to three others on the wide bench seating. A wall of the glass stall was outfitted with an interactive screen that tracked the oncoming buses, providing arrival times. The screen also offered trivia games to keep a waiting person's mind occupied. While very futuristic, I had recently read that they would be installing these at a few locations around the city. So it was the present day then, 2011, evidenced by everything I could see. There was nothing out of the ordinary. Except that there was that man.

The man kept his office near there, just as he had years ago. When the Sanguine look-alike provided the name the day before it had taken me slightly off guard, though I suspected that he would see this charade through to whatever end he anticipated. He has done his research, this fucking guy, I thought to myself. But it wasn't that the address hadn't changed and it wasn't that the name remained the same. It was that man again. Exactly that man again.

The man was Gary Butto. He managed some local acts and handled the booking for two nightclubs in the city. But those nightclubs had been closed for years—a grocery store now stood on Haight Street and a strip club on Broadway.

And yet there was Gary: greased black hair, diamond earring in his left lobe, wide-collared leather jacket, skull ring, and one arm significantly shorter than the other. He was in his mid-forties as he stood talking just then to a young girl whose face was pierced like a human pincushion, as he was in his mid-forties when I so easily proved to Sanguine what he had suspected of his manager thirty years ago.

A day later I sat with Sanguine in my home. As he spoke my body began to feel bloated beyond the limits of the actual space it took up behind my embarrassingly small yet abundantly empty desk. My arms felt twice as thick as they truly were. I was sure that, if he had reached out to touch me right then, I would have sensed his hand on my forearm three inches before it would land on my skin. It was as if my soul–the soul that I do not believe I or any other human being actually possesses–had pushed through the boundaries of my skeletal mass and was now occupying the area around me, a protective layer: a force field activated by anxiety and an unfamiliar brand of fear.

"Why is you followin' 'im anyway? I mean, I hire you to look into this fing with, like, where I'm not being paid what I'm supposed to, and you take to ripping me off as well. That's 'ow I see it, geezer."

When I was young, new and unsure, these exact words, now being recited to me again, had initially killed my confidence, and I wavered in a show of weakness. Now, after following a man that had not aged for three decades, and understanding that the client who sat in front of me, also un-aged, was very possibly who he claimed to be, I spoke to him from a place of unmitigated habit. Rather than breaking down in this man's presence, which may have been the goal of what was surely an elaborate ruse, I summoned the authoritative detective in me, or the one I had spent thirty years fabricating anyway.

"How do I know that you are not who you pretend to be?" I asked.

"What you mean by that then?"

"I'll ask you again. How do I know that you are not who you pretend to be? How do I know that you, sir, are not British? That you've never even been to England or so much as left the United States?"

Sanguine looked startled and then readied himself as if to lie but I put an end to that before it could begin.

"I may not have all the answers, Mr. Youth–and there are clearly many questions here today, many, many fucking questions–but do not tell me how to do my job. I am good at what I do."

We ogled each other for a long while, me feigning a confident manner, Sanguine pulling off befuddled.

"I'm not changing the way I speak for you, mate," he finally said.

"I know," I acknowledged.

I then presented to Sanguine what I had learned over the previous week. The evidence had entirely nothing to do with the time I had spent following Gary Butto, just as it hadn't thirty years prior. In fact, every time I tried to follow Gary Butto this time around, I quickly lost him. Back in the 80's I tailed Butto because it was my first case and that's what private eyes did, and I had looked forward to that part of the job, so that's what I was going to do.

It was dark when I returned home that evening and the flashing light of the answering machine was all I could see. Five messages: one from Al, wondering why he hadn't heard from me in nearly three weeks, and four from potential clients, which is to say former clients presenting cases I had long ago worked.

I returned no calls. I took no jobs. My days still began with café coffee, but I no longer had the time to read the whole paper. I set out each day and did what I had learned to do best; I tailed people.

The first day I followed Gary Butto to the grocery store on Haight Street where the nightclub had once stood. I waited outside but Gary remained in there for hours. As he had never actually seen me there was no harm in entering the store to look for him. I stalked every aisle, over and over, until a pungent, young white man with dreadlocks and a grocer's smock began to follow me, the kid far less skilled in the art. Gary didn't turn up and I returned to my car. Hours later—now night—Gary emerged from the store carrying no groceries, only a guitar case. He flagged a cab and I started the Camry. A few minutes into the drive I was completely flanked by nearly one hundred bicycle riders (a monthly ride they call Critical Mass that I'm told aims to lessen the amount of cars on the roads) and I lost the tail.

That was also the night of the first sighting.

The next day I camped out in front of Sanguine's apartment. He lived on Fulton Street, directly across from Golden Gate Park, not far from my place. Spying on Sanguine would demand all of my acquired talents. Although Sanguine had no reason to suspect a tail, he would notice me if I didn't take precautions. Costumes were always my favorite part of the work. Hippies were the cheapest to accomplish, and they never went out of fashion in San Francisco. I spread a Mexican blanket on the grass under the canopy of an overgrown bush and relaxed in my wig, bandana and tie-dye tee shirt. I looked like Wavy Gravy setting out to take a morning nap.

Hours passed and I felt like an ass for thinking Sanguine would wake up before noon. I pictured him, somewhere across town, in another bed entirely with at least two liberated women, living the life of a rock star.

When you decide to watch someone there's not always a way of knowing for certain if that person is actually in the place you assume they will be. You wait for them to come home some nights and they never do. You begin your day at their office and they don't show up for work. You're committed and it's as boring an undertaking as you could ever consider.

Sanguine walked naked across his living room and peed into a plant.

He lived on the second floor and had no curtains, only a Union Jack flag that dangled from one end of the large bay window. It was nearly 2:00 PM and Sanguine's eyes were still closed as he urinated on the ficus. A pale boy wearing a holey t-shirt and no pants suddenly popped into view and pulled Sanguine down by the shoulders, piss spraying in the air above them as they fell out of sight.

I waited fruitlessly for another three hours and then made my way to my car. As I opened the door I responded to the mad blur of motion coming from my right, jumped into the car, and pulled the door closed, narrowly avoiding a potentially-grave collision with the charging Samurai Swordsman who rode on a WHITE FUCKING HORSE FOR FUCK'S SAKE.

That being the second sighting.

CHAPTER FOUR

Les Missourables

Lewis's bus left the parking lot of McCluer High School and headed north on South Florissant. The first stop was his and he got off last in the group. He crossed the street when it was safe and lingered for a few minutes, picking up rocks from an empty field and tossing them into a woody area, giving the other kids a healthy lead. He started up his hill and Angel cut through the traffic, pulling up next to him.

"You could just walk home you know," she said.

Lewis turned and felt the stammer coming.

"From school I mean," she said. "You don't need to take that bus. Kinda silly, don't you think?"

"Yeah," he muttered.

"How far to your place?"

He pointed up the hill, which was no answer.

"Just your luck. That's exactly where I'm going," she stated and pointed as he had. "Get in."

A 1976 Silver Chevrolet Camaro for your sweet sixteen says your parents *know* high school, know how it works. Angel's folks were what we called key-partiers back then. She said they laughed a lot and played grab-ass so much that it was normal for her.

She barely drove. It was just enough forward momentum to get the car to roll. She turned the stereo up when she saw the kids, the ones who had the head start. Cruising by them, she put her hand on Lewis's thigh as she leaned over and down, greeting the group of boys with a smile as *Whole Lotta Love* played.

"Mmm hmmmm," she purred and proceeded just faster than their advance, which all but came to a halt at the sight of them together. She looked at Lewis whose gaze was fixed on her hand as it squeezed his leg. She smiled.

Marco was on his front lawn and near the edge of the road. He wore a yellow tank top with red piping, green nylon shorts that were cut high and a pair of blue suede Puma tennis shoes. His tan legs and dark hairs made the dainty little shorts appear manly. When they drove by he accidentally flung a Frisbee he had been holding a few feet, his hands having gone up to his sides at the sight of Lewis in the car. Angel rolled the wheels a few more rotations and then tapped the brake.

"Who's that?" Angel asked, looking back through the rear window.

"Marco," he said, controlling the stutter.

"Are you friends with Marco?"

Lewis nodded his head up and down. Angel put the car in reverse and worked her way back.

"Nice ride, Lewis," said Marco as he bobbed his head.

"Yeah, he was nice enough to let me take it out for a spin. Weren't you, Lewis?" said Angel.

Lewis said nothing.

"He's cool that way," said Marco, tapping Lewis's shoulder through the open window.

"Is that your Frisbee over there, Marco?" asked Angel.

"It is indeed, Lewis's young companion," answered Marco.

"Angel. I'm Lewis's Angel."

Marco and Angel did the talking. Lewis just threw the Frisbee back when they chucked it his way and he smiled big and goofy, considering his luck on that handsome afternoon.

"You went to McCluer before us, didn't you, Marco?" asked Angel.

Marco caught the Frisbee and held onto it for a few seconds before sending it to Lewis.

"Everyone around here does," Marco said.

Angel arched her back a little and slit her eyes in the glare of the sun.

"You pitched, right?" she asked.

"How old are you, Angel?" asked Marco.

"Eighteen. Soon anyway. Marco Whitehead, right?"

Marco acknowledged with a stoner's chuckle in a way that showed how uncomfortable the questions were making him.

"Do I know you?" asked Marco.

"It's alright, Marco," she said. "No need to be so nervous. You know you're a little bit famous."

"He famous?" asked Lewis.

Marco shrugged and walked over to the porch and turned a spigot. He let the water run through the hose until it went from the temperature of hot tea to merely warm with a rubbery flavor. He lifted the hose and tilted his head sideways to catch the water in his mouth, never taking his eyes off of Angel.

"No big deal, Marco. My uncle is Coach Romaine," Angel said.

"Shit," said Marco.

"Yeah, he's an asshole, Lewis. In case you hadn't heard," said Angel.

"He's alright," said Marco. "At least he was to me."

"Really? That's not what I remember," she said.

"How old were you then? Nine, ten? It wasn't his fault," said Marco.

Marco hit the hose again and after a long gulp he moved the stream to his hair. He ran his fingers through his wet mane as he dropped the hose and turned the water off. He went to open the screen door.

"I gotta take care of some things inside. I'll talk to you later, Lewis. Nice meeting you, Angel."

Lewis looked at Angel who seemed to take his early departure as a victory.

"Likewise, Marco," she said.

Lewis's father was a big man, as strong as anyone would ever need to be. He put his might to use all day long, lifting the boxes at a Famous-Barr department store and the bags at TWA airlines. The only break Terrence's muscles would get was working security now and then for an events company, but the boxes and bags paid better and were steady employ. He worked long hours at the store warehouse during the week and longer hours at the airport on the weekends; Wednesday through Friday Terrence did both: the unflagging dedication of a single father.

East Saint Louis was always just murder waiting to happen. It would soon enough become the most dangerous city in the nation. It was well on its way when Terrence and his wife grew up there together. After his true love bled out on the floor of the restaurant where she worked, Terrence moved the family of two back into his childhood home, with his mother and sister lending a hand in raising Lewis. They stayed with them for eight more years, finally leaving the noise and the violence of East St. Louis behind when Weebie wanted the serene sprawl that St. Charles had to offer.

Those first weeks there, before Marco had offered him the lemonade, Lewis felt the neighbors' stares. He'd walk the street directly home—his head down but his peripherals at work. They were part-time housewives mostly: women who saw to the early-morning needs of their husbands and children before eventually heading to work in hair salons, K Marts, White Castle restaurants or Grandpa Pigeon's discount stores. What did these women gain from watching him walk to a school bus? If they didn't keep vigil, would he hotwire their cars, break into their homes or rape their daughters? Once Lewis realized that this was a neighborhood of narrow-minded cowards he just felt sorry for them, and in turn felt sorry for himself in his new reality.

Lewis didn't know that Marco was half-Puerto Rican specifically, not until the trial anyway. If he had known it wouldn't have informed much, as Lewis didn't know where Puerto Rico was. Marco's skin was just light enough that anyone who met him may have made him for Italian. If the neighbors had never seen Marco's father they may have guessed as much. Lewis later heard from prosecutors in court that Marco's dad had been a regular fixture on the lawn before leaving his wife and baby, returning to his island home one morning, without a word to Marco's mother. Words about Marco's father, however, continued to populate the blocks.

Denny certainly knew that Marco was half Puerto Rican. He'd said plenty of nasty things to Marco and his mother as part of what passed for jocular moments and what often legally qualified as domestic disputes. Marco said he was raised on harsh words where his absentee father was concerned. According to him, his mother could be as vile in her tone as Denny when it came to the subject.

"Where your real daddy at?" Lewis asked as they sat next to each other on Marco's lawn, on the very same chairs that the toddler Marco and his father used to sit upon.

"They tell me he left when I was around two or three," Marco answered.

"Damn. Where he go?"

"Home. He sent a letter after awhile. Haven't heard from him since."

"So Denny raise you then?" asked Lewis.

"That'd be a mighty generous interpretation of the definition of raise. He was sometimes around."

"He ain't around today, is he?"

"That beating I gave him probably bought me a couple of days. He embarrasses easily enough. Can't see him coming back until the bruises and cuts are gone and he can play it like it never happened."

"Damn. You fight like that with him before?" said Lewis.

Marco shrugged.

"It's hard growing up with one parent, huh?" said Marco.

"Hardly even feel like one sometimes. My daddy have to work too much."

"I bet you miss your mom a lot."

"Yeah," he said, looking down. "You miss your mom, Marco?"

"Ish…," Marco said hesitantly, as if charges could be brought against him for admitting as much. "She had her moments. Obviously she wasn't much for choosing men but she meant well I guess. I think she just had her demons, you know."

"My grandmamma say that all the time. 'Them demons doing evil all over this world.' You think that true? You think it was demons did what they did to my mama?"

"Boy, I don't know. Maybe your grandmother means it a little more literally than I do. I just think there are some shit people who do really fucked up things to other people, not thinking or caring about how much they affect a whole lot of other people."

Lewis nodded his head and mulled over what Marco was saying.

"You ever think what might have happened if your daddy stayed?" asked Lewis. "Or if he come back?"

"My advice is don't live the 'what if' life. It'll drive you batty. Just control what you can, man."

The kid was running a ring around the house, chasing his little friend, screaming, growling and putting everything he had into it. He was deep into character. Emotive. Feeling it. War is primal.

Marco and Lewis sat on their foldout chairs and took in the action across the street.

"I'm no P.O.W.," yelled the teenage boy. "I'll fight 'till my last breath. I'm no P.O.W."

"You sound like an asshole Jerry," said Jerry's dad as he punched the screen door open.

The kid that Jerry had been chasing stopped running. Jerry froze in place.

"I didn't finally take a Sunday off so I could listen to this bullshit. Do you know how fucking retarded you sound? Do you?" asked Jerry's dad.

"God. We're just playing, Dad," he whined.

"Playing? Playing? You're fourteen ya fuckin' idiot. You throw a ball or ride a bike or something. You look at girls. Tits! You don't run around out here screaming like an asshole, Jerry. It's embarrassing."

"For who?" yelled Marco with his hands around his mouth in bullhorn fashion.

Jerry's dad put his hand up over his eyebrows and scoured the terrain ahead.

"The fuck you say to me, boy?" said Jerry to Marco.

"You're the one out here embarrassing the kid. And yourself while you're at it. What kind of an asshole calls his kid an asshole anyway?" Marco said while laughing as Lewis got nervous next to him.

"You wanna talk to me about parenting do ya, Whitehead? Do ya? Ya fucking spic."

"Keep that up, Skinny. Keep talking that and I'll thrash you in front of the kids."

Jerry's dad moved closer to the edge of the road, barefoot and anxious, his eyes tearing up with the emotion that accompanies the threat of violence for some men. Marco wasn't like those men. Never had been. Even back when he knew he was about to take a beating. Lewis knew this about him. Tears are tears. Skinny over there getting emotional, like he was trying to pinch out a stuck loaf.

"Alright, skinny. You meet me halfway then," he challenged matter-of-factly.

"Dad," said little Jerry.

"Get inside boy," Skinny commanded but in a less than commanding tone now.

"You coming or what, chief?" Marco asked as he made his way to the middle of the road.

Jerry's dad held his ground.

"You stay the fuck outta my family business, spic."

"One more time with that. One more time and you'll eat your fucking grass, sport."

"Jerry, what the hell are you still doing out here? I told you to get inside, boy. Take your frank...your fuckin' friend too," said Skinny.

"Talking about it don't get it done, Skinny. When these kids remember this day it ain't gonna be how tough you talked, man. You come out here in the goddamn street and take me on or you get your sorry ass back inside."

"Don't you tell me what to do. You don't tell me what to do in my own yard. I don't tell you and that fat nigger what to do."

Jerry's dad turned out to be fleet of foot, skinny as he was. He ran the ring around his house, Marco making a show of it. Marco's emotions were clearly in check and he seemed to know better than to raise a hand to this man on his property. He pursued him halfheartedly while the kids circled inside the house, looking through the windows and doors at Jerry's dad, the fraidy-cat.

"I'm no P.O.W, Skinny," Marco yelled.

Jerry's dad finally thought to run through his back door. Marco laughed at him through the screen and whistled the theme from *The Andy Griffith Show* as he walked back across the street. Lewis hadn't left his chair.

Jerry's dad went to work the next day and Jerry went to school. Jerry's mother had been out and missed the Sunday exchange between neighbors. Her house now empty, she stepped out of the front door.

When Lewis showed up after school later that day, Marco told him all about Jerry's mother's morning visit.

Marco had had an eye on Mr. Green Jeans and another on the advancing mom. He got off the couch and pushed the knob on the TV. He made it to his door just before she did.

"You come to call me spic, too?"

Her walk had been brisk and she went forth as though she'd been followed there.

"May I come in?" she asked as she slithered by him.

"Goddamn."

"Well, shut the door, will you?" she said.

She stood there, taking the house in. The carpet was a low shag of deep orange, well matched to the brown leather couch and white beanbag chair, which were pretty much the only things in the room outside of a bulbous, blown glass lamp that hung from a chain on the ceiling.

"Why are you standing in my house, lady?"

"I'd prefer to sit," she said.

"Huh. Funny. I never made you for funny."

She sat on the couch and looked at him until he figured out that she meant for him to sit there too. He rolled a barbell out of his way with his foot, the sand shifting in the weights until it came to a halt near the corner of the room. He sat closer than she had probably anticipated he would. Lewis would later describe her as, at the time, seeming much older to him than she actually was. She was pretty, but not possessed of the kind of beauty that appeals to a 15-year-old boy, more the sort that would arouse him in his memories of her much later in his life. He said that Marco had more than once remarked that he found her alluring.

"Tell me what happened yesterday," she said.

"What? With your husband and all that bullshit?"

"Yes. I've heard his version. Now I'd like to hear yours."

"There's nothing to tell. He was being an asshole to your boy and I told him as much."

"That's hardly nothing to a mother, Marco."

"Hey, listen, this is weird, you know. You guys have lived there for years now and you've never said shit to me."

"That's the trouble with having a son-of-a-bitch for a husband. It dampens neighborly relations."

"So what do you want from me?"

"I just want to make sure my kid's safe."

"What? From me?"

"No, stupid, from his father. They don't spend much time alone but I worry when they do. He's not going to lay a hand on him when I'm around, but I don't know what he may do when I'm not there."

"Skinny's afraid of you, is he?"

"Skinny. That's cute. No, Skinny isn't afraid of me, but he is afraid of my brother."

"I got news for you, lady. Skinny is the type that's afraid of just about everybody when it comes down to it. I wouldn't worry too much about a guy like that. I wouldn't marry him either, but hey, that's just my opinion."

"Yeah, well, where were you twenty years ago with that advice?" she said as she patted his thigh.

Pulling out of the parking lot at McCluer High, Lewis felt good at school for the first time since he'd transferred. Any other girl would have been subject to open ridicule had they offered him a ride home. Angel towered above reproach.

Angel's boyfriend was known to be the jealous type, which is precisely why she chose him. She bored easily and looked for ways to make growing up in the greatly predictable state of Missouri bearable. The challenge of doing whatever she wanted, all the while keeping nearly everything she did a secret from her guy, kept her stimulated. She needed someone to set restrictions that she could break and her parents were not about to volunteer for duty.

If her boyfriend didn't attend Hazelwood West High School in the next town over this ride never could have been offered. She had met her fella the year before at a party. His best friend made the introduction, having given up on trying to get with Angel himself, not realizing at the time that his chance would eventually come.

"Can I ask you something?" said Lewis.

Angel had her left arm hanging out the door and her right hand at the top of the steering wheel, head tilted, as they waited in queue for the main road traffic to clear.

"Mmm hmm."

"Why you say Marco be famous?"

"He didn't tell you?" she said. "Hmm. Humble. Maybe embarrassed, though. I probably shouldn't say," she said with a tease in her voice.

"Okay," he said.

She obviously wasn't expecting him to acquiesce so quickly.

"Alright, I'll tell you. Everybody else around here knows. Your friend Marco was a big-shot baseball player when he went here. I mean, I don't give two queefs about sports but this guy was good. Like *really* good. My uncle used to talk about him like he wanted to suck his dick or something."

Lewis was disgusted by much of this statement and made it clear with his sour lemon puss.

"Yeah, right? Creepy. Everyone around here talked about him like he was some sort of God, you know. I think he threw a bunch of no-hitters and hit lots of home runs. I don't know. But the Cubs were supposed to be interested in him."

"So why he don't play for them?"

"Well, now that's the thing, Lewis. He went and fucked it all up."

They made their way onto the main road and headed toward Lewis's street.

"How he do that?" asked Lewis.

"I heard he was downtown one night with some friends and they got pulled over with a bunch of drugs. I think he was tripping on acid or something, acting all crazy with the cops. I hear he hit one. He was arrested and it was in the paper and all. They kicked him off the team senior year. My uncle tried to convince the school to let him play but they wouldn't. So they were shitty without him and my uncle couldn't stand it, started calling him all kinds of bad names. As if it matters, you know. It wasn't my uncle's life Marco fucked up. He did that shit on his own a long time ago. Fucking gym teacher. Right?"

They pulled onto Lewis's block and found Marco mowing his grass. It was another humid day and he wore only the nylon running shorts and Pumas.

"Daaaaamnnnn," she purred.

"What," asked Lewis.

She peeled her eyes away from Marco's shoulders long enough to see that she was dealing with, in every way, a sexually oblivious kid.

"It's just hot, you know. And he's out there cutting the grass."

"Yeah. Damnnnnn."

She pulled the car into his driveway and they both got out.

"Hey," she said as Marco killed the mower.

"Hey, Lewis," said Marco. "Didn't realize you'd be catching a ride again."

"We can't let him take that bus with those losers anymore, can we?" said Angel.

"Yeah, well, that's why I…" Marco looked Angel over and then smiled a little dopey as he looked back at Lewis. "So check it out," he said to Lewis.

Tucked next to an overgrown Yucca plant that covered the corner of his house was a bicycle. He rolled it out backwards and stabilized it against his leg.

"I got this for you," said Marco. "I was thinking maybe you could ride to school and back on it."

Lewis went ape-shit.

"This mine? You messin' with me, Marco? You giving me this bike?"

Marco saw how happy and surprised Lewis was and it triggered his own emotions. His eyes welled up a little and, when Angel saw this hers did, too. Lewis was busy inspecting the bike at first but then looked up in time to notice their softer sides.

"So it's a Mongoose, as you can see," said Marco as he cleared his throat. "I had them get these pads for you across the frame here, like they use for racing. Look, you just peel them off like this," he pulled back on the Velcro and removed the black sleeve that held the foam padding in place. "Pretty cool, right?"

"Very," answered Angel, looking into Marco's moist, near-black eyes.

"You know how to ride, don't you?" asked Marco.

"Yeah. I used to have one from my cousin but I got too big for that one. It don't look like this one though. This one nice, Marco. Where you get it?"

Marco looked over at Angel for a moment before answering.

"I had a friend bring it over today."

"A friend?" she asked in a suspicious tone.

"Yeah. My buddy knows a guy down at that bike shop over in...fuck, where is it?"

"Yeah, where is it?" she asked.

"Doesn't matter. I just knew you could use some transpo so I got you some wheels, man. Like you said, keep him off that short bus."

"It ain't no short bus, Marco," said Lewis.

"I kid. Come on. Take it for a spin."

"Yeah?" asked Lewis.

"It's your ride, Lewis. You can go wherever you like."

The representative from Chicago (The Cub Scout as Marco called him) had let Marco know that there was a path. He could keep up his normal workouts, graduate high school and look to Florissant Valley Community College or maybe U.M.S.L. or S.L.U. if he could pull the GPA up. He could walk on to a team and show everyone that he was remorseful and committed.

Buried near the bottom of a pile in the garage sat boxes of awards, gloves, uniforms, bats and balls, unmolested since the incident in 1969.

When the police called the house the night of the arrest Denny told them, "to fuckin' keep him." One of the other boys thought to alert Coach Romaine two days after the kid's father had freed him from the jail. The coach tried to sit down with Denny and Marco that evening but Denny wouldn't have it and threw a smiley-faced cookie jar at Romaine before Marco was forced to physically remove his coach from the home.

"What'd ya think, you'd be Juan fuckin' Marichal? Huh? Dipshit. You ain't even half a Dominican."

Denny slow-tossed him a spite pitch, and Marco could have driven that thing right out of there, if that hadn't been the harder road.

Within a month of the arrest Marco was finished at McCluer. He dropped out and started dealing. Denny probably figured by setting Marco up with a few suppliers, he would see Marco's dream of playing in the big leagues blighted for good, and he'd also have a scapegoat if the police ever looked at his business.

The bell rang and Lewis squeezed out of the desk, smiling back at the girl that let him into the exit lane ahead of her. He hustled to his locker and threw his science book on the top shelf. He spun the lock on the door and made his way through the bustling hall and out towards the main entrance. He worked the padlock on the chain and freed up the Mongoose.

A crowd was moving oddly at the bottom of the hill where the main parking lot stood. Kids were operating in spurts–jerking, hopping and climbing over backs. Lewis took it slowly and worked his way onto the grass as he came down the slope. Angel's Camaro was stopped in the middle of the lot near the exit and traffic was backed up behind her, but everyone had vacated the cars. She came into view as Lewis made his way off the grass. He camped out between two parked pick-up trucks.

"You're a fucking psycho, Phil," said Angel.

"Fuck you, Angel. Whore."

Phil was bobbing up and down, vacillating between screaming at Angel and watching as his best friend skimmed the gravel-based parking lot under a 1971 Ford Maverick.

"Come out you fucking faggot," screamed Phil.

"Leave him alone, Phil," she said with less conviction.

"Shut up, Angel."

Phil got down on all fours, cut-off jeans and all, and went under the car. He grabbed his buddy's ankle and gave it a yank. His friend skidded closer and Phil switched his grasp to the boy's waistband. He pulled him out into the open and the kids that had moved in closer gave them a wide berth again. The boy flailed as he was being dragged back and he latched onto the bumper of the Maverick with his right hand. Phil got to his feet and ripped at the kid's jeans, pulling them down to his thighs along with his underwear, forcing him to let go of the car. He drew his pants up as most in the crowd laughed at his bare ass, until Phil kicked him square in the balls, inspiring a collective groan and shouts along the lines of, "Oh" "Ouch" and "Not cool, man."

The kid dropped and flopped like a big mouth bass slapped fresh from the lake onto a boat's floor. Phil dropped a knee on the base of his spine and began punching his ear. The kid screamed a lot but he never cried or fought back. He'd fooled around with Phil's girl and probably felt so bad about it (or really, really good) that he had told too many people.

Phil got off him and removed his belt. It was made of thick, light-brown leather and had "PHIL" inscribed across the back between two stars. It had been clasped together with a belt buckle that displayed the name of the band *Boston* embossed over a spaceship. He bent the belt in half and whipped at his friend's back a number of times, the crowd mostly grimacing with only a few spectators approaching the kind of sadism that Phil the Boston fan showed that afternoon.

Phil made his way back to his car—which he had nosed in to block Angel's Camaro—walking like John Wayne and looking every bit as queer, holding his belt in his hand.

"Bunch of McCluer pussies," he exclaimed as he opened his door. The nearest jock took a step toward him and Phil shut the door halfway. "You want some?"

Phil had a naturally tan complexion and coal-colored hair that was owed to his mother's Spanish bloodline. He was six-foot-five and a salmagundi of muscles, looking very much like a swashbuckling villain in a pirate movie. The jock stood his ground and Phil gave him a smug-fucker look before opening the door again and getting in. He started the car, spun it back into an open spot and started to pull out of the lot before stopping. He leaned out the window and called Angel a skank. Fuck you, she said. Fuck you, he retorted, and it went on like that for a little while until he flipped off the student body and spun his tires in the gravel.

There were the two rooms in the back of Marco's home—one a master bedroom and the other half its size. The smaller room contained two safes. Denny knew the combination on one of them, Marco the other. The only bed was in the bigger room.

Denny had told Marco to start sleeping on the couch a year before he had hit the road. He was having a hard time concentrating when it came time to jerk off, he openly admitted; the rooms being right next to one another and the walls being thin.

Marco was sawing logs on the couch, the TV still running. The drugs played hell with Denny's digestive system, so Marco later speculated to Angel that Denny had been waging a midnight battle on the toilet when Angel climbed through the wrong window.

"Shit. Shit, shit, shit," Angel said.

Denny kicked his bedroom door closed behind him and leapt to the edge of the waterbed, just as Angel was standing up.

"Well, hello missy," he said as he pushed her onto the bed.

"Hey. No. No," she said.

He climbed onto her, naked, his member resting on her torso: a bad time for a halter-top.

"Who the fuck are you then?" he asked.

"Marco. Marco. Where's Marco?" she said in a panic.

Denny grinned down at her—displaying the full glitz and glamour of that missing tooth—letting go of her arms and running his hands across his wet hair and face.

"He don't let you use the front door? You gotta be jailbait then. You look it."

"Get the fuck off me," she screamed as she tried to leverage herself but sunk into the bed, the water rolling them gently up and down.

"Marco," he called out. "Marco, goddamn it, get your ass in here, boy!"

"Fuck off," grumbled Marco.

"Help!" cried Angel.

Marco tossed the door back and took in the sight of them.

"Look what climbed through my winda," said Denny.

"Get off her," Marco said as he grabbed the back of Denny's neck. Denny slapped back at his arm and hopped to the floor, displaying his ludicrous erection.

"Jesus Christ, Denny. She's seventeen," Marco said.

Marco helped Angel off the bed and led her out of the room. Denny stood there grinning ear to ear.

"Give her a key if you want. Hell, keep her in the basement. Just don't forget who has the big room, baby."

"Shut up, Denny," Marco said as they made their way down the hall and through the living room. "Come on, Angel," he said.

He grabbed her arm gently and they headed out the front door and toward the main road. His large hands wrapped around her biceps easily.

"What the hell were you thinking?" he asked.

"Well, I didn't know. Lewis said you lived alone," said Angel.

"I do. Sometimes. He's been gone."

"Is that your stepdad?"

"Yeah. No. Not anymore. Don't fucking call him that."

"God. Okay. Geez."

"Why are you climbing in my window anyway?" asked Marco.

"I dunno. I thought it'd be kind of a gas, you know. I didn't think you'd mind."

"Yeah, I would mind. That's not cool, Angel. He's got guns. You're lucky he didn't rape you. Or kill you, thinking you were there to rob us."

They walked briskly until Marco's anger and adrenaline seemed to subside a little. He stopped suddenly.

"What?" she asked.

"I better get back."

"To him? You'd rather spend time with that creep than walk with me? Come on. Let's head over to your old field and you can try for first base."

"No. I can't do that. Go home, Angel."

"You're just gonna leave me out here to walk all the way home by myself? What happened to you being concerned I could be raped or killed? This isn't the best neighborhood, you know," she said.

"Hey, nobody told you to break into my house, man. And you have a car. Where's your car?"

"My parents borrowed it."

"So. You walked here, you can walk back then."

"Come on. I've had a shit day. And that was before your whatever rubbed his gross cock on me. Just walk me down to the main road. Just down to the lights," she said.

He looked behind him, his house just barely in sight.

"Fine. Just to Florissant Road. That's all."

She smiled, grabbed his hand and pulled.

CHAPTER FIVE

Sweet, Sweet Little Ramona

Lindsay hated Pacifica. Madison was her town. Wisconsin had always treated her well and she felt like a fat girl again when she moved back home to the Northern California beach community. She'd stayed in Madison after college and took a daycare job. The kids loved her; everyone always loved her. She drank too much at night, which induced a rosy-red sentimentality where I was concerned, inspiring purplish prose and confessional reminiscences. Our correspondence over the years did not include a single word about Ramona. I knew the subject was off limits. Lindsay never told her mother that she remained in contact with me. It had been nearly a year since her last letter and I imagined she had finally outgrown her desire for a daddy.

This was hardly the first time I'd thought about Ramona. In the years that had passed since she called me a coward I thought about her in small ways almost daily. We had worked together, had been like a family as Lindsay would tell it, but it was the eleven months of coupling that had amalgamated the three of us, and the romantic split that put a quick end to it all.

It has to be pretty bad for Lindsay to have called, I thought, as I drove down the Pacific Coast Highway.

I hadn't expected the affection I would feel when I met my first ocean. I would never surf, swim, fish or sail it, but its presence gave everything in life the calming scale you'd expect it to, I suppose. That day in '81 I had no idea where I was going. I drove into the city over the Bay Bridge, admired the downtown skyline, and kept driving until the Pacific formed a blockade. I greeted it with awe, humbly, as if I was meeting a legend. From there it was a pleasant drive back east some blocks on Fulton until I saw a rental sign at 29th Avenue and searched for a payphone. I felt compelled to take up residence near the ocean. It made me feel Californian. Nothing about my life leading up to that first communion with the sea could have been even generously considered Californian.

Ramona loved the Pacific too. She committed to it years before when she bought the house on the water shortly after the birth of her daughter, having to go it alone when Lindsay's father said that a father was the one thing in life he never wanted to be.

Pacifica sits just below San Francisco, tucked away from the rest of the world. It's a short, serene drive down the coast but most days the fog hangs over the town like a clinical depression.

I pulled into the driveway of the simple one-story house at the end of the block, the one nearest the sea. Lindsay burst out of the screen door to meet me before I could work free of the compact car. She was even heavier than when we'd last embraced. I squeezed hard and Lindsay began to weep.

"Joe Iocca without a Chrysler? And no curb feelers either," Ramona said dryly from the porch, referencing the wheels of my Toyota with a simple flick of the forehead, displaying her keen memory.

Lindsay turned to see her mother and neglected to release me from her embrace, spinning me to the side. I lost my footing where the driveway met the lawn and I fell backwards, taking Lindsay with me. The moment of shock and no small pain gave way to ridiculous laughter, eventually even gaining some ground on Ramona's stern face.

Inside, we sat at the kitchen table and reacquainted ourselves, but we did so like strangers who had been given exhaustive biographies on each other, referring back to the poorly memorized text in our heads when necessary, hoping we didn't get a detail wrong, praying it wasn't an erroneous anecdote, one meant to recall another lost lover from another script entirely. Ramona remembered to be bitter with nearly every word. Lindsay kept with her unsubtle plan and excused herself, saying that she needed to go into town to pick up groceries for the dinner she was to cook for the three of us that evening. I offered to drive her, and Ramona quietly but clearly took it as an offense. Lindsay declined.

"She's not ready for it," said Ramona as soon as the front door shut. "She can't handle it. I imagine that's why you're here. She's calling in the cavalry. Isn't that sad? You're the entire sum of my cavalry, Joe."

"She seems fine to me, Ro," I offered. "You seem fine as well."

"People tell me that as if I don't know when I'm fine."

"I don't mean to insult you. I just mean maybe it's not as bad as–"

"It's Alzheimer's. Of course it's bad. Don't be a fool. And for heaven's sake do not patronize me."

"I'm only saying that you're young. It's better that you're young, isn't it?"

"No, Joe," she said to me like I was an eight year old. "It's worse that I'm young. And I'm not. Neither are you. We're not young anymore."

Eventually I began to wear her down and she had moments when she forgot to be angry with me. This had nothing to do with her deteriorating mind; I had a subtle charm that was effective but took time. For Ramona it had originally taken years. That I'd been her boss had always been in the way, but when we gave in and tried for something more I believe we made each other happier than either of us had ever been before, for a short while anyway.

"You're alone, of course," she said to me.

"How do you know?" I said.

"Because I figured you out, Joe. It took some time and some distance but I put the pieces together. A good PI's secretary."

"Well? I'm all ears."

"It's simple really. Women, family, love: these are things that require solving. They're mysteries to us all, but particularly to men. So what would have happened if you had fully committed to solving that mystery, Joe? You wouldn't know what to do with yourself after. The case would end. And you have no idea what comes after, do you? That's the saddest thing, Joe. What comes after is the good part. You missed the good part."

I summarily dismiss anything new as either useless or detrimental. I've been told that I dress like it's forever 1945. I listen to old records, I follow baseball in the paper only, prefer AM radio, occasionally play the ponies, read no contemporary literature and pay little attention to politics. I enjoy history, though. And I probably watch too much TV. I've never used an ATM, never owned or even borrowed a cell phone. I've found a way to live, a way to work and a way to function in my time—a time I'm convinced should never have been my own.

I know enough to know there have always been people like me, people who feel they were born too late: folks who've decided that they would've been better off living decades before their birth; as if they might have been something or someone other than who and what they are. It wasn't a matter of fate, or some miscarriage of fate, to me. Fate is an ignorant construct, just as my family's religion, as all religion is to me. It was an infinite series of arbitrary events that allowed for me to be born in 1951. It was just a damn shame.

Ramona was born in the 1940's. When she grabbed me by my wavy, black hair that day years ago and pulled me toward her, it was the first time I had kissed a woman over the age of fifty. Her build was in stark comparison to that of her daughter's: she was tall and reedy with small breasts and long legs. Even now she appeared no more than early fifties, her hair not fully gray, her skin still taut, her cheeks as blush as ever.

Driving home that night, I considered what Ramona had said. I wondered if she was right and I thought about what it would take to win her back so that I might care for her in her time of need. I would have done anything to lessen the burden on them both. I could close the business, relocate to Pacifica, and leave the confusion of the previous weeks behind. Maybe find a new line of work and a renewed sense of purpose. As I approached the tunnel that took me back toward San Francisco, I felt warmth in my chest and a great sadness all at once, like the day I left my mother. I embraced the feelings, didn't push them down as I tend to do, and I wondered if in doing so I might cry for the first time since that exodus in 1981. I was on the edge of tears when I saw the object in the road ahead at the mouth of the tunnel. I swerved violently and applied the brakes, skidding to a halt at the side of the freeway. I got out of my car and came in for closer inspection. My eyes darted back and forth between the movement overhead and the antiquated spectacle that remained immobile in front of me. There, not three feet away, stood a horse and buggy. The Appaloosas were bucking and pulling, spooked by the drones that flew like mad bats from the tunnel ahead, drones that buzzed the carriage to collect biological data on the pioneers.

The phone rang, jangling the receiver off its base a little. I have an appreciation for older things and can stare at my antique telephone for long stretches, until the act itself leads me to introspections my listless mind would prefer a quick departure from.

"Iocca Investigations."

"Joe. Joe, it's Al. Julie had the baby! It's a boy. I'm a father, Joe. I'm a father!"

"Oh, Al, that's wonderful news," I offered.

"Can you believe it? I have a son."

"I'm happy for you. And for Julie. Please tell her as much for me."

"Of course, Joe, of course. Holy crap. I'm someone's dad."

The news gave me hope. It reaffirmed life and purpose and wonder and possibility, as children (or more specifically the idea of children) can do. It warmed me to hear the joy in Al's voice. There I sat, imagining the road that lay ahead for Al and Julie and their newborn. I began to consider the ways in which the world had changed in the years since my own father had called a friend to announce the birth of his son. I pictured myself through the eventual grown eyes of Al's child, when the boy would reach that age where he understood that the world was now his, and that my time had passed, leaving only traces of what I had learned and done along the way. That's the hardest part about that baton: when you're gassed from your leg you still have a good view of the next guy, and you watch him run it out, until your view begins to fade, not always knowing whether or not you've truly won.

Buzz.

Buzz.

Fuck.

I got out of bed and put on my robe, a gift from Ramona that was now worn down to the edge of tattered and several sizes too small. It fit well once, but as I grabbed the belt ends to cinch it just then, a two inch stripe of my bulging belly was left exposed.

That fucker was out there again. I didn't need to wait to confirm his perfectly cadenced doorbell routine. It was him. I knew it was him. I was glad it was him. I wanted to give him a piece of my mind.

"Special delivery for Mr. Joe Iocca, Private Investigator, PI, if you will, detective for–"

Clap.

I put my hands together loudly and startled him. He looked at me blankly, frozen, a lifelike toy that had abruptly run out of battery power mid-sentence. I reached out to touch his bicep. He must have added 25 pounds of muscle since his first delivery attempt. But that was only days ago. This kid must be juicing, I thought.

"May I continue?" he asked.

"You may not."

He began blinking in an exaggerated way, actually moving his head in a slight nod with every blink. He didn't take his eyes off me. His neck was turned toward me, his body hugging the box, the machine in his left hand. If I had to hazard a guess I would say this tactic was to annoy me into letting him perform his bit. I wouldn't budge.

"How heavy is this thing?" I asked, giving it a knock.

"Quality," he said.

"Quality is not an answer to that question."

"Highest quality."

"You're quite young, aren't you? I wanna call you dumb as well. Are you...touched?"

"Special delivery for Mr. Joe Iocca, Private Investigator, PI, if you will, detective for hire, dick for short, care of the Northern California Association of Integrated Technologies for the Betterment of Humankind, with a home-base in St. Louis, Missouri, for your convenience, maximizing the services of AFTERCARE!, fully bonded,

LLC, providing goods guaranteed to survive in any conditions, even the most grave of conditions, sincerely, CEO, COO and President for life, of the Northern California Association of Integrated Technologies for the Betterment of Humankind specializing in sturdy encasements, air tight and waterproof, equipped with sonarific apps, lab tested to ward off critters and creatures, the slimy variety and burrowers alike, entirely worm-proof to coin a phrase, firewalled, wifi –ready and, might we add, spacious and not at all frightening."

I let him do the whole spiel. I wanted to see if he would repeat it verbatim.

"Whaddya think happens next, kid?" I said.

He transferred the machine from his left hand to his right. He hit a button or two on it as he was extending it toward me. He turned the device to face me, literally pushing it in my face. I could smell the thing. It had a sulfuric odor.

"Your signature is required," he stated.

I looked at the machine he had placed only inches from my eyes. I stretched my neck around it and looked at him. He remained expressionless. I took one last peek at the screen of the device. Without my glasses I couldn't be certain but I believe it said *Proper Goddamn Recipient Signs Here_____.*

"And if I don't sign?"

"I cannot relinquish the item if you do not sign."

I looked again at the machine.

"How would I even sign? There's no pen."

"With your finger."

I gave him a sign with my finger alright. It was not the proper goddamn recipient sign.

The gardener opened the automatic gate and hauled a Rubbermaid trashcan out to the street. He disappeared around the corner, heading to where his truck was parked to dump the clippings. I walked onto the property through the open gate and made my way around back. The driveway doglegged right and ended at a freestanding garage. Fortunately for me Muriel had parked the K car at the end of the drive. Why would she park a shitty Chrysler in a garage? More to the point, why would a woman of such means own a 1981 Reliant in the first place?

I produced a pad of paper from my shirt pocket and slid a pencil out from behind my ear. I peered over the windshield and into the dash, pulling my reading glasses on from the thin chain around my neck. I looked over the glasses for the gardener, relying heavily on the stereotype of a slow-footed Mexican landscaper. I saw that the drive was clear as far as I could see and I began to take down the VIN number.

Phillip came running at me from the lawn that stood opposite the driveway on the other side of the massive brick house. He was screaming and he wore nothing but tight, white underwear and brandished a snub-nosed 38.

"Get down, motherfucker. Get down," he yelled.

Phillip turned the gun sideways and pulled it back to his chest before thrusting it into my temple. As my head thrashed back, but before I went dark, I caught the Mayans miming laughter and applause from a set of bleachers to my right.

I came to in the garage, on my back, my wrists each tied crudely with thin, white extension cords that pulled me over the hood of a pristine 1984 Jaguar, the other ends of the cords lassoed around the mirrors of the car. My glasses were now broken at an arm and the chain was strewn across my chest, with half of the spectacles caught in the low pocket of my sweater. The garage door was open and Phillip was nowhere to be seen. The gardener stood watch over me, holding a pitchfork in his hand and eating an apple he had picked from a tree on the grounds.

I heard Muriel's panicked voice as she ran down the driveway, her slippers flip-flopping closer and closer.

"Why didn't you just call the police, Phillip?" she asked. "You could have been killed."

Muriel came around the corner with Phillip running sideways next to her, looking maniacal in his attempt to win his mother's approval, still sporting nothing more than the tighty whiteys.

"Oh, my Lord. Joe?" She stopped at the hood of the car and turned to Phillip. "What have you done?"

"Aw, fuck it," screamed Phillip, throwing his gun down into the grass. "This is why I didn't want to come back here goddammit," he said as he turned and headed back up the drive. "Nothing I ever do is good enough for you people."

"Phillip," she pleaded as she began to follow him up the driveway. "Phillip, come back."

I eyed the gardener who continued to nosh on the Granny Smith.

"Little help here buddy?" I said.

The gardener didn't understand a word.

"Can you just...por favor. Just untie," I said as I struggled with the cords, shaking my hands but getting no closer to freedom. "English?"

The gardener shook his head no and laughed at me like I was fucked.

Ten minutes later he now sat on the hood of The Reliant, still staring at me and chuckling occasionally. I had dry blood stuck to the right side of my face.

"So what's my play here, pal? When they come back that is. Because believe it or not I hadn't really accounted for this specific possibility," I said.

Another ten minutes went by and Muriel could be heard flip-flopping her way down the drive again.

"Oh, dear Lord, Joe. I'm so sorry. Senor, please. Por favor."

She motioned for the gardener to help her untie my hands and he pointed to himself, shooting her a quizzical look before sliding down off the K car.

"My God, look at your head, Joe. Can you hear me? How are your faculties?"

"I'm alright, Muriel. Just a big misunderstanding is all."

They freed my hands and I went to rub my head but that was a stupid thing to do and I winced at the pain.

"Let's get you inside and clean you up, Joe."

We walked together, the three of us, up the driveway. Muriel supported my left and the gardener my right, as the headshot had made me woozy and unstable. The gardener continued to giggle and judge.

"I should explain why I was here looking at your car, Muriel. There's this other case, totally unrelated to you, of course. An urgent matter. It needs to be solved. I can't break with confidentiality here. I'm sure you understand."

"Yes, yes, of course. Let's just concentrate on getting you fixed up so you can help me find Phillip."

I wanted to be that guy they banged around, over and over, case after case. I grew up reading those books and watching the old movies about PI's that took it on the chin a bunch but still ended up solving the mystery, getting the girl. I thought, "That's how it'll be out there in Frisco." Then I got here and one of the first things I learned was not to call it Frisco. Later I learned the job wasn't gonna be exactly how I thought it would be.

I'm no idiot. I realized that was fiction and they don't show you or tell you about all the boring stuff: the mundane tasks, the tedious work, and the long hours waiting for things that don't always come. What surprised me the most was the things people hired you for. Yeah, it's true it used to be a lot of cheating spouses or the occasional missing person. But fellas kind of specialize and maybe you get a reputation for being this kind of guy or that kind of guy and soon enough you start to see a pattern. I got the feeling I was getting the jobs nobody else wanted. I imagined somewhere there was a group of detectives having a healthy laugh at my expense; talking about the case of the missing Cabbage Patch babies (true story) or the time those Pac Height's yuppies had me dig up dirt on their kid's seventy-eight-year-old teacher because she had failed the child on his fifth grade English exam. But I've always been a good connections man—you gotta be. If the cops like you and the girls down at the DMV take a shine and you remember all the names of the folks working in city records you'll do all right. But physical confrontations? Most of my work is behind the scenes. I never solved a murder or rescued anyone. That's not the job really. But the job was always good enough for me, and it beat the shit out of laying brick. I felt like I served my community, met a purpose in people's lives. I gave my customers answers, information they needed, and, in the best cases, some relief, or at least what everyone now refers to as closure. And then it all went and changed overnight it seems.

It wasn't just Al. Ramona was always reading me articles or making suggestions on classes I should be going to or pushing this gadget or doohickey that would change the way I worked. I know they meant well, but when someone tells me I can order a tracking device or GPS or whatever off the internet and just stick it on a car and wait to see where a schmuck goes, I'm just not seeing the work there. I figured other fellas were doing things like that. But it's not like I hung out at a bar for Dicks, talking shop and trying to keep up with one another. It's a solitary gig. I was mostly in my head all day, just how I like it. I didn't need a big, fancy agency with all the hassle that comes from working with people. I had my girls, so to speak. I liked having someone who helped me keep the days straight and made sure people paid me when they were supposed to and maybe a little chitchat around the water cooler.

Nowadays there are loopy goddamn stalkers out there who have more technology than me. They can track you better than I can. They know how to call you and make it look like it's coming in from another number. They can find out where you're going that evening by just looking at your online activity somehow. They can bird-dog you and fuck with you and make you long for the days when privacy meant something—when a person had to have the dough and the inclination to hire someone like me when they had their suspicions about someone, or they just needed a bit of leverage. But just because a woman can look on her computer and find out if her husband is emailing some broad, that shouldn't make me expendable.

And this thing with the insurance companies? Sure, I can tell when a person's lying most of the time and I got the mind to figure out how things really went down, but we're talking about cars here, and mostly newer cars at that. I never turned down much work when it walked through the door but to me that's like taking the same shitty case over and over until you croak.

CHAPTER SIX

Wentzville: a Shit-shack

Weebie had left a few things on the walls: a macramé owl that clutched a tree branch, a velvet painting of a toreador, a framed photo of Eisenhower, and a flock of metal birds in flight. The garage was full of old nails, washers, bolts and the like, as well as a stash of dirty magazines that Lewis had imagined might exist, given that there were two hairy-bush centerfolds pinned to the back wall.

Lewis sat with his father at the kitchen table on a Sunday morning, eating Fruit Loops together, Lewis staring at the owl.

"We'll take a walk down there this morning," said Terrence.

"Come on, Dad. We have to?"

"Just wanna talk to the man, see why he give it to you."

"Cuz we friends."

Terrence crunched his cereal and inspected his boy.

"Never had a friend just give me something cuz we was friends like that, Lewis. Folks have reasons. So you and I just gonna go down there and see about the man's reasons is all."

Terrence reached out to pet his hair. Lewis pulled away playfully. They finished eating and Terrence told Lewis to get the bike from the garage and meet him out front. Lewis pushed his bike as Terrence walked next to him. An old man tended to his rose bushes, glaring up at the two of them as they made their way past his house. Terrence gave him a tepid nod and the old man answered back with even less. Lewis got on his bicycle a house away from Marco's and rode up the walkway, dumping it in the grass near the stoop.

"Marco," he called out through the screen.

"Hey, Lewis. Be right there."

Marco opened the door.

"Marco, this my dad. Dad, this is Marco."

Terrence walked up the path and put a hand out. Marco gave him a smile and the handshake.

"Good to meet you, sir."

"Terrence."

"What brings you by?"

"My dad just want to meet you since you give me this bike and all," said Lewis.

Terrence watched his son interact with Marco, likely sizing up the relationship as best he could.

"Yeah, of course. I understand, man. It's no big deal really. I got this buddy down at a bike shop," Marco said.

"Is it stolen?" asked Terrence directly.

"What? No, sir. I just thought Lewis might want something to ride around on."

Terrence nodded his head.

"Okay," he said.

"I'm glad we're finally meeting," said Marco.

"Lewis say he spends some time over here. I wanted to see for myself."

"Yeah, he's a great kid. We just toss the football around, you know. Talk."

"You play?"

"Not much," answered Marco.

"He play baseball, Dad. He the best."

Marco threw up his hands in a show of humility.

"That right? I played some back in school," said Terrence.

"Yeah, me too. Haven't played since, though," said Marco.

"So what you do now then?" asked Terrence.

"Um. Just working on the house right now, really."

"Construction?"

"Yeah. Just my own thing here."

"Okay then. Don't mean to take up more of your time."

"Well, it was really good to meet you, sir."

"Sure," he reached out to shake his hand again. "I thank you for getting that bicycle for my boy."

"Happy to do it."

"Come on, Lewis. We got to head over and see your grandmamma now."

"Bye, Marco."

"See you, Lewis."

Denny opened the screen door as Marco waved goodbye. Terrence turned for a brief moment to see Denny shoot him a patented shithead Denny look.

"Who that?" Terrence asked Lewis as they came to the road.

"That Marco's step daddy."

"Oh, yeah?"

Denny waved at them and danced on the stoop a little like a rodeo clown, Denny probably thinking he was making more like an ape just then. Lewis saw this as he walked away. Luckily for Denny, Lewis's father did not. Marco pushed at Denny's chest and worked him inside.

Lewis pedaled up the road, pulling onto the driveway and braking right next to Marco. Denny was leaning on his orange Dodge Swinger. Marco was watering the lawn, and when Lewis got close Marco splashed him. Lewis took in a ton of air. Marco laughed, as did Lewis when he caught his breath. Denny looked disgusted with them both.

"When's the last time you left this damn house, boy?" said Denny to Marco.

Two years, two months and thirteen days.

"I don't know," said Marco. "What do you care? Just go about your business and leave me alone."

"That the bike he got for you?" asked Denny as he stalked around the thing.

"Yeah. It's nice," said Lewis.

"Yeah. It is nice. That was mighty nice of you, Marco. Nice of you to do such a thing for a friend like that."

"Knock it off, Denny," said Marco.

"What? I'm being genuine here. That was a nice thing you did for this boy. And sometimes it feels good to do nice things for people, now don't it, Lewis." Lewis shrugged and Denny continued. "So I'm thinking maybe you could repay my family's kindness here today. You see, Marco here won't leave the fucking house for nothing. And here I am in need of a companion on a short drive I've got to take out to Wentzville."

"I said knock it off," said Marco.

"Well?" said Denny. "Somebody's got to go with me. So either you get your ass in the car or the kid comes with.

Or maybe I call the law out here and have them put your ass out of my home. Huh?"

"It's Saturday. You know I've got things to attend to around here. How we eat and keep the fucking lights on."

"Oh, yeah, right. The *boys* come by. The boys that I set you up with. That's right. Now, you gonna test me, son? You wanna test me. Do ya?" Denny bent down and put his hand on the neck of the bicycle. "Yeah, I thought so. Well, then. Looks like you and I gonna get to know each other a little better, Lewis."

Lewis waved to Marco as they backed out of the driveway. Marco was clearly panicked but trying to put on a face for the kid.

"What's in Wentzville?" asked Lewis as they drove.

"Good times. Good fuckin' times are in Wentzville."

They turned left onto South Florissant and made their way to the Highway 270 onramp.

"You ever been out there?" asked Denny.

Lewis shook his head no.

"You even know where Wentzville is at?"

He shook it again.

"Well, I only brought ya cuz I figured you knew how to get to where we're heading."

Lewis looked at him like he might not have been kidding.

"Relax, boy," said Denny.

Denny was a straight-up asshole. Lewis might have been green but he wasn't stupid and he knew an asshole when he met one. Denny was the kind of guy you thought for sure would go away and die somewhere alone but you look up and it's twenty years later and he's still there, still taking in air somehow. But the thing about being fifteen and kindhearted is you haven't yet learned that some people are so fucked up you can't un-fuck them with a kind word or two or even a gesture, like taking a ride out to an all-white shit-shack of a town, even if you didn't know what kind of shit-shack town you were headed for.

Before development would eventually push that far north and west of St. Louis, Wentzville was the kind of place you could live thirty minutes from, as they did, and never have occasion or need to see. Denny had people out there, some kin among them, but just like everywhere else outside of his mother's womb, Wentzville was a place that didn't particularly care for Denny.

"Why is it since I got back Marco don't seem to leave the house no more?" asked Denny.

"I dunno. I never ask him."

"All the time you spend over at my house and you never seen or cared how he don't leave the fuckin' property hardly?"

"I dunno... I... I... I... na na..."

"Oh, settle down, kid. I ain't giving you no third degree. Just asking if you could figure that boy out. I sure as shit can't."

They headed west on Highway 70, crossed the Missouri river and passed Old Town St. Charles on the right. Lewis saw the town sign and thought about Weebie.

"You be knowing Mr. Weebie?" Lewis asked.

"What?" said Denny. "Weebie? That shit-for-brains lives down the street?"

"He live here now. St. Charles. We live in his house."

"Well, it all makes some damn sense now, doesn't it? I mean, that old boy had himself a colored girlfriend awhile ago. This is back when Marco's mama was still livin'. We used to see him driving this colored girl down to his place. Used to tell him, we did, call out to him, 'the blacker the berry the sweeter the juice, Weebie.' Aw, now, don't you give a shit what I say, boy. I'm just talking. I ain't never laid a hand on your kind. Ain't a fair fight anyhow. Y'all got monkey strength, don't ya now? Heh heh heh…"

They drove into Wentzville, Denny lighting up a Pall Mall filter-less as they worked through rural stretches the likes of which Lewis had never seen. He tipped the pack toward Lewis and grunted but Lewis declined. They pulled down a dirt road and up ahead was a line of cars, trucks and motorcycles. Smoke came from a barbeque around back and a half dozen or so people hung around out front.

"You stay here now, boy. You wouldn't want to be coming to this here party," he said as he opened his door and walked toward the crowd.

"That's a damn Jap bike right there, faggot," said Denny loudly. "What you doing sitting on that abomination?" he asked as he grabbed ahold of the man's shoulder, snatching his beer out of his hand before running wildly toward the back.

"Fucking Whitehead," grumbled the man to his friends.

The men looked back at Lewis who remained in the passenger's seat of the Swinger. The man on the bike took a long drag from his cigarette and fixed his gaze. Lewis began to rock back and forth.

Night fell and Lewis's nerves had finally settled enough to let him sleep. He was spread out on the front seat, his head tucked underneath the steering wheel. Denny opened the door and startled Lewis, slamming the door shut to fully wake him. Lewis slinked back to an upright position in his seat and Denny got in the car.

"Fuck it. You drive. Ah heh, heh, heh, heh, ah heh, heh."

"Damn," Lewis said, rubbing his eyes. "Why you be gone so long?"

Denny searched each pocket for the keys until finally locating them in the breast pocket of his Hawaiian shirt.

"Youshutthefugup," he slurred as he stabbed at the ignition. "I've kilt before, you know."

Denny started the engine and turned his head to slowly back out of the long, dirt drive. He made it about fifteen feet before bumping into a tree.

"Azzholetree," he mumbled as if he had a working relationship with the Hickory.

He drove forward and tried again.

There was a store located on the side of the road just before the freeway entrance. The sign out front read: Liquor and Ammo. Denny somehow made it that far and pulled in.

"Okay, time to earn your pay, tubby," he hiccuped or burped, possibly both. "This is why you're here. Now..."

There was the long pause of a drunk, the moment you're sure they are swallowing their own vomit.

"I'm gonna leave the car running. And you just honk the horn if anybody pulls in," instructed Denny.

"What?" said Lewis.

"Honk it, honkey. Heh, heh, heh."

Denny got out of the car, stumbling of course, and commenced a series of starts and stops, his hands out to balance him, his head on a swivel, looking for anyone that might get in the way of his plan. He made it to the glass door and gave the flat metal bar a good yank, so much so that he went flying backwards, landing on his back.

"Oh. Oh. Fu—" he murmured through a chuckle.

Lewis opened the passenger door and started to get out of the car. Denny saw him (although it was upside-down-Lewis from Denny's vantage) and Denny pointed and ordered him back with a hushed yell.

"You do your job and I'll do mind. Mind, that is. Don't mind if I do," he rambled and cackled as he got to his feet.

Denny made it through the door this time. Lewis was rocking so hard in the car that it was creaking at the struts. The parking lot was completely empty but lit up like a spaceship hovered above, as if aliens had arrived and were reloading on Canadian Mist and buckshot.

Lewis felt like he was under a spotlight. He worried about what Denny may do in his condition. He jumped out of the car and went to the door to watch and listen, quietly pushing his way in and stopping in the front of the store near stacks of hunting clothes. Denny sashayed toward the counter. A damp and portly man with a crew cut, Elvis sideburns and aviator-style reading glasses watched him make his way.

"I help you, pal?" asked the man.

"Lemme see that ammo," said Denny.

Behind the man: ammo. In the glass counter under him: ammo. Next to him: boxes stacked high: ammo.

"You gonna have to be a bit more specific."

"That one. The red one," Denny said, pointing to a box of .45 calibers on the shelf behind the man, just below where the booze started climbing the wall.

The man turned to grab the box but never took his eyes off of Denny. He placed the box on the counter.

"Yeah. Those are them," said Denny as he grabbed at the box and pulled back the top, spilling rounds all over the counter, some falling to the floor at his feet. He bent down to pick them up, pulled a .45 out of the his pants that had been tucked under the front of his oversized festive shirt, and began to attempt to load his gun.

Click.

The portly man stood now. The floor of the counter was a full two feet higher than the rest of the store. He leaned over the glass and pointed his .38 at Denny's head. Denny sat silly on his ass with an unloaded gun.

"Alright. Alright," said Denny in surrender. "No need to point that thing at me. I was only testing these bullets, seeing sure they fit."

Denny held his .45 out to his side and dropped it.

"Look. I'm unharmed. Armed," said Denny.

"Number one," said the man, "I spotted that piece sticking out your shirt when you came walking in. And B: I got a phone call from my brother just now, sayin' how some idgit was bragging at some party how he was gonna waltz in here, get some ammo and a fifth of bourbon and rob the place."

Denny stared up at the fat man with a well-don't-that-just-beat-the-fucking-band look on his face.

"Still wanting that fifth, chief?" asked the store operator.

With the fluorescents flickering, the radio crackling, some hard-soled shoes walking the hallway in the back, Lewis buried his head in his chest and thought of the scenarios. If everything fell just right, this day could be for the best. Denny locked up, Marco rid of him, Lewis drinking iced tea and tossing a football, Angel a newly single girl. Lewis's mind didn't operate that way for long, not under that kind of tension. He slumped in his chair at the policeman's desk and he pondered a life without his best friend.

"Your father the hothead type, son?" asked the cop. Lewis shrugged and began to sway in his chair. "I ask because I'd like to be prepared."

The officer peered up at the large clock on the wall, the kind that always adorns police stations, schools and courthouses. It was officially Sunday morning, well into it, officially.

Terrence came through the front door, not bullish but clearly full of nerves, a man looking around at places and things where nothing was to be gained by view. He spotted his son in the back of the narrow station. He didn't seem sure if he was allowed to push the oak gate that separated himself and his boy, so he raised a hand and motioned to the officer who sat across from Lewis.

"You're the father, sir?" asked the policeman.

"I am," he said.

The officer stood and waved him in. Terrence entered and took his place behind his boy, resting a hand on Lewis shoulder, Terrence looking bewildered, Lewis sullen.

"Now, we don't think your son had anything to do with what went down here tonight," said the officer. Terrence nodded fervently as the cop continued. "He seems like a good kid, maybe just got caught up with the wrong kind of person. I've taken his statement and there's no need for him to stay here any longer. But I did want to ask you, sir, if you were aware of this relationship your son has going with Mr. Whitehead?"

"That Marco?" Terrence asked Lewis.

Lewis kept his head down.

"Well," said the officer, "the one we all know around here is Denny Whitehead. Him and some others. Cousins of his mostly I believe. He's the one Lewis was with this evening."

"Why you all the way out here with this man, Lewis?"

Lewis shook.

"Come on, boy," said Terrence. "You got to talk on this."

"Denny say he want me to come with him today," said Lewis.

"For what?"

"I dunno, dad. He ja…ja…just say he needed someone and ma…ma…Marco say he couldn't come."

"So you just come with him. Just like that then?" said a now angered Terrence.

"Listen, sir," the officer chimed in. "What's important here is that you get to the bottom of this thing he's got going with these men. I won't tell you how to raise your son, but my experience with the Whiteheads out here tells me these aren't the kind of people I'd want my own kids associating with."

"I hear you. We gonna talk about that. Ain't natural you to be hanging out with these people anyhow."

Lewis jerked his neck up and pleaded with his eyes, unable to say what he felt just then.

"So that's it then? I can take him on home?" asked Terrence.

"Sure," said the officer as he stood. "We may call if we need more from Lewis to make our case."

Terrence kept his arm around the boy as they walked out to the parking lot. Lewis was surprised at how little Terrence had to say to him on the way back to Ferguson. Lewis wasn't the kind of kid a father would ever think to prepare himself for a drive home like this, a drive home from a police station in the middle of the night. Their silence was of a stunned nature.

Everyone in the neighborhood knew that Skinny got two weeks vacation every year. He was a goddamn braggart, as if paid leave made him the king of Inner Mongolia. They'd been to the Wisconsin Dells, Meramec Caverns, Lake of the Ozarks, Centerville, Branson and Cape Girardeau, the latter to visit Skinny's cousin and his "bunch of Hoosier kids," as Skinny called them. They always tried to get a day in at Six Flags if possible. This year it was camping in

Steelville, where Skinny and Jerry would take in some bass fishing with Skinny's brother-in-law.

Sunday arrived and they loaded up the Chevy Caprice Station Wagon—hideous green with woody sides. Terrence and Lewis walked up the street, much the same as they had the previous weekend, but Lewis was without his bike this time around. Marco burst out of the front door.

"Well ain't this the convention?" Skinny said loudly to his wife as she packed a red and white Coleman cooler full of Hamm's in the back of the wagon.

"Hello, sir," Marco said as he exited the porch.

"Hey, Marco," Lewis said in a pout.

"Need to talk to you about yesterday," said Terrence.

"Okay," Marco said.

"The police call you?"

"What? No. What the hell happened?" he asked with genuine surprise.

"That man, your stepfather, he took my boy out to some place in Wentzville, then he try to rob a store."

"Jesus," said Marco. "Really, Lewis? God, I'm sorry. I don't know what to—"

"Yeah, well, you should be sorry. Lewis say you the one supposed to go rob this place with him but you sent him instead."

"What?" responded Marco, his face squinting and his eyes blinking in an exaggerated manner at the accusation.

"I ain't say that," said Lewis.

"Now listen, sir, I didn't know anything about a robbery. Denny just said he wanted company for a ride. I'd never let anything happen to Lewis."

"Well something did happen, motherfucker," yelled Terrence.

As built as Marco was, Terrence made him look like Skinny when he stood next to him then, stepping in close and tilting his head, a finger in his chest.

Marco took an immediate step back and put his hands up.

"I hear you."

Lewis saw Skinny slap at Jerry's arm and point across the street as he grinned. Lewis was keenly aware of the quality of the audience that was witnessing his heartbreaking event, and it made him angry to go along with the sadness and the fear.

"What business you got spending time with a fifteen year old anyway? You ain't got no friends your own damn age?" said Terrence.

This was the way Lewis had imagined it would go, the way it had to go.

"I understand you're upset," said Marco.

"Man, fuck you. You don't understand nothing about me. You and your racist ass step-daddy. I see him looking at me the other day. I know what he thinking. Motherfucker. He lucky he sitting in that jail right now. You hear me?"

"Okay. Let's just—" Marco began.

"Fuck this. Come on, Lewis." Terrence spun and started walking but quickly turned back and got even closer to Marco this time. "You stay away from my boy. Hear me? I catch you 'round my boy again—"

"Dad," screamed Lewis, tugging at his massive arms.

They walked back down the driveway. Skinny, Jerry and Jerry's wife now stood at the end of their drive, having watched closely as things got heated. Terrence grabbed Lewis by the shoulder and pulled him to get him to walk faster.

"The fuck y'all looking at?" he yelled across the street, sending Skinny's family scattering.

CHAPTER SEVEN

Roger Croon Returns in the Night

The fella who lived downstairs from me was a bass player. When he plugged in I could hear and feel every note. To make matters exponentially worse he gave lessons, and the icing on the shit-cake was that he only attracted beginners and the occasional intermediate. For years we had done the cordial nod, the rock-n-roller and I. He didn't ask anything about me and I freely returned serve. We kept roughly the same professional hours, so when I had worked downtown his means of putting food on his table hadn't been an issue for me. Now, after a few weeks of home office, I wanted to immolate this man in his sleep.

I couldn't make out the conversations the bassist had with his students. From where I sat every hour-long session went something like this: the teacher played a line, gave some quick but muffled instructions to the student, and the student then proceeded to murder the piece of music for a few anguishing minutes.

And repeat.

If I were "lucky" and the pupil was vaguely competent, they would go back and forth, like a call and response, the master laying down the riff perfectly, the answer coming back to him slightly off the rhythm and choppy, fingers crossing over frets here and there, truncating the notes with only the slight resonance of their metallic little deaths.

The bassist favored a bass solo from Fleetwood Mac's *The Chain*. He tried to teach it to everyone. It was ten notes. The first one rang out and held for a long moment while the next nine came in at a hasty pace, landing on a long sustain. I'm not much for music recorded after the 1940's, but what they now call classic rock was unavoidable in St. Louis in the 1970's. Rock radio stations were particularly popular with my cousins at the brickyard and on our jobsites, so I knew the song well enough to know what was supposed to come next. After two bars there would be a build-up. The drums were softly on their way in. The guitar was joining the party. A man named Lindsey and a woman named Stevie were soon to be singing, "Chain keep us together" over and over. This was the emotional crescendo, the real reward of the tune. But that moment never came in my house. I got the ten notes followed by the ten notes followed by the ten notes followed by the ten notes followed by the ten notes, but never the satisfying climax.

On this day, on the thirty-third round of a particularly horrific exchange between two disparate musicians, the door buzzer was the payoff. I removed my hands from my ears and made my way toward the foyer, noticing the red marks on each side of my face as I walked past a mirror and stopped to take inventory. I shook my head back and forth to wipe away any remnants of the terrorized look that had been painted on my face like Edvard Munch's *The Scream*. I opened my front door to see the delivery boy sidled up against the box, the kid's arms above his head and behind his back a bit, gleefully playing air guitar along with *The Chain*. He now looked like Mr. Universe.

There was a baby I had not met, a fact that hurt Al's feelings. I could not continue to hurt Al's feelings. The sightings, or "occurrences" as I kept track of them in my head, were coming with greater frequency now. I didn't understand what they meant but I knew what they could mean. I kept quiet to the few people that were still in my life, an easier feat if I never actually saw those people.

We all met at AT&T Park: me, Al, Julie and Jackson, the now six-month old boy—baby's first ballgame.

"Joe, would you mind taking a picture of us in front of the Willie Mays statue?" Julie asked me.

We walked to the front entrance where the monument loomed. Al showed me how to work Julie's digital camera. I took two photos and Al scrolled back and was pleased with both. I noted privately how the Roman soldiers that had been in the background also appeared to me in the viewfinder.

We took our seats and Al began to talk baseball minutia. Today's pitcher had an inflated ERA, with three of his starts having come at the bandboxes in Philly, Houston and Arizona, Al informed. I missed talking baseball with Al. It had been an unexpected development when I first gave him a job, as was so much about Al.

I had originally hired a young woman named Heather in 1983. After she left a year and a half later, "because this is totally boring me," I tried temps and went for a few years without an assistant while the business suffered, before finally hiring Ramona. When Ramona walked out I reacted immediately, placing an ad in the Bay Guardian and settling instantly on Al, because Al is just the kind of guy you're sure about as soon as you meet him, character-wise.

I looked down the row that was directly in front of us and one by one each fan turned to me and showed me what was in their hands. The first man presented a bronze cast of my baby booties. The woman next to him was holding my notebook from grade school with poorly sketched drawings of *The Three Stooges* on the front. The next woman held a plate of Italian cookies that the women of my family made every year from a secret recipe that I could only tell you included oranges. Another man gazed longingly at a high school yearbook photo of a girl I dated back on the Hill before she moved to Connecticut. I looked at the people and back at Al. He studied me and seemed concerned.

"How's work, Joe?" asked Julie as she bounced Jackson on her knee, never actually looking at me as she spoke.

"It's alright," I said. "Hey, is this one of those throwback games? Matt Cain looks like Christy Mathewson out there in that old jersey."

Julie continued to play with her son. She was an eminently modern and singularly gorgeous woman: mid-thirties, short and messy blonde hair with a pink highlight across the bangs; she was tall, with a sturdy build and emerald green eyes that never seemed to look directly at me. She had no reaction to my answer or question. I knew she thought of me as a silly sort and paid the minimum required attention. Al, however, gave me a look.

"Old jerseys? Those are just the home whites," said Al. "Same as last year. Remember?"

"Oh, yeah. Sure," I stated unconvincingly. "I think I still expect them to run out there in those ugly things they wore when I was a kid sometimes."

"Christy Mathewson? He was a little before your time, wasn't he?" said Al with a small laugh.

"Knock it off, pal. You'll see. One day you're in your thirties and bouncing babies, then it's hello, old age. Boom."

"Boom," said Julie, still talking directly to the kid. "Ah, boom, boom, boom, boom ah, boom ah, boom ah, boom," she continued, making up a little song on the spot that seemed to do the trick with the formally nonplussed boy, happiness-wise. I inspected the child, elated to be bounding along in life as he was just then. I returned my eyes to the field of play and saw that the 1905 Giants were still tossing the ball around as their hurler took his last warm-up pitches. The Brooklyn Dodger hitter dug in and Christy poured in a big, slow curve, stealing strike one.

The next morning I sat in my local café looking at a box score from the game. Reading a statistical account of a game you saw in person the day before should be a dull event. But words did not betray me. There was comfort in the text that was shorthand for the story of a perfectly lovely afternoon. It was all right there: Matt Cain going seven strong, the bullpen holding the lead, solidified by the closer, a position invented within the game not so long ago really. Knowing with certainty that I was seeing things— things that apparently only appeared to me—well, it didn't frighten me then. It galled me as a man who didn't like change. I had to make sense of what was happening to me. I needed to investigate. Somewhere in all of this there were answers. And I was pretty good at finding the truth.

A pinkish woman with a perm and large glasses threw open the café door and pointed at me.

"You," she yelled.

I looked up and identified the woman. She marched over in stout, neon blue pumps.

"Why aren't you returning my calls?" she asked.

"Ma'am?" I said.

"Answer me."

"How did you know I would be here?" I asked.

"I hired a private investigator to find you."

"You hired a private eye to find a private eye?"

"Yes," she stated.

"Why?"

"You weren't returning my calls," she screamed.

"This never happened."

"Well, it's happening now," she said.

"No, I mean, you came to my office manic, sure, and I disliked you for some reason that escapes me now, but this thing with another PI?"

"Whatchu talking 'bout, Willis?" she said.

And there it was. The reason she had grated my nerves like stinky French cheese all those years ago. I knew then that, if I took this woman's case again, I would suffer through countless pop culture references. There would be calls in the middle of the night wondering "where the beef" was in her case, her "pitying the foo" that kidnapped her precious poodle.

I still took the job. Aside from my desire to look for resolution in "The Curious Case of My Current Fucking Condition," money was tight. I had found that, as with the Sanguine Youth detail, money paid from 1985 clients spent just fine in 2011. The pink woman had been an easy assignment back in the day. It was a hate crime before there were hate crimes. Her neighbor despised the pink woman and her well-groomed yapping dog. So the neighbor stole the pedigreed pooch from the pink woman's backyard and delivered it to his uncle in Berkeley, whom he also detested. I retrieved the canine and in return was paid my rate. I had attempted to curb her many crazed phone calls and visits throughout the week that it took me to locate the dog this time around, insisting that she follow some ground rules I set from the beginning. I came to find that, while I could change the past in many ways, that competency did not extend to altering who she was at her core, and so the calls came in regardless.

After two successful cases I hit my stride. The jobs were easy, the pay was decent again and I knew precisely why I was getting out of bed each day. The clients continued to come in order but with many absent, for reasons I couldn't figure. I began to write down thoughts on why this might be—looking for reason and purpose behind the visitors—attempting to solve the larger case as it were. I noted that the more I took on old cases, the more the present time (time not spent in the presence of former clients) became populated by the silent historical and future types, as I referred to them in my detective's log.

I was in bed and listening to a Blind Roosevelt Graves record, *Dangerous Woman*, part of my collection of blues 78s. My socks and chinos were crumpled on the hardwood, while my cardigan and button-down shirt covered a mid-century rosewood chair.

"JesusfuckingChrist," I screamed.

A thin man whom you'd have to label disabled when he ambled came out of the darkness and stepped into the doorway of my bedroom.

"I'm going to sit here," he stated, removing the shirt and sweater from the chair and placing them on the bed next to my bloated feet. He pulled the chair close to the bed but left room for his crossed-up legs.

"How did you get in here?" I asked.

"You're seeing clients, aren't you?" he said.

I knew the man as a late 80's case, one that to that day remained sharp in my mind. He was an odd and memorable man. Nothing of his face or body made any practical sense as a total body of work, so to say. His nose was buttoned while his eyes were mere slits. His hair curled tight and black but his skin was like paste with ink in it, splotchy and unorthodox. He was disproportionate in limbs, so much so that I was always troubled in his presence by the curiosity I held for the size and shape of the man's penis, a wondering I had never considered with any other fellow. I imagined few others had given much thought to his genitals over the course of what had to be a troubled and painful existence, so I reconciled these wonderings as a form of flattery I would never actually utter aloud.

"I was nearly killed. The police seem to have given up. I need you to find the..." He paused long enough to change his word, "people who did it."

These weren't the kinds of cases that made up the bulk of my resume. The man, Roger Croon, had been the near victim of a formerly all-too-common act of violence: he was walking down a San Francisco street when a car slowed and began shooting. What Roger hadn't seen in the seconds before the shooter unloaded was that a young man, the real target, had apparently ducked into an alleyway between tenement houses. The gunman continued to shoot as the driver sped through the block. Roger froze in a contorted position—his arms curling above his head and his legs unable to move except to buckle and tremor slightly, all the while wetting himself and moaning, incapable of letting fly with a full scream.

They had missed him entirely. People poured out of the projects and the police responded to the scene. Roger gave his statement surrounded by men, women and children, many pointing and laughing at the piss stain across his white slacks. I knew I couldn't take Roger's case again. I hadn't solved it the first time. I couldn't imagine solving it now.

"I'll find those niggers myself then," Roger announced as he moved queerly out of the chair and back into the darkness beyond my bedroom.

In late 1989, after months of working with the police and ingratiating myself into the low-income housing units of that area, I had produced nothing to take to Roger or the authorities. Drive-by shootings were increasingly commonplace in American cities then, and most of the time you would read about someone like Roger it would be as an innocent bystander, killed or critically injured by gang members fighting over turf. Roger Croon was spared that fate. The police assured him that he should have been dead. Croon couldn't accept that night as some sort of mixed blessing, instead obsessing, feeling powerless and craving revenge for an act not fully perpetrated against him. One morning in 1990 I got a call from a lieutenant, informing me that Roger Croon had been gunned down by police officers responding to 911 calls in the middle of the night, describing a white man with a gun who was shooting into apartment buildings in the projects. Croon had fired indiscriminately into the rooms, one of his bullets striking a three-year old girl as she slept.

CHAPTER EIGHT

Angels Walk

Arching, feet touching carpet, fingers bending at the wall, her forehead certain to leave a sweaty, temporary indentation. It was like fucking a rock star, an icon Angel had spent her youth admiring, some famous actor spread out on a bearskin rug, hairy and complacent, repugnant and seductive all at once.

"How do you go about cleaning a bean bag chair anyway?" Angel asked, now sprawled on the shag and feeling their juices on the vinyl above.

"Never have," Marco answered.

"Gross. So that was a first?" asked Angel.

"Wouldn't have thought to before now. I was happy with the couch anyway."

"Beats that waterbed," she said.

"Yep."

"You don't go out much, do you?"

"Nope," he answered.

"Because this town is stupid and boring as shit?"

"Yep."

"Nope," she said playfully as she pulled a little at his fur. "That's not it."

"Alright."

"Asshole," she said through a laugh. "Tell me now or I bug the crap out of you until you do."

He pulled himself off the floor and walked to the kitchen, pouring a glass of water for himself, drinking it and then offering her one as well.

"Yes, please," she said bitingly, annoyed that he had put his own needs before hers.

He came back into the room and took a seat on the floor next to the chair, handing her the water as she propped herself up next to him.

"You don't like to talk about yourself," she said as she pressed her finger into his stomach with every staccato word.

"Thought you already knew all about me."

"Ah. Now we're getting somewhere," she said as she popped to attention. "You're one of those, 'Everybody thinks they know me but they don't know shit.' people," she said in a deep but childish voice.

"Like that's not true?" he said.

"So you think that everyone around here spends all their time thinking about you - is that it? Poor Marco, how he messed up his life."

"Whatever," he said, standing up, grabbing his pants off the couch and sliding them on.

"Don't be a baby. I'm trying to get you, man."

"What's to get, man? I hang out around here. That's that. I like it here."

"Here? In this house? With your stepdad? You hang around, you deal drugs. Yeah, shocking, I know about that, too. Like everyone around here doesn't? Even Lewis knows that."

"Cuz I fuckin' told him."

"Big deal. You never took him anywhere. You don't think that kid would have loved to go to the drive-in with you or gone bowling or skating or something?"

"What the fuck, Angel? Why are you riding me? I didn't ask you to come here."

"You didn't have to ask, dumbshit. I want to be here. Just tell me why you can't bring yourself to leave the damn house."

Marco sat on the couch, looking at her. She was seventeen, naked and completely unselfconscious standing there.

"These people around here," he began. "They always looked at me like I was just some half-breed. Until they saw how good I was at baseball. 'Oh, we're so proud of

113

you. You're gonna be a star.' And the whole time I was just, fuck, man, it was just such bullshit, you know? My mom was dead, my dad was long gone. And Denny?" Marco rolled his eyes as he uttered the name. "I didn't give a shit. I did what I wanted, man. And I paid for that."

"You could've—" she said.

"What? You weren't there, man. The shit they said about me? I couldn't fight them all. Fuckin' wanted to. Trust me, I tried. Just walking home. Always someone there to run me down. 'Well, look at you now, hotshot.' Denny splits and it's just me, finally alone, not hearing it in my own goddamn house. It felt right. Felt easy. No one in here to run me down. Nothing or no one to give a fuck about. I got real used to that."

She dropped to her knees before him. She ran both of her hands up his arm and kissed his shoulder. He looked at the curtains and lifted his hand toward them.

"And then I see Lewis, walking this street, all sad and alone, probably feeling scared and judged with every step by these motherfuckers. Broke my heart, man."

Marco didn't actually see Lewis again for weeks. Angel gave Lewis rides home when she could, Lewis explaining to her what had happened in Wentzville that first day back at school. She'd drop him off and park a block over, walking to Marco's nearly every afternoon. Marco respected the wishes of a good father, and Angel protected the feelings of a good kid.

A Saturday came, and Marco had decided on a change. He told Angel his thoughts for the future. He made his usual deals with the men that day. He also made his plans known to them. Saturday went, uneventful; and Sunday came. Marco had begun to share the details of his days with Angel. It spoke to the growing depth of their feelings for one another.

Go Way had approached the door and knocked the way he always did—that idiotic knock some people do. Everyone called him Go Way because he was the kind of man you'd have to shoo off, particularly back before he began dealing, back when most conversations ended in him asking to borrow money. Of all the men Denny had set Marco up with, Go Way was the closest to being cut from Denny's cloth. He was a bigger, younger, thicker Denny, stupider still.

"Hey, man. Come in," said Marco as he gave his usual scan out front. Go Way didn't actually like to be called Go Way, so as Marco had forgotten his real name long before, he used many substitute salutations.

Marco shut the door behind him and asked his guest to wait on the couch, which was customary. Marco went to the small room in the back and spun the lock on his safe. When it was open he took out a large baggie of pills and removed the masking tape on which he had written "Go Way - $300." He pressed the tape against the inside of the safe and shut the door, spinning the lock before calling him in.

"Alright, pal. Come on back," he called out, shifting Lewis's dusty bike from one side of the room to the other.

"What do we got?" asked Go Way, inspecting the bag as Marco handed it to him.

"Mostly Christmas Trees. One new one called White Crosses. Most of them speed. Some painkillers—those are these big ones here. Three hundred for the lot."

Go Way reached into his army-green Wranglers and pulled out a cold wad of bills. He bent down and began laying them out on the floor, counting out loud as he did.

"…Three hundred. There you go, Marco. All there. You can count it."

Marco already had.

"That's fine. I trust you, buddy."

Marco swept his arm out toward the door of the room. Go Way had some heft and he lumbered a bit as he walked past him.

"Where's your little friend?" he asked as they made their way back to the living room. "Haven't seen him around here lately."

Marco didn't like things to get personal between him and the buyers, but he knew not to be as rude as to spell that out for them. The interactions were awkward enough as it was.

"Dunno," Marco said.

"He's a good kid. I always like seeing him."

Marco reacted with a *yeah-well...* look that included the raising of his eyebrows.

"So listen, man, I need to talk to you about something."

"Sure," Go Way said with excitement tingeing his voice.

"This is gonna be it for me. I'm not gonna do this anymore."

Go Way went from delighted to dismayed in seconds flat.

"You're cutting me out?" he asked.

"No, I'm done."

"Well, what the hell am I supposed to do?"

"What do you want from me, a letter of recommendation? I don't know, man. I'm just telling you what it is. You dig?"

Go Way fumed and began to stomp his way around the room. His feet were large and his big body made thumping noises with every step. He didn't say anything for a minute or so, Marco just staring at him, considering when to ramp things up.

"Wait, what about Denny? I can just get stuff from Denny then, yeah?"

"Not from jail you can't," said Marco.

"What?"

"Denny's locked up."

"Then you can't do this to me. You can't just cut me out. That's not the deal."

"Oh, I can't, can I?" asked Marco, now stepping closer to Go Way in the middle of the room. "What fucking deal do you think we have, you and me? I sell to you if and when I want. That's the deal, man. And now I'm done selling to you."

"So you *are* cutting me out then."

"Fuck you're thick, man. I'm not cutting you out of shit. I'm fucking done. Hear me? And I don't give a shit what you do, but you need to get the fuck out of my house now."

Go Way brushed past him, pulled at the entrance door and flipped the screen door open.

"You'll pay for this, Whitehead."

Marco went after him.

"What the fuck did you just say to me?" Marco said as he grabbed him by the back of his broad neck. Marco pushed with his legs, driving him out toward the street.

"Did you just threaten me, you dumb son-of-a-bitch?" said Marco.

Jerry's mom came out of her house and watched as Marco plowed the man to the road, giving him a shove at the edge of the property. Go Way jumped right up and looked over Marco's shoulder. Marco shot a quick glance back, thinking someone was advancing on him from behind. Go Way's Gremlin sat parked in the driveway.

He walked back to his car and got in, looking at Marco the entire time, sulking: the look of a man struggling with a calculation. He backed out and slowed down when he had turned the car onto the street. Through his open window he pointed and began to speak. Marco ran at the car full speed, prompting Go Way to hit the gas.

Jerry's mom stood on her porch, the screen door kept open by her backside. She looked disgusted with him, like a jilted lover. Marco shook his head and turned and went back inside.

A deep Missouri winter came. It strangled life, slowed it to the pace of a dying animal, made the most basic of tasks Sisyphean. School cancellations dominated morning radio. Plows cleared the streets, trucks salted the main roads and children took to the outdoors as if these days had been bequeathed to them specifically from on high. Snowdrifts piled steep on the sides of houses and kids shimmied up trees and jumped onto pitched roofs from which to plummet, forging tunnels, bludgeoning their way back to daylight and air. Sleds of all fashions were used on even the slightest of declines: disks, flat rollouts, wooden plank and metal runners with handles that turned them. A short army of snowmen stood guard on every block, with their vegetable noses and their button eyes. The kids took reign o'er kingdom, exalting for eight triumphant hours as their parents went on with adult life, the grown-ups not bestowed the autonomies that were snow days.

Lewis opened a second box of value pack cereal and poured its sugary lode into his bowl. When the man on the radio said McCluer North he heard a perfectly synchronized shrieking cheer come from the twin sisters who lived in the house next door.

The driveway his father had spent twenty minutes shoveling at 4:30 AM that morning was already two inches deep. His moonboots hit the concrete porch and slid forward, the aggregate in the slab too far below ice to give tread. He grabbed the wrought iron handrail and sidestepped his way down the four steps. When sure-footed knee deep in the yard, he scrutinized the landscape: his neighborhood completely alabaster.

He trudged through the property and reached the road. A plow had been through an hour before, surely to the chagrin of the kids on the block, no doubt fearing it an indicator of their fate on that school day. But out there in the rest of their town, many roads still required attention, roads where buses could not safely travel.

Lewis walked the street in winter wear bought at an employee-discount rate. A snowball hit him in the back of the knee. He turned to see a ten-year old girl whose face was covered in a ski mask and whose body was encased in a one-piece snowsuit. She laughed in a sweet and silly manner through brightly knitted cotton. Lewis gestured to her with his huge mitten. She waved back.

When he got to Marco's mailbox he swiped the snow off the top and rolled up a snowball as he walked closer to the window. It was fogged over and snow congregated over a foot high at the sill. Ice sickles festooned the roofline, dangling ominously from the gutter. He stopped ten feet shy of the house and threw at the window as hard as he could.

"Hey, Lewis," said Marco.

"Hey."

Marco spent seven minutes inside, adorning himself with the appropriate vesture. He appeared again on his stoop wearing a dark stocking cap, gray corduroy jeans, brown suede hiking boots with bright red laces, and a denim jacket that had an off-white lining and collar. He had grown a winter beard and his hair was well past his shoulders now. It winged under his cap and tickled at his neck in the light wind that blew the flurries sideways.

"How've you been, buddy?" he asked Lewis.

"My dad at work," Lewis said.

"Did he say it was alright for you to be here?" Lewis pulled his right leg out of the snow a little and then dropped it back down. "I've been thinking about coming by and trying to talk to him again," Marco continued. "What do you think of that idea?"

"I dunno. I think maybe he still don't want me coming here no more."

"Well, possible I can change his mind on that."

"Yeah. He still working all the time though. I was thinking maybe it's okay for me to just come by."

"And not ask him? I don't know, man. I mean, I'd love to have you around again, but I don't want to cause any trouble for you with your dad."

Lewis couldn't look him in the eye. He just stared at the coverlet of fresh white that sheathed the area where the lawn chairs once were.

"I think it's okay now," said Lewis.

They threw a few snowballs at each other and went inside. Marco made hot chocolate with marshmallows while Lewis watched a glitzy daytime program on the television.

Angel counted down the days until graduation, secretly wanting to make one of those colorful paper chains to mark them, as she did with Christmas when she was a child.

Marco suggested Denver or Aspen but Angel convinced him of Boulder. A family friend had attended college there and she remembered the photographs the girl had shown her. It looked clean and uncomplicated, yet exciting all at once: a new frontier. They both liked the idea of big skies, mountain ranges and room to move.

At first Marco had said it was best to tell Lewis everything. Angel was in a better position to anticipate how Lewis might take the news, having spent more time with him at school than Marco had since they began seeing each other. Phil, Angel's now ex-boyfriend, had made it a ritual to stop by McCluer almost daily, his appearances ranging from belligerence to what he considered courtship.

When Angel got in Phil's car one afternoon after school, Lewis looked on, devastated. Angel knew exactly where Lewis's heart was on the matter of Angel.

Angel was getting to Marco. She worked hard on him. The payoffs came in time and were more than enough to counter the boredom she felt for life in her hometown. Their first outing was to a pool hall in nearby Florissant. Angel picked Marco up in the morning and they drove through the slushy roads to the next town over. Marco had at one point been a regular in the poolroom. They shot a little here and there, breaking to drink forceless coffee and recount exaggerated tales of former glories. They hit the drive-through at a White Castle on their way back to Marco's and ate their lunch from the kitchen counter before making better memories for Angel on the waterbed.

Marco set an alarm and when it went off at 2:45 he went outside to warm the car for her. They kissed goodbye and Marco waited for Lewis to come up the road. When Lewis went home for the night Marco called Angel and twenty minutes later they were making waves on the bed again, neither of them aware that she was pregnant at the time.

Marco worked the combination on the safe and took out a thousand. He'd saved a lot of money in three years. The plan was to call Denny's nephew in Wentzville the day they hit the road. He could get word to Denny that the house was his when he got out. If it caught fire in the meantime, who gave a fuck?

Angel picked him up at noon, skipping out on her afternoon classes, and they took a drive out to St. Peters. Marco found a Chevelle on the lot and talked the man down to eight hundred on it. They followed each other back to Ferguson, stopping to walk the old brick roads along the Missouri River in downtown St. Charles.

Marco sprung his new car on Lewis that afternoon. He didn't share his plan to leave it for Lewis when Marco and Angel would head for Colorado in her Camaro early that summer. Marco and Lewis drove down to the Schnucks grocery store, a couple of miles away.

"How's school been?" asked Marco.

"It's alright."

"Any girls you like?"

"Nah. I talk to some but nobody I wanna be asking out or nothing like that. Not like Angel."

She had changed everything. Kids began talking to Lewis immediately after he was seen with Angel. She spread the word that he was a good guy and it became widely accepted as truth. There was still a distance between him and many of the students there, but they looked at him now, engaged him in brief, convivial conversations during classes, said hello when he passed by in the halls. It was the reason Lewis loved Angel.

Lewis and Marco pulled into the parking lot and Marco gave the kid his first driving lesson. Lewis was a natural. They went inside the store and Marco pulled from a list he had compiled with Angel earlier that day. Marco told Lewis to add whatever he liked.

"You ever play pool?" he asked.

"Nuh-uh," Lewis answered.

"There's a hall over in Florissant I like. I'll take you there tomorrow."

Twenty minutes later they pushed a cart full of bulging paper bags out to the Chevelle. Lewis couldn't wait to get back to Marco's place to mix up some strawberry milk.

"What's up, Marco?" asked Go Way as they walked the parking lot.

Go Way and two other guys were leaning on a Pacer parked a few spots ahead of Marco's car and they were drinking beers and smoking pot. Marco nodded and kept walking, opening the trunk as they reached the car, quickly loading in the groceries.

"I heard you're leaving us soon, Whitehead," said Go Way.

Lewis looked at Marco and Marco signaled for him to get in the car.

"Heard you been screwing some high school chick, too."

Lewis stopped, his hand on the handle of the door.

"Yeah, well, you heard wrong, Go Way," he said as he worked his way around to the driver's side door.

"Aw, we ain't friends no more, Marco? You don't wanna stick around and have a beer? Like friends," he said, throwing a can at Marco, hitting him in the neck. The two men behind Go Way got into position next to him. They weren't big but they were as lit as Go Way and likely to be as full of bravado just then.

Marco looked back at Lewis, his eyes growing wide, trying to convey to the boy to get in the damn car. Looking back he caught Go Way advancing. Go Way meant to shove him but Marco went into a crouch and charged back, picking him up from the waist and tossing him to the pavement. One of the others took a swing and landed a stinger against Marco's ear. Marco answered with an elbow to his face thrown backwards from in front of his chest. The other man danced around, no doubt nervous now, as he had cause to be. Marco kicked Go Way in the side of the head with his heavy boot and the other man finally found the courage to jump in. He grabbed Marco by the back and tried to pull him down. Marco drove backwards and dropped him on the trunk of the Chevelle, spinning around and throwing a wild succession of punches about the man's face. Go Way and his other friend clutched at Marco. Lewis barreled over and knocked at them all, doing just enough to throw them off balance. From there Marco stepped it up. By the time security made it over Go Way and his friends were a bloody state of affairs.

The security guard tried to stop them from getting into the Chevelle. Marco pushed him aside and instructed Lewis to get in the car. They pulled out of the lot but there was traffic getting onto the service road. Marco became visibly impatient and finally pulled into the oncoming side and spun his wheels, moving across the road and heading back toward his house. They made it another half mile before the cop car appeared in front of him. He lost control and the car slid through the wet road, colliding softly into an embankment that was completely covered in black and gray slush.

"I saw you play," said a cop with a giant red mustache and an unlucky horseshoe haircut. "My son went to McCluer same time as you. He was JV when you were pitching. You picked it clean at first, too. Swung the lumber like no kid I ever seen. Ever wonder which position you would have played, had you gone pro?"

Marco was obviously having a hard time concentrating on what the officer had to say. Lewis sat across the room, rocking back and forth, staring at him like he had never done before. Lewis was putting everything together now.

"Uh, yeah, I liked hitting too, so—" said Marco.

"National League then. Pitch and hit, like it's supposed to be."

"I'm sorry I drove out of there. I was just trying to protect the kid."

"I'd say you did a fine job of that," said the cop with pride and admiration in his voice.

"Yeah, well…"

"No reason to run off like that is all I mean. Those boys were down for the count," said the cop.

"It was self-defense."

"We've seen these louts a fair amount around here. Leslie, the bigger one, he's been picked up for just about everything stupid under the sun."

"Les-lie," Marco said. "*That's* his name."

"Security guard already had an eye on them and had called it in. He saw how it all went down."

"So can I go then?"

"Yeah, sure. The boy's got to wait for his dad to show. He's having a hard time getting out of work."

"He just lives down the road from me."

"Wish I could, Marco. The dad was all fired up about him being with you. Says he's not supposed to be. From the sound of it you may want to steer clear of this family for a while."

Marco thanked the officer and gave one last look over to Lewis as he headed for the front door of the precinct. Lewis shook his head and pouted with some anger behind it.

She grabbed at him. She punched at him. She screamed at him and the tears came hard and wild. Her words were primitive utterings: every time she tried to say his name the hardness of the consonants failed and the vowels rang out through the modest home. The door was partially open still but the screen door had shut behind her. Jerry's mom came out of her house with Jerry clutching at her blouse like a six-year old.

Angel dragged inch by inch. Her bottom scraped through the thick carpet and her feet dug into the arid blood. She reached back to open the door wide and jabbed at the metal handle on the screen door. She pushed her weight into it and fell backwards onto the porch, landing flat on her back with Marco between her legs as she screamed up at the new morning's crisp and bluing sky.

Skinny's wife ran over to help. Angel slapped at her as the woman tried in vain to pull Angel away from Marco's inanimate body. Neighbors made their way onto their lawns. More came, closer and closer, as the sirens stirred them from slumber or early morning communions.

Police milled about, asking questions of the residents. More official vehicles made clamorous voyage up the normally serene suburban road. Help was called in from near townships. Photographers took pictures inside the house. Men dusted for fingerprints. The safes were hoisted and carried out to a police van. Guns were tagged and bagged up and removed from the residence. A baseball bat—assumed to be the murder weapon for reasons of bloodstains and proximity—was handled carefully and put inside the trunk of a cruiser, along with several other items. Marco's body was put on a gurney, covered and placed in an ambulance after detectives gave their okay.

Two uniforms scoured the back yard and garage. They searched through the stacks, setting aside awards, photographs and personal documents. They pulled birth certificates, lien and mortgage information, letters and everything they could find to make clearer the picture of who exactly their deceased was beyond a mere name and address, and who might have had a connection to him.

Others moved through the master bedroom, finding nude polaroid photographs of various women—including Marco's mother—stashed under a dresser, presumably taken and put there by Denny years prior. They noted the broken locking device on the sliding window in the room, one officer speculating that the lock hadn't functioned properly for some time, his hypothesis dually noted in the police report.

Angel gained no composure over the hours that passed. A paramedic suggested that she be sedated, but she refused now knowing she was with child. Policemen took turns approaching her, each of them getting nowhere with their questions. The most anyone could gather was that she had come by on her way to school that morning and found her boyfriend's body on the living room floor. There was some debate over whether there was clear evidence of a struggle, as there was so little in the room to disturb. At first it seemed like a robbery, until they took a closer look and found no signs of forced entry, many valuables untouched and the safes not tampered with. Marco had been felled by a single blow to the head and died slowly on the floor in front of his couch. The police canvassed the neighborhood and asked for names or descriptions of possible suspects.

Lewis stayed in bed. The commotion couldn't be heard from his bedroom. Terrence had gone to work, well before Angel made her discovery that morning. Angel's parents were summoned to remove their daughter from the crime scene. Children were escorted down to bus stops or driven to grade schools, middle schools and high schools by panic-stricken parents.

Two officers eventually knocked on Weebie's door. No one knew the names of the renters. *They live down there. The blacks. Weebie's place.* The officers knocked again. One wrote a note on a small piece of paper from a pad and taped it to the front door.

Lewis stayed in bed.

CHAPTER NINE

Poor Little Girl

Los Angeles, CA, 2011

City buses are for the wretched. They are cheap transportation and they add to a healthier planet but you're going to see, smell, touch, hear and taste the worst we have to offer each other. Little Girl didn't take the bus. It was a rule. When the rule was broken it was always owed to electrical problems. Squatting next to the Triumph motorcycle she loved, Little Girl regretted her decision not to put in a battery eliminator system. She'd installed most of an original 1950's wiring harness, and now something somewhere was shorting out the system and draining her battery. She'd have to smell the worst we had to offer just to get back home.

There was a long, heavy chain slung like a sash across her narrow body, parting her breasts and making them pronounced. She took it off and wrapped it through the spokes of the back wheel. She pulled the ends of the chain together around the leg of a mailbox that was bolted to the sidewalk, and she closed a padlock on it. Pulling her phone from her pants pocket, she opened up the memo app and typed a note to remind her where the bike would hopefully still be later that day: Melrose and Hayworth.

She made her way to the bus stop and waited for the RTD. When it arrived she paid the fare and walked towards the back of the bus where she stood with a few others, as the seats were all taken. She was a sweating mess inside her leather jacket, jeans and riding boots. She held her open-face helmet in one hand and used the other to grip the pole in front of her as the bus began to jump and jive down Fairfax Avenue.

There were three people sitting directly in front of her and two of them were napping. The third person—a teenage girl from a Catholic school as her uniform announced—fidgeted in her seat. They were sitting in a row that ran parallel with the long walls of the bus. The girl made a face and then shielded her eyes with her hand and mouthed the words, "Oh my God." Little Girl shifted across the bus to get a look at what was troubling the teenager. Sandwiched between two large Mexican women in their golden years was a tall, thin white man. He was in his forties, balding and masturbating. The old woman sitting to his left looked out the window with a purpose. The immigrant to his right alternated between staring at the ceiling and the floor, quietly reciting the Our Father in her native language. The public masturbator had locked his gaze on the sophomore, seemingly oblivious to everyone else.

"Put it away," said Little Girl loudly.

The thin man peered at Little Girl just long enough to give his *I'm fucking annoyed* face and looked back at his young prey. Little Girl held out her helmet and pointed it at him as she walked deeper into the bus toward the back row. She came face to face with the man. The exhibitionist raised his ass a few inches off the seat, gyrating his penis at her.

"You like that, bitch?" he said, looking back and forth between her dark eyes and his pasty hand as he stroked away.

Little Girl drove her helmet into his testicles.

He screamed and frantically tried to grab at the helmet, but he was no match for Little Girl, who kept it firmly in place, pinning his dick to the hard molded plastic seat. He grabbed at her jacket and she slapped his ear with her left palm, just missing the praying woman. She hit his ear again and again, as he flailed his arms to ward off her blows, finally covering both ears with his hands. Little Girl swung fast and hard, delivering a stabbing blow to his throat. He struggled to breathe, then began to wheeze and cough.

A passenger behind her said, "Fuck, yeah!"

Little Girl jerked her helmet from the man's crotch and put it on the lap of the woman next to him, much to the woman's disgust. Little Girl then grabbed the thin man by the collar with both hands, yanking him onto the metal floor, where he landed face-first. Grabbing him by the back of the coat, she tried to pull him toward the back door, but he punched her weakly in the crotch.

"Jesus. Little help maybe?" she said to the other passengers.

A few people giggled and one said "damn," but no one volunteered until the Catholic girl stood up. She raised her hand as if offering an answer to a biology question in class, but immediately kicked him hard in his side with the bottom of her school-approved footwear, her hand still in the permission requested position.

Together, they dragged him down the aisle. The man seemed resigned to his fate and went limp. The bus driver watched in the rearview mirror as they reached the back door and Little Girl hit the button for the next stop. The man was crumpled on the exit steps, propped up against the doors.

"Door don't open if you leaning on it," yelled the bus driver.

Little Girl reached down and began to pull the flasher again but he leaned forward enough on his own for the doors to activate. Little Girl smiled seeing the opportunity this presented. She grabbed ahold of the pole with her left hand and pushed at his chest with her boot and all of her weight. He tumbled backwards onto the sidewalk. A teenaged boy stepped over him nonchalantly, as if it were a part of getting on every bus.

That is the way she imagined it could have gone. That is the way she imagined it should have gone. Someone needed to speak up. Someone needed to do something. But people rarely do something. It wasn't in her to be confrontational in this manner. It was once, or she believed in a past version of herself in which it was, but either way it lay dormant inside her. She had averted her eyes when she saw what he was doing, just as everyone else had. The schoolgirl had gotten off at the next stop, probably several blocks before her destination. Soon the back of the bus was nearly empty except for him. He continued to please himself, wearing a strangely distant and maniacal look on his face, his head tilted back as he now stared at no one. Everyone looked away. Everyone pretended as though it wasn't happening. Little Girl shook her head in disgust and made her way to the front of the bus, having seen the worst we have to offer.

Little Girl watched as the tourists made their way toward Venice Beach early that Sunday morning, the visitors having come upon the "Distinguished Gentleman's Ride" by chance. They waved and hollered at the riders who were dressed in their Sunday best, many with a classic style. A hundred-plus motorcycles rumbled, most of them elderly and venerable models: the high-pitched two strokes, Hondas, Suzukis and Yamahas; the sonorous roaring of the Moto Guzzis, Ducatis, Benellis, Harleys and Indians; the shot-sounds of Triumphs, Nortons, AJS's, BSAs, BMWs, Nimbuses and rarer models still.

Her phone rang just as Little Girl was about to kick-start her engine and join the ride. She dug the phone out of her pants and brought it closer to her face. She saw the caller ID she had assigned to the number long before. It read *NOPE*. She declined the call and shoved the phone into her pocket.

Little Girl was among the last riders to exit the meeting grounds. She didn't bother wearing a suit and tie or an ascot, as she couldn't pass for a gentleman on her worst day. She was small-framed and had long, pressed dark hair and anthracite eyes, with nearly all of her olive skin covered in colorful tattoos. Her features were decidedly feminine, in spite of what the uninitiated may have considered an effort to masculinize her looks. She wore what she typically wore when taking her 650 Thunderbird for a scoot: vintage leather jacket and jeans.

She'd retrieved her Triumph from the Fairfax district, rolling it with her friend, Biker Billy, into the back of his 1960 Ford pickup. She spent days completely rewiring the motorcycle. The bike would have been unrecognizable to the men that had originally crafted them a half century before. It was her first bobber, a bike she'd pieced together over the years, originally coming by it as a basket-case motor only. She used a later-model frame, removed the swing arm and installed a bolt-on rigid rear end, effectively lowering the bike to accommodate her smaller stature, and to look fucking cool. Beyond the unlogged hours she'd spent rebuilding the engine was an equally innumerable measure of time submitted to swap meets, EBAY, Craigslist and the obsessive perusal of dozens of bookmarked vintage Brit bike websites, seeking that perfectly worn, original Bates seat or structurally sound Wassel tank to complete her piece of functional art. She'd painted the tank and the chopped rear fender in the garage below her apartment, giving a chemical odor to the entire building for days. Every bolt had been polished and turned by her hands. She could look deeply into the powder-coated frame or the beads on the battery box she had welded from sheet metal and she could inspect the imperfections and know they were hers and hers alone.

Little Girl headed east and caught the day's first strong ray of sun off the gold, candied paint of the gas tank. With one hand working the throttle, she pulled her tinted welding goggles to her eyes from atop her helmet. She squeezed the clutch lever and toed the gear shifter with her right foot, weaving from the back of the pack toward a pre-war Harley Flathead that carried a sidecar with a Mastiff in a leather aviator's cap, the wind marking the dog with a communicable smile.

Riding down Santa Monica Boulevard, she spotted a Triumph Daytona sputtering a few lengths ahead. The rider was struggling to keep his composure as the bike lunged and lost power alternately. He put his hand on one of the carbs as though an adjustment could be made that way. She rode up next to him, advised him to pull over and hoped it wasn't an electrical issue.

"It's never done that before," said the young man.

"You mind?" asked Little Girl as she began to inspect the Amal Carburetors.

"Aw, thanks," he answered.

She kicked the bike over and gave it some gas.

"When's the last time you synched these carbs?" she asked him.

The young rider was a slight kid with strawberry blonde hair, blanched blue eyes, and the kind of bone structure you would surely remark on when describing him. He wasn't as young as he appeared, but he was convincingly outfitted to look like an established 1920's barkeep that day. The boy hesitated to answer Little Girl's question about his carburetors and then started to but laughed inelegantly instead. Little Girl grinned and walked behind the bike to where she had parked hers. She pulled a standard screwdriver from a shabby leather tool case that hung on the frame just behind the seat springs. With the bike still running she began to adjust the throttle and mixture screws, bringing the idle up and down, killing the engine at times and restarting it until she heard the sound she wanted.

"That should get you by for now. Bring it by my garage some day soon and I'll clean and adjust those carbs for you. Unless you do your own wrench," she said.

"No, obviously not. I mean, yeah, that'd be great."

"3000 Grayson Ave. Here in Venice. Easy, right? Weekdays. Not before 10:00 or after 7:00. K?"

"Yeah, thanks," he said.

"Happy to help. I'll let you go first and keep an eye on you for a bit," Little Girl said as she walked back to her bike. "Open it up a little."

The ride ended with a barbecue at a Motorcycle Boutique Store, a place that sold espresso, retro gear and overpriced tee shirts: a new fashion beginning to catch on in moneyed urban areas around the world. Little Girl had been to the inaugural ride, taking her 1974 Suzuki GT550 for the run last year. Running the Brit bike for that long of a stretch was much more difficult. She'd fallen in love with the make (the rat-a-tat-tat of the pipes alone had done her in) but she was a good enough mechanic by then to understand why the Japanese bikes had such a hand in killing the English manufacturer's sales. The boy wasn't the first customer she'd pulled from a vintage bike ride; she felt like an ambulance chaser at times.

"How's the Triumph holding up?" asked Indian Jim, known as such, not for his native bloodline, but for his brand loyalty to the first incarnation of Indian Motorcycles.

"Better than my ass," Little Girl stated.

"Yeah, these rigid frames will work your tailbone. Make you miss those shocks."

"You ever *own* a bike with shocks, Jim?" she asked.

"Hell no, Little Girl. I don't love myself enough for that kind of pampering."

She gave his white and gold beard a tug as though she were back on Santa's lap. The corners of his hairy mouth were stained orange from the recent meal.

"Remember, old man, it was you who got me into these ancient fucking sleds. I curse your name every morning it takes me ten minutes to get out of bed," said Little Girl.

Indian Jim supplied her a grin so big the yellow of his teeth made a rare entrance into daylight and he leaned in and nuzzled his colossal head next to hers.

"You give me a call anytime you need help getting out of that bed, little missy."

She grabbed his nipple through his t-shirt and gave it a light twist.

"When you giving up that dream, old man?" she asked.

"Three days after I die, Little Girl."

The young rider rode up at 10:00 AM the next Wednesday. Little Girl had hired Biker Billy to paint a Union Jack on the passage door to the garage, and there was a stencil-sprayed motorbike depicted in the middle of the British flag. Above the bike it read "3000." This was the closest Little Girl had come to settling on a name for her business.

The boy knocked softly.

"Hey," she said as she opened the door.

"Hey," he answered back.

She paid an extra $300 for the garage on top of the $1400 she ponied up every month for the one bedroom apartment above it. Her landlords lived up in Oregon and didn't know she'd converted the garage into her shop. Toward the back stood a waist-high table she'd constructed from an old door and below it was a ramp for rolling the bikes onto the homemade workbench. She'd welded a tire boot out of steel and bolted it to one end of the table to stabilize the motorcycles as she worked. Her formal education in the trade ranged from small engine theory classes at City College to Mig/Tig welding courses at a school of the arts. What she didn't learn in schools she'd picked up haunting small repair shops over the years, as well as the trial and error work she'd done on her own bikes and those of generous and reckless friends who were willing to risk catastrophic engine failure, all in the service of her incremental improvement.

There wasn't a square inch of bare wall or ceiling in the 15'x20' space. She'd spent nearly two years adorning the unpainted sheetrock with spare parts, punk rock posters, pin-up girl photos, and vintage tin and porcelain signs—most all of them motorcycle subject matter. She said that some days the predictability of the place nauseated her like the thought of a "Hang in There" kitten poster in some accountant's cubicle.

"Wow. Is that a '74 Commando?" the boy asked, spotting the Norton up on the table.

"'75. You see the shifter on the left side there? And the electric starter, of course. That's how you can tell," she said.

"Oh, yeah, of course," he answered.

She detested the smug, know-it-all-biker-delivery and an alarm went off in her whenever she heard herself give information in this way.

"It's hard to tell from year to year, though. So similar. Great bikes, right?" she offered enthusiastically.

"Aw, man," he said nodding.

"I feel stupid. I never got your name," said Little Girl.

"Oh—Henry."

She paused as her hand was reaching out for a delinquent formal shake and acknowledged the incidental humor with a wry smile.

"I'd been calling you *Boy* in my head since that day. You look younger than you are I'm sure. Everybody calls me Little Girl. Probably why I thought of you as Boy," she said.

"Yeah, I heard that from some of the guys on the ride. That's cool. And I'm glad you were thinking of me, Little Girl," he said with a flirty confidence she didn't expect.

He had said her name right, just as she had, and she liked that: Little Girl, with the emphasis on 'Little' so that that it didn't sound dirty, so it sounded like an Native American name, as if it were one word.

"I'll open up the big door and you can roll her in then," she said.

"Sounds good."

Little Girl rooted around in one of her toolbox drawers and grabbed the wrenches she needed. She placed a foam pad on the floor of the garage next to the bike, knelt down and began to remove the left side carburetor.

"Is it okay if I watch or should I take off?" he asked.

"Nah, stick around. Not sure how much you know about these Amals, but I'm happy to teach you a few things."

"Really? That'd be awesome," he said.

"It's good to know the basics."

"For sure. Most mechanics seem like they want to keep all that stuff a secret so you'll keep coming back, though."

"Oh, you'll be back, Henry. Trust me, this isn't the last problem this Triumph will give you," she said.

Little Girl saw Marvin walking in and she wished she'd thought to shut the doors.

"Little Girl," Marvin crowed in a froggy, gravelly tone. It startled Henry.

Marvin was a sixty-six year old Filipino, retired from something he never did say. Little Girl said she thought of him when that smug alarm went off: don't be like Marvin.

"Oh, Daytona 500," said Marvin. "Stock, too, except for those handlebars. You like those aftermarket bars, kid?"

Henry began to respond, obviously not realizing what everyone who had ever met Marvin knew: almost every question Marvin would ask would be rhetorical by default; Marvin rarely waited for answers.

"I like stock bars. You should get those. Little Girl, you got any stock bars 'round here?" Marvin said.

Marvin went straight to the back of the garage and began to search through a cubby full of handlebars.

"Don't mind him," Little Girl said to Henry in a hushed tone. "Marvin, this is Henry. Henry's just here for his carbs."

"Whatchu doing? Cleaning? You know the trick to synching, donchu?" asked Marvin.

"Yup. We're full of tricks around here," answered Little Girl with a smile as she looked at Henry.

"You should switch those out anyways. Give him new ones. You should use them concentric ones Amal make now. Premieres. Those new ones they make are passivated," Marvin stated with great excitement.

"No one knows what that means, Marvin. Even you," said Little Girl.

"You know, Little Girl. You know. Means they hold up longer," Marvin said.

"Marvin here is just waiting for me to cut him a check, Henry, put him on my payroll," Little Girl said.

"Heck yeah. I'm honorary mechanic around here. You need to honor me with some money, Little Girl," said Marvin.

Thomas walked up and stood just outside of the garage.

"Hey," said Thomas.

"Hey," answered Little Girl.

"Thomas. Come on in, man. How you been?" yelled Marvin.

"Good, Marvin. How 'bout you?" he asked, waving but remaining in the driveway.

"Aw, you know," answered Marvin in brief complaint.

Henry had been squatting next to Little Girl as she was pulling off the carbs. He turned to see Thomas, a well-formed man in his early thirties.

"Just wanted to say bye. Heading in to work," Thomas said.

"Where you work, Tom?" asked Marvin.

No one called Thomas "Tom" or "Tommy," and he hesitated in the way that some people do when someone shortens their name, as if it were so unfamiliar to them that it wouldn't register immediately: a passive-aggressive pause.

"Uh, Zerpa," answered Thomas.

"Oh, yeah?" said Marvin.

"You know it, Marvin?" asked Thomas.

"Oh, no. Sound cool though, man," Marvin answered.

"Yeah. Okay then," said Thomas looking directly at Henry. "I'm Thomas by the way."

"Hey. I'm Henry," he said as he waved a little.

"Hello, Henry," Thomas said, waving back. "Okay then. See you tonight, babe?" he said to Little Girl.

"Yup. Dinner at 8:00?" she said, as she continued to work.

"Sounds good," said Thomas.

"See you later, Tom," Marvin squawked.

Planning your masturbation schedule seemed a decidedly male enterprise. Little Girl looked up at the clock and calculated her time. She could fit in the minutes it required if she waited to call the client to let him know his Ironhead was properly timed. Harley Davidsons weren't normally one of her brands, but the rent was due that week and the customer a former coworker. She put the points cover back on and went through the motions the owner had shown her the night before when he dropped the bike off. She primed the carb with three easy, partial kicks before turning the key and pulling the choke on top of the S&S. She put her left knee on the solo seat and hovered over the kick-starter with her right foot. She came down on the kicker with all her weight but the resistance was too much to cycle down.

She tried again, fully committing her fall, and got about halfway down before the high compression of the rebuilt motor stopped her. On the third attempt, she was able to send the kick-starter through its full throw. The motor turned weakly and the S&S let out a puff of white smoke. Sucking in a breath, she pounced on the kicker again and it ratcheted through without any resistance and her knee hyper-extended.

"Jesus fucking Christ," she said in agony.

She called the client from her apartment above and told him the bike was ready. She put ice on her leg and popped four aspirin.

Almost anyone can kick start a Brit bike from a straddled position with ease. Even a 105-pound person could do it. Harleys are another proposition entirely.

She scrolled through the pictures on her phone to a photo of herself in Day of The Dead make up. She was looking for a good memory, something that might put her in the mood, something to jumpstart her libido, which currently had its needle nearing empty. Henry appeared in her thoughts and she broke into a pleasantly stunned smile. She slid her right hand down her pants. Her phone rang in her left. The caller ID read: *Absolutely Not*.

There was a café near the end of the block and Little Girl had heard enough good things about the place to endure the line that spanned from the counter to the entrance door. She scrutinized the packed house and the complete repetition of type there: bunch of fucking hipsters.

"Little Girl. Hey. How are you?" Henry said.

"Oh. Henry. How's it going, man?"

Henry had been tucked away in a seat near the window and had literally jumped up when he saw her standing in line. Little Girl caught this leap in her peripheral and it pleased her. She had begun to doubt that she would see Henry again and wondered if she had misread his interest in her.

"Good. Good. You? What brings you to Hollywood this morning?" asked Henry.

"House call on a buddy's bike. It won't make it to Venice. Do you live here?"

"Yeah, this block actually. It's really cool. I just moved here last winter. Plus my job is just around the corner."

"Where do you work?"

"The Bemusement Park," he said. "You know that place?"

"Yeah, it's some kind of natural science museum or local circus but with, like, I don't know…"

"Yeah, exactly," he said with a laugh. "You should come by some time. I could give you the tour."

"The tour?" she asked laughing. "Is it that big?"

"Well, no, not really. It's really just a couple of floors in an old building."

"Right on. How's the Triumph running?"

"Aw, great. Just great. Thanks again. You really dialed it in."

"I figured since I hadn't seen you back at the garage everything must be good," she said.

"I wanted to come by. I mean I know you have a boyfriend and all." Little Girl gave Henry a look that was a blend of confusion and amusement. "Thomas is your fella, right?" Henry asked.

"Fella. That's rad. No, he's not my fella. Thomas is the gay neighbor who acts like a protective boyfriend."

As Henry smiled widely, a cell phone rang from the skinny jeans pocket of a twenty-something man directly in front of them. The man answered the call and began talking loudly. Little Girl had recently read an article detailing the science behind the annoyance of hearing a one-way conversation. Henry continued to grin at her, even as he rolled his eyes in acknowledgement of the impoliteness of the man's behavior. The man's voice grew louder as they inched toward the front of the line. Little Girl gave Henry a can-you-believe-this-guy look. The conversation continued, even as the man placed his order. The barista pointed to a sign that read *No Cell Phones Please*. The man laughed and told the person on the other end about the sign. He nuzzled the phone between his chin and shoulder as he collected two coffees. He turned to see the disapproval on Little Girl's face.

"Oh, fuck you," he said to Henry and Little Girl. "No, not you," he spoke into the phone. "Talking to a couple of little bitches."

"Sir, you need to leave," said the barista. "Now."

He turned back to look at the counterperson.

"This place is full of little bitches, bro," he said to the person on the other end of the call as he pushed past Little Girl on his way to the exit.

"Wow," Little Girl said to Henry, wearing a stunned look on her face.

They sat together and watched as people drank hand-pressed coffee and ate thick pieces of toast with marmalade. They discussed what they agreed was a recent uptick in rude behavior by much of a formally civilized society. There had been an awkward moment at the counter where Henry had attempted to pay her bill. Little Girl refused and Henry accepted her decision, but not before explaining that he had been taught that a gentleman always offers.

CHAPTER TEN

It's a Little Girl

Before she was Little Girl she was Deborah. Deborah was the thirteen-year old who, with the help of the nice man from New Hope, MN, had convinced her mother to move to Minnesota for hockey.

The nice man hadn't seen Deborah play. They didn't actually scout the rest of the country for young talent. If she was promising he could not have spoken to it. He'd talked to her coach on the phone and heard some pleasant words and best-guess statistics. The nice man ran a camp, the camp took both girls and boys and the camp ran on money.

When the deposit was paid on the apartment, when the first day at the new school had been recorded in a journal, when the license plates had been switched from *Show-Me State* to *10,000 Lakes,* it became clear that Angel had been played by a thirteen year old girl.

Bill hadn't called as he said he would, and the glee in her daughter's eyes told the story. Angel had seen Deborah in victory before—in nearly every thing she'd attempted—but this was a sucker-punch betrayal.

"Deborah, come back here a minute," Angel instructed.

Elation carried Deborah down the corridor and by the time she made the kitchen it was obvious she was working hard to control the muscles in her face.

"What's up?" asked Deborah.

Angel looked up at her daughter from the table they'd scraped across the slatted wood floors of a rented moving truck just two weeks prior. Deborah was flush in a quizzical cast. They inspected each other.

Little Deborah had seen an ugly future only five months prior, and since that moment she had moved quickly to recoil from that course. It had been there, right in front of her, where Bill made his true nature known through little more than a simple and execrable look. Her mother, more lovely than ever and barely thirty years old, had excused herself to her kitchen where she would soon return with a homemade coffee cake. It was Bill's first evening in with his new girlfriend and her child. Deborah was uncomfortable with her mother's exit and kept her eyes trained on the television as she sat on the floor directly in front of it. She heard the swishing of fabric on the couch above her. The screen went dark for a few seconds and she saw Bill's reflection in the TV. She turned to look back at him and received his grin. His hand moved a measure of inches on his inner thigh between his knee and his groin. As he moved it further she turned back and noticed how her ripped-neck tee shirt slightly exposed the smallness of her cleavage from above. She felt his socked foot brush lightly against her shoulder blade. She sprung from her place on the floor and walked into the kitchen. Her mother seemed a completely new person to her as she beamed over a moderately successful confection.

"Told you I could do this. Who says I couldn't be a good wife?" she whispered as she walked by Deborah, nudging her with an elbow as she carried the dessert into the living room.

A good wife hadn't previously been in Angel's lexicon. She had spent a dozen years balancing a career, a strong desire to be an attentive mother and sporadic yearnings for sexual gratification, the latter of which she exorcised on the rare evening out. Her parents were always available to watch Deborah, who had been born and raised until age five under their roof before Angel found work in the personnel department of a gross polluter on the river. Angel was an indulgent young mother but careful to watch for the signs that she may be raising a selfish and entitled only-child, something she grew to openly admit about herself as she had aged. She set out to raise the most well-rounded person the world had ever known. She settled for unwavering support in whatever piqued Deborah's interest, no matter how fleeting the enthusiasm or at what personal sacrifice. Deborah made her path clear at an early age— with skateboards, sports and racing of all species. Angel told her she was her father's daughter through and through. She made it a point to pass along the tales of Marco's greatness to her kid. She even went as far as to enlist her uncle, Coach Romaine, in this effort, as he was the only other member of her family that had known Marco.

The planning and execution of what would be their exit from St. Louis had consumed Deborah after that night on the couch with pervy Bill. She was fresh off a regional championship in which she earned the MVP award for the tournament in spite of being kicked out of two games, one for a hip check and the other for fighting. At that point she was good enough to attain those honors with a half-hearted effort, her interest in the sport waning as it was. In the early 1990's St. Louis wasn't known for its hockey programs at any level, so the first deceptive conversations with her mother were aimed at expressing her dissatisfaction with the competition and seasonally limited training. Deborah noticed her words being met with a fractured attention span and she came to know this as the first indication of a woman in love.

"Mom. Mom. Are you there, Mom?" Deborah asked as she waved her hands in front of Angel's face across a record aisle at Vintage Vinyl.

"What? Sorry, Deb. What did you say?"

"I said I'm really bummed the hockey season's over. I feel like I don't know what to do with myself."

"You'll manage," Angel said curtly as she flipped through the LPs. "What am I even looking for? I don't know what you like any more. It changes so quickly at your age."

"Some things change. Not everything. Some things are more important, Mom," she said.

"Okay, let me ask you this then. Do you think you'll feel so strongly about Mudhoney in a year?" she said, pointing at her daughter's concert tee shirt.

"Fuck yeah," she answered.

Angel shot her a disapproving, motherly look: the one that she typically reserved for public cursing or the passing of gas in her presence.

"But I do know there's a difference between what band I like right now and what decisions might affect, like, my whole life," Deborah said with the dramatic verse of a newly-minted teenage girl.

"Deborah, seriously? I mean I know you like to play hockey but really?"

"You don't know. I could win a scholarship. We may need that. You don't know," stated Deborah.

"Worry more about not flunking the 8th grade."

"That's my other point. Kids don't do well in school if they're not happy."

"Since when are you not happy? All of the sudden you hate it here and you think we're just going to pack our things and go live in an igloo up in Canada?"

"Minnesota. The camp is in Minnesota. Not Canada," said Deborah.

"Same thing."

With the seed planted in her head, Bill was now faced with a slightly distant Angel, one who was unwilling to talk about their future together. Deborah never said an unkind word about Bill. She had entered into it with a chess player's calculated approach, while Bill was pounding the board, trying to jump everything in his way.

Angel gawked at Bill's head as he chewed a triple-decker burger with an open mouth. His head hair was stiff, kinky and disarming to the touch. She took in her surroundings. Bill had insisted on Dairy Queen again, in spite of Angel's earlier request that they spend the evening at a well-reviewed beer garden restaurant downtown, as early spring had birthed a splendid night.

"Too far," he had said upon his arrival at her apartment in Bellefontaine Neighbors. "It's right here, they got outdoor seats too and it's cheap."

Bill was thirty-six but over-exposure to the summer sun and a soda-based diet made him appear a man in his mid forties. He worked as a framer for a disreputable contractor. He had no kids of his own and had yet to marry. Angel found him attractive the moment they met, and had spent much of the time since tending to the mystery of why that was.

"You gotta be careful with her at that age. That's when they start lyin,'" Bill said to Angel.

Angel placed both of her hands on the red metal table and leaned in a little, looking him in his eyes.

"I'm not saying she's a liar," Bill continued. "I'm just saying that's when you can't trust 'em. Not like when they're little."

Angel had sat at this exact table many times before, mostly after a game of some kind. Deborah's first choice for any celebratory meal had always been a Brazier burger, highly salted fries and a chocolate shake. They'd sit outside together at the round tables with the fixed canopy umbrellas and they'd talk about Deborah. When Deborah was young she would ramble on and on about what she did in her soccer match or what some boy at school thought was funny but she thought was retarded. She would giggle or blow the wrapper off the straw with her nose or roll her tongue over her lips so it looked like her mouth was thicker and Angel would laugh loudly and Deborah would roar even louder and with a surprisingly deep rasp.

Bill said he'd move to Minnesota in the winter. He said his work slowed then and it would be the perfect time. He said he'd call every day. By the time the postal service began forwarding Angel's mail from Bellefontaine Neighbors to New Hope, Minnesota, Bill had stopped calling. Deborah had scored her latest victory, but it came at a price.

There was a network among Little Girl's biker friends. Everyone was always reaching out, across the country at times, looking for that rare or mint bike for a deal. Some bikes were barn finds, long ago abandoned to some cobwebbed corner: the kind of motorcycle that often required a master mechanic's knowledge to put back on the road for any kind of profit. Others just needed a new battery, spark plugs, maybe a quick clean of the carbs and some fresh gas through the tank. The Internet changed the likelihood of getting a bargain. Grandsons and granddaughters simply punched in their dead grandfather's make and model and the computer told them what an old, rusty, oily bike was currently fetching.

Biker Billy, one of Little Girl's better friends in the community, told her about a BSA Rocket 3 up near Bakersfield. He couldn't afford to buy it, even for a quick flip, so he suggested she head up that way and grab it before someone else caught wind of it. The original owner of the 1969 Rocket 3—the "speed triple"—had passed away a few years back. His stepdaughter was charged with clearing the home and garage so her aging mother could sell the house and enter assisted living. The stepdaughter worked retail with a girl that was good friends with Biker Billy's sister. She told them it ran when it was put away nearly twenty years prior. The bike was her stepdad's pride and joy and no one was allowed to ride or touch it. It was parked under a cover in the garage.

Little Girl took a Greyhound bus to Bakersfield. Based on the story she was confident she could revive the bike and ride it home. She packed the necessary tools to get it back on the road, as well as a charged battery and a few sets of plugs. When she arrived she paid the stepdaughter $900 in cash which was $100 less than they had agreed upon on the phone when the woman still thought she could locate the title. It took her less than forty minutes to have the bike scooting up and down the roads of rural Weedpatch, California.

It was a hundred mile run back to LA. She spent the day riding the bike around the area, adjusting it when needed and learning to trust and understand the motorcycle. She prepared to leave her hotel at sun-up, thinking it best for the machine to avoid the mid day heat. Thirty-seven miles into the ride home the bike lost all power. She pulled over on Interstate 5 and got as far from the freeway as the small shoulder would allow. She tinkered with the BSA as cars buzzed by. The wind from the automobiles blew her back and she had to reposition the bike so the kickstand was on the other side, keeping it upright when the semi-trucks came through.

Her nerves were racked and she was getting nowhere with the repairs. Whatever had gone wrong couldn't be sussed out in those conditions. She needed to get it home, get it on the table, and get it apart. She needed different wrenches. She needed specs from the Internet. She needed help.

It was hot enough that her jacket had been peeled off as soon as the bike had conked out. She wore a white wife-beater tank top with The Misfits skull logo on the front. She'd never hitchhiked in her life. It was a rule, much like her policy on city buses.

A semi-truck was making dust of the gravel for a long stretch of road directly behind her. She thought it might come in too fast so she backed up until she hit what remained of a wire fence that was badly leaning. The truck driver pulled in with half his tires touching the dead, brittle grass. He stepped out from the driver's side and, although he was on the north side of middle aged and a portly man, he quickly ran around the front of the truck.

"Golllll-ly," he said. "That wind's fixin' to take your skinny butt flying."

They loaded up the bike into the back of his truck. The entire trailer was empty. They strapped the Rocket to the wall of the truck and when the traffic was slow for a moment they made a run for the cab.

"Maybe just the nearest stop," she said as she was now inside.

"You said you were heading to LA. I'll get you there. Not to worry."

They drove in silence for a few miles and the trucker clicked his turn signal to get off the highway.

"Need gas," he said.

She had been staring out of her window and hadn't seen a sign indicating that this exit had a station or anything else for that matter. It was desolate – the very definition of desolate as far as she knew it. She straightened herself in her seat and looked over at the door handle.

"I know a place. Just over here. Diesel only. For truckers," he said as he slowed to merge onto an empty road.

When he began to turn off onto an even smaller and more remote path she grabbed the handle. Before she could pull it he reached over and grabbed her by her hair.

"Uh-uh," he said as he guided the truck down the road at a slow pace.

She threw a punch across her body and grazed his nose. He was fat but strong. He kept his big hand in her hair and pushed her head to the dash. Her forehead hit and she bounced back, immediately dazed and woozy. He laughed and yanked her toward him. She flopped down, head to knees.

Parked on the side of the road, she pulled herself back up and began to lean toward the door again. He grabbed her by the back of her thin neck and pinched until her eyes went blind for a few seconds. He turned her head to face him and when she could focus she saw that he now held a gun in his left hand, pointed only inches from her face.

"Take those fucking clothes off," he said.

She saw that he was shaking slightly.

"Please," she said.

He laughed and moved the .50 caliber Desert Eagle up and down, directing her to take her top off.

"I'm gonna do it, man, just get that fucking gun off me. You're going to shoot me."

"He grabbed at her shirt and pulled until the top half of her bra was exposed.

"Put it down," she yelled. "I don't want to die."

He pushed her shoulder and she hit the door, which had been locked since she got into the truck. He set the gun on the dash in front of him and pulled a hunting knife from the sleeve in his door.

"Don't plan on killing ya, bitch. But I'll slit your fucking throat if you don't get those clothes off," he said.

She watched as his eyes darted between her own and the rest of her body. He touched himself for a minute and then took the knife and slid it between her skin and shirt. He grabbed her with his other hand and tried to stabilize her enough to cut the strap at the shoulder. She grabbed at his curly salt and pepper hair, trying in vain to move him from her body. He bit her neck and pulled back so he could finish the cut without slitting his own throat.

She began to cry a little and he slapped her face. He took his free hand and grabbed her crotch as hard as she had ever been touched. She screamed and he fumbled with his left hand on the buttons of her jeans.

"Fucking wait," she cried. "Just let me do it."

He smiled and leaned back in his seat. He opened his pants and pulled his penis through the zipper. She began to slowly unbutton her jeans as he touched himself.

"Usually they put up more of a fight. You must want it. Fucking whore. Ya ever seen one this nice?" he said as he looked down and stared at his erect cock.

She swiftly grabbed his dick and squeezed as hard as she could. He let out a yelp and his hand opened around the knife's handle as he moved it toward her, fumbling the blade, dropping it to his feet. She lunged across him and grabbed the gun from the dash. She hit him in the temple with the side of the handgun and quickly moved as far back toward her door as she could. She pointed the firearm at him.

"Let me out," she screamed.

He rubbed his head. He reached down for the knife and clutched it tightly again, bringing it up to show her but not moving any closer.

"It ain't loaded, you stupid cunt," he said.

She pulled back on the trigger and the explosion pushed her into the passenger's window. His shoulder was immediately red and wet. He had dropped the knife again with the impact of the bullet into his upper arm. It landed on his foot, cutting the top of his big toe. He clutched his gunshot wound. She saw the head of his now limp dick sticking out of his jeans. He leaned toward her and reached for the gun with his blood-soaked hand. She pointed the gun at his chest with two hands this time and braced herself for the impact. She now knew what large caliber weapons felt like when they kicked. She shot the gun into him until the magazine was empty. She couldn't hear anything.

The cab of the rig, the whole world: just a blurry, ringing, bloody mess. She threw the gun at his corpse and laughed wildly at him.

CHAPTER ELEVEN

It's a Big Boy

You think much about death? That's a silly question; everybody thinks more than enough about death. I could've talked about it though, maybe with Al. We really should've been talking about it. His words have always been so calming to me. If anyone could take the dread out of an eternity of nothingness, it'd be Al.

Until that day in 1981, I had lived with my mother in the same house on the Italian Hill for my entire life. From the time I was in my late teens, girls were presented to me by friends of our large family, or my dead father's former co-workers, or fellow parishioners of our local Catholic house of worship, and by scores of dark-haired neighbors: men and women who hoped to control their daughter's fate. This felt ridiculous—the wrong kind of old-fashioned as far as my tastes were concerned—but it was always the 1940's on what everyone in the area either called Dago Hill or simply The Hill. When you dated an Italian-American girl, you knew the deal. Respect is the first multisyllabic word we learned as toddlers, and in our family's native tongue it's got three syllables so it's that much more difficult to say. In all my time in that neighborhood I only once went all the way with an Italian girl, when I was just out of high school. After I called it off a few predictable months into it, she left for Connecticut; apparently I had disgraced her honor by being uncertain of how the rest of my life was going to pan out, and which lucky girl would be joining me for the next seventy-odd thrilling years.

The women in my family rode me about finding a wife. The men followed the lead of the women. Females really are the stronger-willed, more resolute of the genders after all. It became a tormenting chorus of idiocy, and that idiocy became to me what just *had* to be a lie. It was like Shakespeare in Little Italy: an olive-skinned mob protesting too much. I privately mocked them all, knowing that every day in which I failed to take action—failed to take a wife—was another victory against the oppression of a big idea about the biggest of things, an idea that was not my own and simply did not feel right.

Nana was the lone exception. She knew not to prod me. She was always so happy in her role as my de facto spouse. My grandmother had been a widow since the day I was born, her husband suffering a massive coronary as his eldest daughter fought eleven hours to bring his first grandchild into the world. They said I was the light that led the way through the gloom of those days. The superstitious among my family believed that my grandfather's spirit in some way inhabited me. But Nana knew her husband didn't live on in the body of her grandson. She said she enjoyed my company far, far more.

I had finally mustered the nerve to leave and condemn my mother to live out her days alone as a perpetual mourner. I tried to remain a good son, visiting her at least once a year from San Francisco until she died at the age of seventy-four, just as her mother had four months after I had originally left The Hill.

My Ma, my Nana—it's not like I didn't see what drew them to thinking that there's something that comes after this life, especially those lives that are eighty kinds of struggle to every one damn smile. When I was a kid Nana would tell me how we would all meet in Heaven, the whole family and all these people that came before us, people just like us. She was big on that point, excluding a lot of God's children in her otherwise sweeping portrait of the Promised Land. But I could see what that idea did for her. It gave me awful nightmares and had me thinking the dead watched my every move on earth, yet it seemed to work for my grandmother. Later on, when I started to believe it was all a bunch of horseshit, I remember feeling like I was lied to, duped by the ones I trusted the most. "I'll show them," I thought. And then it dawned on me: if I'm right I won't even get the opportunity, and if they're right I'll go straight to hell before they can say I told you so. Sometimes I wish I *were* wrong, just so they could get what they wanted. It's a nice enough thought to hold I suppose.

I just didn't get why it was *these* people who were coming back to visit me. I mean why couldn't it have been my family? I could not remember the last time I had a dream about my dad. Maybe that was it. Maybe I just couldn't remember enough about the details to conjure them up anymore, if I was even the one that was in charge of this madness.

I wondered how Croon would have reacted had I just confronted him. You're dead, Roger. Been dead a long time now. So let's talk about THAT. Maybe I should have looked into it and seen if any of these others had passed on. I wonder what would have happened if I had went to the pink woman's house unannounced, prior to her showing up at the café that day. What would she have looked like standing at her door? Would she have aged or would this specter that had come back to haunt me with her unoriginal catch phrases be waiting to greet me? The dog should have been dead at the very least.

I remember being forty and thinking, well, the first ten years were kind of a blur and I'm guessing the last ten will be in their own sad way. Any way you looked at it, I was seeing about half of it gone back then, if I'm even that lucky. There I was, now sixty-plus and staring down what would likely be my last good decade, and I had to drag these fucking people along with me.

With over thirty years in my line of work, I hadn't met many corpses. On a bus from St. Louis to Champagne, Illinois, in my late teens I fell asleep and missed my stop, waking up just before Chicago. I sat on a bench for what would be less than an hour's wait for the next bus back, and it was in that hour that an indigent man quietly died next to me. That was the last lifeless body I had seen, the one that had slumped onto me, the simple death I should have missed.

Standing over this dead body, I performed the duty upon which I was called to do.

"That's her," I spoke evenly.

When I excused myself to use the bathroom, a room that felt as cold and drained of life as the morgue itself, I vomited and wept.

It was Ramona that had shifted the culture of my office, or gave it some I should admit. She charged the place with talks of dead singers and writers and their impact on the world. Our friendship and eventual romance was forged in these exchanges. It was through some dated-cultural-icon osmosis that Lindsay came to share our love for these artists from other eras. At times in Madison, her memories of the three of us dancing to Big Band records into the night were enough to move her to put pen to paper, reminding me in those letters how big her love for me would always be.

I gathered myself, exited the restroom and made my way down the hall and out into the chill of the Pacifica night, considering all the while whether to tell Ramona that her only child was gone.

"Uncle Beer Belly."

Ramona threw her hands up in the air as she sat on her recliner. Her niece, Mindy, had opened the door and escorted me into the living room. Mindy and I had spoken on the phone and met briefly at Lindsay's service that morning. Mindy paid her respects at the funeral home and returned to look after Ramona, while I drove to the cemetery with the sparse procession.

"Uncle Beer Belly's here. Hey, Uncle Beer Belly," said Ramona.

"I don't know where she gets these names," Mindy muttered to me as we entered the room.

"Hi, Ro. How you doing, sweetie?" I asked.

Ramona waved her hand to shush me away and went back to watching TV.

"Joe and I are going to sit outside, Aunt Ramona," said Mindy. "You just yell if you need us. We'll keep the screen door open."

Ramona didn't acknowledge Mindy as we walked through the kitchen and out onto a ground-level deck. Mindy closed the sliding glass door most of the way and pulled the screen shut.

She was a large woman, just as nearly every woman in their family but Ramona was. Her nasally accent was close to the one had I left behind in St. Louis. When she spoke I relinquished my investigator's clout and accepted her honest nature in the way that cult followers submit to a leader.

"Thank you for coming, Joe. I know it might not seem like it but Ramona is glad you're here."

"I haven't seen her in a while. Maybe longer than I'd thought. She wasn't like this the last time I was over."

"I spoke with Lindsay just a few days before," she said to me. "Oh, God."

I pulled a deck chair out from a table and helped Mindy into it. I took a seat near her and allowed her to gather herself.

"Thank you, Joe. I'm still in shock. She was my baby cousin. I just can't wrap my mind around it, and now with her mom the way she's been."

"I talked to her doctor yesterday," I said. "Told me her memory is in and out. Said it was getting worse. Ramona still doesn't know about Lindsay?"

"We've talked with the physician about it. I'm not sure what to do. I'm not sure what to do about any of this. I just keep praying for guidance. And my mom is much older than Ramona, and she's in assisted living back home already. We hardly have what it takes for that. It's just too much all at once."

"The doc said they'd put her in a home, but I don't know. You've been with her. Seems to me like she deserves to stay in her own place for as long as she can if it doesn't do her any harm. She loves it here."

"If I could stay I would. In a heartbeat. I just have so much…"

She broke down, trembling and weeping so much that I pulled the stranger in. I hugged her and said, "there, there" as people do. I realized then what needed doing, knowing it would only be a matter of time before Ramona would have to move to a place that was better equipped to handle her. It seemed important that she have her hours spent in the comfort of her home on the water, even as she was losing her ability to recognize the life she had built there.

The child ran imbalanced, pin-balling from wall to chair to bed and to wall again. He bullied his way through the clothes in my closet and emerged with a wooden cigar box, pumping it up and down and up and down again like a mad monkey, spraying the contents onto the floor. As I gathered my artifacts and placed them on the nightstand, the kid chucked the box over his head and stumbled like a drunk into the living room, caroming off a small table that was home to a photo of my Nana as a young bride, and only for a moment more.

In over four decades of adult life I had not gained any experience with toddlers to speak of. What I did know about young children always relieved me of tendencies toward that particular life's regret.

"Jackson. Come to daddy," said Al.

"How old is that boy, Al?" I asked.

"A year now, and already walking. Can you believe it?"

I could not.

When I'd find myself unsure of date and time I would consult the paper and confirm that the day was always as I suspected, or damn close to it. I'd know it was May of 2012. Accounting for time—lost time—well, that was another enterprise entirely.

"Are you okay, Joe? I don't mean to pry but we haven't seen much of you lately and you seem...I don't know..."

"I think it's just Ramona and Lindsay," I said to Al.

"Of course. But..." he seemed to choose his words carefully here, "I just wonder if this is the wisest way to go. With Ramona I mean. For both of you right now."

"I get what you're saying. I can't let her end up in one of those places, though. Not yet. I think she's better off in her natural environs. You know what I mean?"

"I do. I really do. And you're a wonderful friend to take this step for her. I just worry about you losing income. Business is still just so-so?"

"I'm fine. I could use a break from that racket, to tell you the truth."

Al studied me and I knew he felt helpless. I wasn't confiding in him the way I always had before. That hurt us both.

"Well," he said, "we could always set up your phone with a message service so you could check in and not lose out on jobs. Or finally get you a cell phone. If you decide you need the work, or just—"

"I'll be in and out of here daily. We've got a girl coming in to help with Ramona. I know you're worried, Al. I just need a rest right now. I need to do this. I need to help."

Mindy would control the money, what little there was. Lindsay's last will and testament called for Mindy to be the trustee of both Lindsay and Ramona's savings, set up that way recently after Lindsay had taken legal control over her mother's estate and affairs. Mindy would send a check every month and I would see to it that groceries were bought, doctor visits were kept, prescriptions were filled and Paloma was paid.

Paloma came by recommendation–a hell of a good housekeeper. She'd worked for Martha's Cleaning Crew, the company that handled much of the north side of town. A woman suggested Paloma to us at the funeral, after she learned that Paloma had a nursing background in her native Colombia.

Ramona thought Paloma was Uncle Beer Belly's sister. She called her Val and poorly pretended to like her, making faces behind her back and running her down to me at every chance.

"Your sister is on drugs. I didn't want to be the one to say it but she gets them from the painters. That's why they never come inside. They just hover around out there, pretending to work and feeding her drugs. I imagine for sex."

I removed most of Lindsay's belongings from her bedroom over the first few nights there, as Ramona slept. I loaded everything into the garage out back and installed a padlock. Ramona never went to the garage. I set Lindsay's bed and personal items up just as they had been in her room. At the end of each night I would sit on the edge of her bed and cry.

Paloma's English wasn't bad. She tended to call everyone "he," men and women, including herself. "He go to pharmacy now. He get Epson Salt for Ramona's feet." I was too polite to correct her but at the same time I worried that she would be angry with me for not teaching her earlier if anyone ever did.

It was a house of calm in those first days. I feared Ramona would have trouble adjusting and that at any moment she would ask for her daughter. Ramona seemed to take it all in stride, as if things had always been this way. Uncle Beer Belly lived in the room next to hers and his druggie sister often came to visit.

The disease had begun to ravage Ramona's appearance. She had lived her entire adult life looking much younger than she actually was. Now she seemed a woman in her mid-seventies. The doctors had preached the benefits of what they termed *environment enrichment*, suggesting that a stimulating setting increased her chances of maintaining her ability to perform basic functions. Paloma and I spent many hours encouraging Ramona to engage us in any way she liked. We played simple games, watched Public Television, learned much about South America from Paloma, and took Ramona on walks down the beach.

It was over a week in and I started to believe that my visitors were again in the past, precisely where they belonged. I limited my exploration of the outside world and noticed fewer oddities when I did leave the home. Paloma made a good cup of coffee and I had plenty of time to read the paper, often out loud over breakfast with the women as my semi-captive audience.

"Is there somewhere we might talk in private?" asked a neatly coifed man as he stepped onto the driveway.

I had been lost in the meditative act of watering the plants and could not say from where the man had appeared.

"I'm sorry. I don't remember you," I said.

"We've had no cause to meet," he answered.

The man was handsome, broad-shouldered, with a large nose that was framed by a square jaw, and he displayed his wealth with every word, mannerism and inch of his frame. I held up a finger, signaling for the stranger to wait there on the drive, as I peered through the screen door to confirm that Ramona was indeed asleep in her chair. I waved to the man to follow me as I opened the gate and entered further into the property until we came to the padlocked garage. I took out my key, worked the lock, opened the door, and led the man in.

He stood at a shabby white dresser and began studying the contents that were neatly organized on top. He at first spoke without turning around to face me.

"I've a delicate matter that requires strict confidence and an ethically ambiguous participant."

"Well now, I always provide the first part but I'm going to have to take offense to the latter," I said.

He turned to look me in the eyes and spoke. "The man has yet to be born that is offended by a large sum of money, Mr. Iocca."

"I'm not sure where you're getting your information from, sir, but I'm just a PI, and a semi-retired one at that."

"I imagine you might easily graduate to a complete retirement if you were to fulfill my needs, Mr. Iocca."

"Hey, listen here, you've come around, unannounced, and not so much as told me your name—"

"I will not. If you've any skill you'll learn everything about me on your own. The important things about me, that is. Who I am, where I come from, what I want. If you're any good."

"So you expect me to take whatever you consider to be a big amount of cash to do something illegal obviously and—"

The man turned and put his finger up just as I had on the lawn.

"I would appraise you as a man who reads people and situations quickly and astutely, Mr. Iocca. So with that in mind I will now leave you in this place to consider my offer."

The man made his way briskly past and out the garage door.

"You haven't even *made* an offer, pal!"

He continued down the drive and out the gate. When he turned right at the end of the driveway I kicked off my shoes and ran light-footed down the length of the house, stopping at the neighbor's bush and peering through the branches to see the man walking up the block. I watched him until he turned onto the first crossroad.

Where I had spent nights sobbing, where the stranger had made his overtures the day before, where nearly all of the possessions remained of a girl I had privately considered my own daughter, I now had sex with Ramona's nurse.

Paloma was in her late thirties. She was a widow, had three children at home a few blocks away, and was paid twelve dollars an hour in cash. One day she confided in me that, "he had a things for older mens." She also said something along the lines of how she admired me for the selflessness of my actions where Ramona was concerned.

She had agreed to a dual position as Ramona's nurse and housekeeper. I'll admit that I enjoyed observing the many tasks she approached with a slightly bended waist. When she caught me staring that day, much to my surprise she smiled, took my hand and walked me to the garage as Ramona snored on the recliner.

I enjoyed her mix of English and Spanish words as I took her from behind. After a few minutes she made the switch to Spanish exclusively and her arms began to flail next to her in short spurts. Her face was now supporting her body entirely. She grabbed at the burlap sack over the window and yanked out the tacks that held it at the header. Light came into the dark room from the backyard and the clear vision of her quaking cheeks did me in. She turned her head in the pillow and I saw how happy she was. We panted together like Malamutes and I pictured our life together for a brief moment. I kissed her moist cheek and looked out to see the pack of Huns cheering the event.

They were out there: jesters, Neanderthals, the Chinese that built the railroads, the slaves who constructed the Pyramids, astronauts, the artists of the French Salons, street gang heavies, spry women that moved through the air like hornets. I'd sit on the couch, maybe for weeks, months—I'm not sure. I'd sit and look out the living room window and I'd watch them. They wanted me to see them. So I saw them. They were everywhere.

Ramona would look at me and nod to the lawn with the slight smile of a psychopath, as if to communicate, "Yeah, you see them too, don't you?" Paloma would grin from the kitchen or behind the recliner and sometimes grab her breasts and shake them at me a little. It turned out all she wanted from me was occasional lovemaking.

It all finally became too much for me to handle. I headed for downtown Pacifica. I made my way through scores of strange humanity. Natives donned war paint and danced menacingly. People touched the air they breathed and screens appeared, telling them where to find cafes, the library and restrooms. Topless, elastic bodied women passed by me as men in colonial garb and wigs seemed not to notice them. The whole skyline renewed itself every thirty seconds and the advertisements alternated between anxiety medicines with names like *Apoplectic* and *Ambivalence*, and scented dog shit bags. I saw groups of men building shelters from grass, branches and whatever other natural materials they could source on the lawn of a municipal building. Blacksmiths with huge, curly black mustaches forged their metals in the middle of an intersection. Small girls walked and giggled and worked their phones furiously with tiny fingers. There were Inuits drawing plans for a new society in the dirt, making do without the snow. Even the Mongols simply let the others be. It was maniacal and peaceful all at once. We had finally achieved a harmonic, utopian civilization. Unfortunately it was likely only in my heavily burdened and compromised mind.

I returned to the house and went straight for the car. I drove back to San Francisco, taking 19th Avenue, passing by the State University and a busy mall. I inspected the crowds on the sidewalks as I waited at long lights. I couldn't determine if these young people were from the future or of the day.

I made my way through Golden Gate Park and entered the Richmond District. I passed my café and saw that it had been renamed *The Has Bean*. I wondered how long I had been down in Pacifica.

I turned the corner from Fulton onto 29th Avenue and saw a line of familiar people waiting outside my door, a queue that stretched down my stairs and onto the sidewalk.

They came at me like children to an ice cream truck. "Are you Joe Iocca? Are you Joe?" Sanguine was there again and so was the pink woman. "Are you Joe, " she asked. "Where have you been?"

I pushed past them and made my way up the stairs. I opened the gate, kicked backwards like a donkey and caught a big Samoan. They continued to yell for me, some saying, "Help me," while others only my name. I opened the front door and walked directly to the bedroom. I fell to the bed but the babel of the crowd still terrorized my ears. I propped myself up and slid my legs over the side. I stood and rammed my way through old clothes in the closet, my head buried in Pendleton sweaters, Penguin shirts and the Sears line of winter coats, my ass presenting itself to the mob that now gathered behind me.

One fucker pulled me out. He grabbed at me by the belt and yanked me so hard that my wallet fell out of my pocket. I didn't even recognize him. He looked like a hobo, straight from hopping freights. He could have been an aged version of someone I had once helped, or someone I had forgotten, or he may have been a character from a movie

I saw when I was a kid. I couldn't say. They screamed at me and their faces morphed, some of them turning from one ex-client to another, and then back again. Some were cheering as they watched the man going through my pocketbook. "Get our money back," said one. "He's a fraud," said another. I had four dollars in cash on me. He took out my credit card and said, "Joe Iocca," as he read my name. "Yeah, that's him," said a client. "Fuck you, Joe Iocca," said the one with my card in hand. He grabbed a wedge from an antique set of golf clubs that I kept in my room for no good reason; I'm no golfer. He hit me on the shoulder but I didn't feel a thing. I grabbed the club and yanked it right out of his yellow fingers. I stood up quickly and began swinging. I clocked him good several times. When the others saw my Arnold Palmer rage they began to scatter and I chased them down the hall. I hit Sanguine with a hard one but it didn't seem to faze him. He was probably too hopped on goofballs to feel a thing. He made it to the door ahead of the pink woman. She turned back to look at me, to judge me. "Get the fuck out of my head," I screamed, before falling to me knees.

CHAPTER TWELVE

Rebel Deb

The police had asked Little Girl her name. She said they should call her Deborah. One officer, a female, had put her hand on Little Girl's shoulder and asked, "Can I get you anything, Debbie?" Little Girl requested black coffee and not to be called Debbie. She'd had many names in three decades; Debbie was one she'd moved two thousand miles to mercifully surrender.

Thomas, her protective gay neighbor, couldn't be reached by phone. He would have had to have borrowed a car and driven for over an hour to the station, something Little Girl had never seen him do and wasn't even sure he was licensed or capable to perform. She wanted to keep word of this incident from the people in her scene, so she couldn't call Indian Jim, Biker Billy or any of the Sweaty Betties, the slightly official name of her all-female riding club. Then she thought of Henry.

Little Girl sat next to the policewoman as the officer dialed. Little Girl wore a softball jersey with the Lebec Police Department insignia across the back along with the name of the team's cleanup hitter. The shirt nearly covered the bloodstains that were caked into her favorite pair of Levis. The officer looked over Henry's business card and punched in each number. After confirming that she was speaking to Henry Blue, the officer began to fill him in on the reason behind the call. Little Girl had been in a daze and even considered it part of her defense somehow that she maintained the look of someone who was still in shock, like a kid at the school nurse's office holding her stomach to illustrate the discomfort that was all just a hoax. When she heard the officer repeat her given name for the third time she touched the woman's forearm gently and leaned in.

"Little Girl," she said.

The officer looked confused and put her hand over the mouthpiece.

"Ma'am?" asked the policewoman.

"Little Girl. He calls me Little Girl."

The officer uncovered the phone and spoke the words as if she'd been given a secret password, hoping that it would unlock some good fortune.

"Yes, she's fine, all things considered," said the officer to Henry. "We'll release her soon. She gave us your contact information, asked that we call you. Are you able to head up this way and see to it that she gets home safely?"

Henry told the officer he would leave immediately and then asked if Little Girl needed anything. Little Girl shook her head no and the officer thanked Henry and told him they would see him soon. A corpulent sergeant with an amber mustache approached the desk, palming a football.

"I've read your statement, ma'am, and, as I understand you've been informed, we've no reason to keep you. The gun was registered in his name. Everything seems pretty obvious. We're still trying to contact the deceased's next of kin, but that shouldn't concern you. It's clear you acted in self-defense. He had a record, some history with violence where women are concerned. You may want to have a lawyer look into why this animal was employed with this trucking company. That's between us and the pigskin here, of course, but with the book we've got on him I'm having a hard time understanding why this individual was paid to drive our highways, looking for victims like yourself, ma'am."

Little Girl had been called a victim once before, many years prior. It didn't sit well with her. She didn't feel like a victim at that moment. She felt like a hero. She had done the world a favor. She didn't need the driver's personal history or criminal record to tell her as much.

"What about my bike?" she asked the sergeant.

He looked down at the woman officer and creased his eyes.

"Her motorcycle, sir," said the officer. "She'd broken down on the side of the freeway when—"

"Oh, yeah, it's in the trailer, right?" he asked Little Girl.

"Yeah," she said.

"Afraid the truck will go to evidence today. May be some time before it's signed off on. We'll give you a call when it's free and clear."

Henry drove his pickup down through the grapevine back toward LA. The winds were heavy, as they always are there, and Little Girl looked out the window and considered herself relieved in a way that she no longer had to negotiate those strong gusts that would throw her off her line, toss her into the next lane if she didn't fight back hard enough.

"Was it a problem getting out of work?" she asked.

"No, of course not. Don't worry about that, Lil."

"I like that you call me Lil, Henry," she said.

"Good. I'm glad to hear that. I'd hoped it wasn't too forward of me."

"Where are you from exactly, Henry? Somewhere they teach manners but no accent. Colorado maybe."

"Close. Kansas actually," he said.

"That's funny. I'm from Missouri. Right next door to you. But Colorado never felt close to me. Colorado felt a world away," she said.

"Are you alright, Lil?"

"Yes, Henry," she said softly. "I'm still alright."

"Sorry, I don't want to keep pestering you. I guess I'm just in shock. And angry."

"This is you angry?"

"I'm just so sorry this happened to you."

"Nothing happened to me. I did what I had to. I need you to not treat me like something terrible just happened to me. Can you do that?"

"Sure, of course. I understand," he said.

"You don't have to lie to me and tell me you understand. I could say something stupid like, 'shit happens' or, 'it is what it is' and you'd get my general meaning. How I don't give a shit about that piece of human garbage. How I'm glad he's dead. Glad I got to be the one to kill him in fact. I'm sorry if that scares you."

"No. I'm sure that's a natural way to feel about it right now."

"I'm not traumatized, man. And if you still know me a year from now, ask me how differently I feel about it then."

Henry smiled.

"What?" she asked.

"Nothing," he said.

She knew he was thinking about the two of them a year from the day when he had rushed to her aid, before he had ever touched her, before they had even kissed.

She was wrenching on a Yamaha RD, learning more about two stroke engines, when the call came in. Little Girl still hadn't listened to any of the messages she'd received in those past few weeks. She had begun to feel poorly about ignoring her innocent grandmother as part of her larger plan to avoid her mother and grandfather. She looked at the phone as it again read "Absolutely Not." She put down the Allen key and accepted the call.

"What?"

"Jesus, Deborah, there you are."

"Yeah?"

"We've been trying to reach you for weeks."

"I know," said Little Girl.

"You can't do this to me," said Angel. "It's not fair."

"Did someone die?" asked Little Girl.

"And what if someone has? You'll have missed the funeral by now, you know."

"Is Bill dead?" she asked.

"Go to hell, Deborah."

"Why are you calling?"

"They're letting him out."

"Who?"

"Your father's killer."

"Okay," she said.

"Okay?"

"Good," she said again.

"You don't even care, do you?"

"Do I plan my life around preparing for the next parole board meeting? No, I don't. So I guess you care more than me then. He's been in jail for over thirty years for something he probably didn't even do."

"I'm not going through this again with you, Deborah. I know you do this to get back at me. I thought you should know your father's murderer would be walking the streets in a matter of days now. That's all. Great talking to you, sweetheart," she said just before hanging up.

"Fuck you," said Little Girl too late to be heard by her mother.

Henry walked up to the open garage door just as she had yelled into the phone.

"Everything okay, Lil?"

"Jesus, Henry, is that always going to be our thing? You're going to ask me if I'm okay, over and over, until I can't stand the sound of your voice?"

"Well, I'm sorry, but when I hear you screaming epithets into your phone—" he said.

"Epithets?" she said with a slight laugh. "The way you talk, man. I'll give you that."

"May I please come in?" he asked.

"Seriously, Henry, we're in California now. No one is that polite. Get in here."

He entered the garage and cupped his hands together and shook them slightly as he spoke.

"I wanted to ask if you'd like to have dinner with me tonight."

"Sure, Henry. Sure."

LA nights, specifically those warm evenings enjoyed in the outdoor sections of restaurants, always reminded Little Girl of the beer gardens back home in St. Louis. She sat with Henry and watched as people walked the beach path next to their table. There was no anticipating the kind of person you might see in Los Angeles. For all the stereotypes of bleach blondes, augmented breasts and men who said the word "dude" twice in every sentence, LA was home to all walks of life. There were tourists everywhere and transplants from across the country, like Henry and Little Girl. People brought their culture, their food and their way of life from around the world. Little Girl and Henry ate flavorful Shawarmas, talked and looked out at the Pacific Ocean on Venice Beach.

"You must come down here a lot," he said.

"When I first moved here we used to drink on the beach at night. Cops would usually find us and we'd make a run for it. Especially when someone got the bright idea to do a bonfire."

"I used to go to Redondo and Hermosa when I first came out here," said Henry. "Mostly I stick around Hollywood now."

"Was there a girl?" she asked.

"Yeah. We met skiing in Colorado actually. I then made the brilliant decision to drop out of Kansas State a few months later to be near her."

"And that lasted…?"

"About six weeks."

"Ouch. Poor Henry. Bet your folks give you a hard time."

"No, I'm pretty lucky, I guess. They never tell me what to do or how to live my life. Just happy-if-I'm-happy kind of parenting."

"Lucky for sure," she said.

"What about yours?"

"My dad died just before I was born. My mother raised me pretty much on her own. She got married when I was sixteen to some shit-bag. I split a year later to come out here."

"How did your dad die? If it's okay to ask?"

"Dude, yeah," she said while chewing. "Obviously I never knew the man. He was killed. Supposedly by a neighbor."

"Supposedly?"

"I don't know. It's weird. The guy is getting out, apparently any day now. My mom's always been convinced he did it. She went to high school with the guy's son and they were all friends I guess. I saw him once at a parole hearing. My mother dragged me there as a prop. Like, 'Look at what this monster did. My poor little girl lost her daddy before she ever got a chance to meet him.' Except that my dad was a drug dealer and there was a shitload of dudes who probably wanted him dead. But this guy was black and had threatened him in front of the neighbors over something with his kid. So the white police decided the only black suspect was good enough for them. Least that's what I think. I dunno. I wasn't there."

"Wow," he said. "So maybe this guy spent decades in prison and he didn't even do it?"

"Yeah. Awful, right? When I was sixteen I asked my grandfather to look into it. He hired a PI and there seemed to be a lot of red flags. I fucked up and told my mom what we were doing in the middle of some stupid fight. She got my grandpa to call it off and that was that. I was pretty pissed at both of them. I can't understand how they could let this guy sit in jail if there was even a chance...," Little Girl dropped her fork onto her plate and shook her head side to side. "You know what, this isn't first-date conversation. Let's just move on to hopes and dreams."

They ate their Mediterranean meal and drank a bottle of wine between them. People strolled next to their table, with only a short, iron fence keeping folks from bumping into them. As Henry let it be known that he had enrolled at USC that fall, now that his residency was kicking in, and that he was interested in law, possibly criminal, an obese young woman walked by dragging a four-year-old child by his wrist.

"Come on goddammit," the woman said, as she pulled hard at her son's arm. "I'm not gonna tell you again."

The kid broke free of his mother's grip and sat down on the pavement just in front of Little Girl and Henry. Henry looked uncomfortable and began to assay the rest of the restaurant. The boy cried loudly as Little Girl looked on. The woman came back and stood over her son.

"Get the fuck up right now—hear me?" she said to him.

The kid crossed his arms in defiance and closed his eyes tightly.

"I said get up," she yelled close to Little Girl's ear.

The lady grabbed the child by the elbow and yanked him so hard that he came off the ground. She lost her grip and he fell back on his ass. He sobbed harder.

"Fucking cunt," said Little Girl as she stood. "Don't treat him like that."

The fat woman turned and yelled at Little Girl, moving her neck back and forth as she spoke.

"What the hell you say to me, bitch? Don't you tell me how to talk to my child."

"You're not talking to him, you're abusing him, trailer trash," said Little Girl as she leaned over the railing and pointed her finger toward the boy.

"Who you calling trash, you fuckin' tattooed slut?" she said.

"Hey now, lady-" said Henry.

"Blow me, faggot," she quickly answered back. She grabbed her child again and lifted him up to his feet. "Get up, boy. Not standing here listening to the likes of these two tell me how to handle my own damn kid."

Little Girl grabbed at the woman's giant forearm and squeezed until she loosened her grip on the child. Using the arm to leverage herself, Little Girl jumped over the barrier and now stood between the boy and his mother. The child wailed.

The woman pushed at Little Girl who went easily backwards and bowled the child over. Little Girl struggled to get up without further hurting the boy. She managed to get back to her feet and took a run at the woman, but this was an immovable object. The woman boxed Little Girl's ears and twisted her tit while shoving her stumpy finger up Little Girl's nostril. She fought like a Mexican wrestler. Henry ran to get the manager. The woman punched Little Girl in the stomach and pushed her backwards again. The child was on all fours and Little Girl fell over him. She got up, with less concern for the kid this time, and came right back at the woman. Little Girl was punching her on her multiple chins just as the policeman rode up on his beach cruiser bicycle.

"There was a recent thing up in Lebec?" said the cop as he spoke from his desk with Little Girl and Henry.

"That was self-defense, sir," said Henry. "She was nearly raped at gunpoint. How do you even know about that?"

"What does that have to do with anything?" asked Little Girl.

"Maybe nothing," the cop responded while studying her.

"This woman was physically abusing her child," she said.

"We're talking to witnesses right now," said the cop. "We'll know soon enough if what you say is true."

"It is," said Henry. "I was a witness. I've told you exactly what happened. The lady was pummeling her."

"No she wasn't," said Little Girl to Henry.

"She really was, Lil."

"Oh, how would you know? You ran away," she said.

"To get help," said Henry. "I could still see you, though."

"What, *you* couldn't help?"

"I don't hit girls," he said. "That's a rule, right?" he asked the cop.

"You don't restrain them either?" said Little Girl to Henry.

"I'm not sure I could have," he said. "You saw her, officer? Ginormous."

"Well, you've obviously got a pony in this race, son," said the officer. "So we can't take your word for it alone. We'll see what the other patrons have to say and take it from there. The woman has already said she'd like to press charges. I've got an officer who witnessed you assault the woman, ma'am."

"She pushed me first," said Little Girl. "Right into her own kid. You need to get child protective services or whatever down here and take that boy away from her. No one deserves a mom like that. Mothers are supposed to watch out for their kids, supposed to take care of them and keep them out of harm's fucking way."

Angel had gotten word from a girlfriend back home in Missouri that Bill had started seeing someone shortly after she and Deborah had left for the small town outside of Minneapolis. She was a white-hot combination of totally inconsolable and completely infuriated for several weeks before the morning she signed Deborah up for hockey camp.

Coach Wayne Ranier, the man who ran the camp, had played several seasons in the American Hockey League and was even called up for a cup of coffee, as they say, with the Blackhawks near the end of a forgettable season for Chicago. He was an enforcer, taking more penalties than shots on goal by a wide margin. He was from Western Canada and had married a Minnesota girl, staying on in New Hope after their divorce. He shared custody of Keith, his fifteen-year old son, seeing him on the weekends and at his summer camps.

Wayne was a chisel-featured, strapping man with a build and skin tone similar to Marco's. He reminded Angel of Marco, in fact, and she found herself flirting that first day as she filled out the final paperwork in his office.

"Treat her like a boy. She prefers it," she told Coach Ranier as if Deborah wasn't sitting in the chair next to hers.

"We don't body check, of course, and we discourage any heavy contact. I heard you like the physical game," he said to Deborah.

"Yeah, I can dish and take," she said as she smacked away on chewing gum. "You don't have to worry if things get chippy out there on the ice."

"You and I are going to get along well, Little Debbie," he told her. "You remind me of my son."

"How old is your boy?" asked Angel.

"Just turned fifteen. He's a good kid. I think. He's been testing me lately. His mom and I split a while back. That probably plays a part, eh? Same for you?"

"Her father passed before she was born. It's just us. I'm single, I mean," she said.

"Sorry to hear that," he said to Angel and then paused to smile at her before clarifying the comment. "About your dad, Debbie," he said.

"It's cool," said Deborah.

"Not about you being single," he said to Angel.

The adults laughed together for a moment and Deborah smirked and shook her head at the two of them before loudly popping a bubble from her gum.

It didn't bother Deborah that her mother was soon dating the camp instructor. She didn't see the potential for preferential treatment as a bad thing, particularly considering that she was one of only three girls at the camp. The other females were two years older and veterans of the program. They were there to prepare themselves for college-level hockey with the hopes of one day representing their country in World Championship competition, which had always been dominated by Canada. Deborah stretched the truth with these girls and stated that she shared their aspirations. As a result of her little white lie she soon felt like a little sister for the first time in her life.

Playing with the boys made the sport fun again and, at the same time, far more challenging. She skated fast but not nearly as fleetly as any boy over the age of ten there. She enjoyed the camaraderie that quickly developed. The only kid she didn't feel an immediate bond with was Keith, her coach's son. Keith was in high school so their paths didn't cross when she began her studies in the fall. When Angel and Coach Ranier began spending more time together, including time at Angel's apartment, Deborah was pleased to see her summer instructor as often as she did.

By the following summer camp Angel and Wayne were together every day. Angel came straight from work each afternoon to catch the end of the long day of drills, which typically culminated in scrimmages. Keith had put off skating in his father's camp at the beginning of that summer, and it was only through weeks of riding him that his father was able to convince him to rejoin mid-session.

Keith's quick temper was gaining a reputation on the ice. He was developing into a thickly built young man, taking after his father in that regard. In those first days back to camp, Keith's father had to whistle the play dead often to pull his son off of skaters that were significantly smaller. During an all-boys scrimmage, Deborah asked an older kid if she could take his place on his line, and he jumped at the chance not to be hip-checked into the boards by Keith. Coach Ranier didn't notice that she had taken the ice.

As she followed the play as the "third man in," just as her coach had always preached to his forwards, Keith lined her up just past the blue line. He skated a direct route toward her and crosschecked her into the end boards, lifting his feet off the ice as he came in, driving her hard into the wall. He had hit her squarely in the numbers and she hadn't seen it coming. As she lay on the ice, not moving, everyone in the rink came to her aid, including her mother.

The moment she came to and began to stretch her body, Wayne skated hard and fast from the assembled group, finding his son who was exiting through the door on the opposite side of the ice. He reached him just in time to pull him down by the jersey, snapping his head onto the cold surface. The boy got up and skated as if drunk, falling to one knee, attempting to regain his composure and falling onto his back again. Coach Ranier screamed at his son.

"What the fuck are you thinking hitting her like that? You know better, goddammit," he said.

Keith removed his helmet and looked up at his father.

"I should…I need…we're a hospital," he said.

Within minutes the ambulance arrived and they loaded both Deborah and Keith into the back of the van. Their parents rode together to the emergency room, where the police questioned Wayne for twenty minutes about what exactly had happened to his boy. Eventually Keith could tolerate the symptoms of his concussion well enough to poorly explain how he had fallen during a pick-up game, and that the accounts they were given regarding his father were inaccurate. Keith and Deborah were released with headaches and painkillers. Neither of them ever played hockey again.

The morning that Angel and Wayne let Deborah know they were engaged, Deborah's first thoughts were of Keith. It had been over a year since the incident and she had managed to go without seeing him even once. They ran in very different crowds: Deborah with her grunge friends, Keith now focused entirely on baseball. Angel and Wayne thought it best not to force their reconciliation. They hoped Keith would exit his phase of unpredictable rage and they could address it down the line. But Deborah was starting high school and would soon pass Keith in the halls.

"This is awkward for all of us, I know," started Wayne over dinner that evening. "Keith would like to finally apologize for his behavior on the ice that day to you, honey."

Keith looked up from his plate of Fettuccine long enough to say he was sorry for what had happened and that he hoped they could move past it. Deborah said it wasn't a big deal and they should all just get over it. Her mother let out a laugh of relief and they went back to eating their pasta. Deborah noticed that Keith's eyes darted back and forth between his food and her chest.

"Well," said Angel, "obviously Keith is going to stay with us on the weekends and maybe next summer, so you two will be acting like siblings before you know it."

Angel and Wayne found a four-bedroom townhouse near a small lake. They told the kids that the spare room would double as an office and guestroom but Deborah knew they were planning on trying for another kid. She didn't know how to feel about Keith or the prospect of living with him for forty-eight hours every week, but there was something about him that interested her. He was moody in a prosaic way and wore polo shirts, and yet she began to realize she was attracted to him.

Still, when the weekends came they largely ignored each other. The house was split into two levels and their bedrooms were on the lower portion, while Angel and Wayne slept in one of the two rooms on the top floor. The living room was just outside of Keith's bedroom and when Deborah stayed up late one Saturday night watching music videos with a girlfriend, Keith came out of his room in nothing but his underwear.

"Can you turn that down and lower your voices, Deborah? I've got a game in the morning," he said.

"Yeah, sure," she said.

When he turned to walk back to his room, her girlfriend hit her with the back of her hand, slapping her in the thigh.

"He's hot," she whispered to Deborah.

"You think?"

The underwear parade officially began that night. From that day forward, every time Angel and Wayne retired to the upstairs, the downstairs became well traversed with half naked teenagers. Their tone hadn't changed with each other—it was still very much removed—but now while they passed as near-strangers there was clearly intent behind their choice of limited attire. It went on for months and it became something Deborah looked forward to.

Late one Friday night, Deborah emerged from her room wearing an oversized Green River tee shirt that she had cut the sleeves off of. Just before walking out of her bedroom she inspected herself in a full-length mirror. The shirt nearly covered her panty line but left the sides of her breasts mostly in view. She walked out and saw Keith on the couch with his hand down his boxers. Keith looked up very briefly, likely long enough to see the skin of her left breast as she walked past him and into the kitchen. She turned the faucet on and poured a glass of water. She stood over the sink, looking into the living room as she drank. The back of both the couch and Keith's head faced her and she could see that he was watching a soft-core porn movie on cable. She finished her water slowly and then walked toward her room. She turned back to look over her shoulder just before she reached the hallway, only for a moment and only slightly. Keith's hands were now at his side and his erection stretched his underwear.

"You should do something with Keith this weekend. Maybe go see a movie," said Angel as they strolled through a skywalk in downtown Minneapolis. "I feel like you two aren't making an effort to get to know each other at all."

"Leave it alone, Mom," said Deborah.

"I don't know what you're feeling, hon. I never had a stepbrother or had to deal with my one of my parents getting remarried."

"You weren't married to my dad," she said.

"That monster took that chance from me."

"It's no big deal, Mom. He's seventeen. He'll leave for college soon enough. Wayne says he's practically already got a baseball scholarship somewhere back east. I don't need a brother, Mom. I never asked you for one, did I?"

"Just try. I know you're very different people but I think he's come a long way from that day at practice. His mother's a piece of work. I know she runs us down to him. That's what Wayne tells me."

"You'd probably do the same thing in her shoes," said Deborah.

"Hey-"

"You're right, mom. We are very different, Keith and I. We're civil to each other, though. Don't push it."

Deborah took the bus home from school almost every day. She had a friend—one of the girls she'd originally met in camp and who was now a senior—and Deborah would occasionally get a lift with her. She loved those days. Deborah didn't care for the school bus. She was a year away from driving and Wayne had already promised to give her lessons on the weekends. Wayne had bought Keith his Ford F150 for his sixteenth birthday and Deborah was hoping he'd do the same for her when the time came.

Keith pulled up as Deborah was leaving the school.

"You want a ride home? It's Friday so…" he said.

Deborah looked in the truck and spoke through the open passenger's window.

"Your dad been bugging you, too?" she asked.

"Your mom actually."

They drove through town and Keith said he needed to stop at a liquor store. She remained in the truck and could see him talking to another kid that she recognized from school. The boy was working behind the counter. After a few minutes Keith came out and was holding a brown bag from the cardboard handle of a six-pack of bottled beer.

"You want one?" he offered.

"Nah. My mom would know immediately."

"Suit yourself," he said as he popped the cap and took a swig before starting the truck.

"How'd you get beer anyway?"

"That guy back there is my catcher. His dad owns the place."

"Aren't you worried about getting a DUI?"

"Nope. I'm a star in this town. They celebrate athletes like me. I can do whatever I want," he said as he turned to look her over.

They drove for a few minutes and as they were nearing the house she told him to take a lap around the lake. She reached in the bag to grab a beer, and she struggled with the cap.

"Here, give it to me," he said.

He took out a lighter and popped the bottle cap off. He handed it back to her and then reached across her body to open the glove compartment. He pulled out a pack of cigarettes, turned back the flip top and looked inside. He found a joint and popped it to the top of the pack and then into his mouth. He lit it.

"Dude," she said looking outside of the truck.

"Dude," he said as he inhaled.

"I didn't think jocks smoked pot," she said.

"Well, now you know."

"Now I know."

He stuck the joint in her face.

"Go ahead," he said.

"No fucking way, " she answered.

"You've never smoked dope?"

"Dude, I've never even had a beer before today," she answered.

"Well, look at you, Rebel Deb."

A boy from her class asked her to go to the school dance that weekend. He had always been nice to her in Algebra and she thought of him as someone who had the potential to become cool, probably around his second year of college. Every time she wore a concert tee he'd inquire about the band, wondering if they were any good, as if she'd wear the shirt if they were not. He showed up wearing an R.E.M. shirt one day and she thought it was sweet that he was at least trying.

The kid suggested his dad could drive them and she instructed him to meet her there instead. She got a lift with a friend and was having a surprisingly good time. The boy seemed to gain confidence with every dance and witty comment or joke. He kissed her as they slow-danced, something she expected would happen when she finally agreed to take the floor for a romantic number.

They walked out arm-in-arm. Keith and two of his friends came toward them and Keith bumped into the boy as they passed.

"Watch where you're going, faggot," said Keith.

They kept walking and Deborah felt the boy's confidence dip again to previous levels. His dad pulled into the parking lot and Deborah said hello and took him up on his offer for a ride home.

She had never considered "going steady" with anyone. She wasn't sexually active and didn't feel any pressure to become so as she roamed the halls with her new boyfriend. They went to the mall together, saw some movies and hung out with a group of guys and girls strikingly similar to him: naïve and ready to be pushed into alternative cool. Deborah turned the group on to what she called *real music*, not the crap they force-fed you on the popular radio channels, but the stuff you'd find late at night on the college stations. Once, they all trekked into Minneapolis to go to an art opening at her suggestion. She was now spending most of her weekends with her new steady guy, coming home late and going directly to bed. She no longer took strolls to the kitchen in her underpants.

One Friday in early spring she made her way out the school's front door. Keith was waiting in his truck and offered her a ride home. She got in and he said he was going to make another pit stop at the liquor store. She was less impressed with him now and practically counted the days until he left for college. She thought it would be amusing to make a paper chain and remove a link every day until he was gone. He came out of the store with his bag and sat in the car staring straight ahead.

"Well, what are we waiting for?"

"Steve," he said.

"Who?"

"The catcher," he said without looking at her.

Steve the catcher walked out of the front door with a bag of his own. He opened the passenger's door and slid into Deborah, shoving her into the middle.

"My old man's gonna be so pissed," said Steve.

"You get the retard to watch the shop?" asked Keith.

"Yeah," laughed the boy. "He don't even know how to run the register. Just push a broom. I'm so fucked," he said, laughing.

"What are we doing, Keith?" asked Deborah. "I need to get home."

"Why?"

"Because."

"Well that's not a good enough reason," said Steve, always laughing as he spoke.

"Take me home, Keith," said Deborah.

"Relax, Rebel Deb," said Keith. "You got any weed, bro?"

Steve pulled out a pipe from his pant's pocket.

They drove for a while, filling the cab of the truck with smoke. Deborah became light-headed from the contact high that she couldn't escape, particularly when one of the boys purposely blew smoke directly into her face. They pulled into the empty parking lot of Wayne's camp. Keith stared long at the building with a vacillation of anger and disgust on his face, as if the building was insulting him. Steve grabbed a can of beer from his bag, took out a pocketknife, poked a hole into the can and popped the top, shot-gunning the entire beer into his mouth within seconds. Deborah was leaning back in her seat, trying in vain to remain clearheaded. Steve pulled out another beer. He looked at Keith as Deborah glanced back and forth between the two of them. Quickly, Keith grabbed at her cheeks, forcing her mouth open as Steve popped the top on the can and hit it with the knife. Beer poured over Deborah's face and into her mouth.

A few months later, when she testified in juvenile court, the defense lawyer asked her to describe what she wore those nights walking between her bedroom and the kitchen.

CHAPTER THIRTEEN

A Blue Chair

I awoke in a blue chair. It had a loose cushion on the seat and another tied to the back–both blue– and there were wide wooden arms, also blue. My back was killing me and my shoulder was throbbing.

It was the middle of the night and the mystery room was dim, lit only by what few rays sprayed through the small window in the thick door and crept under the two inch clearance at its bottom. Ramona's face was in shadow, but the whites of her eyes were framed in fluorescence and shone with the disaffected gaze of koi swimming a foot deep in murky pond waters. She stared at me in perfect silence from what seemed to be a hospital bed. I feared for my life without sound reason.

"What the hell have you done, Joe?" she said in even cadence.

"Where are we, Ramona?" I said, my voice breaking.

"What a failure you are."

I tilted my head like a chastised dog caught licking himself again. Her lucidity was chilling. Ramona seemed suddenly more aware of me–of who I truly was–than she'd ever been in all our years together. Her languid eyelids were owed, not to the ravages of her disease, but to an intense, clear and cold contempt.

"I'm not sure what you mean, Ro," I said softly.

"Don't play stupid, Joe," she said.

"Why are you attacking me?"

"Poor Joe. Fuck you," she continued without inflection. "Poor, poor Joe. As if you never had a choice in anything."

"Jesus, Ro. Take it easy. I've been through a lot lately."

"Oh, have you? Have you, Joe? Well, fuck you. We've all been through a lot lately. *Lately* is all the goddamn time."

"Please stop."

"What kind of detective can't handle confrontation? Here, I know, let's play a game. I'll ask what kind of a detective cannot, and then I'll fill in the blank, and when the answer isn't Joe fucking Iocca, you get to speak. Okay? Here we go. What kind of detective thinks reading a few books will make him God's goddamn gift to gumshoes? Joe. Fucking. Iocca. See how this works? What kind of detective skips college, spends thirteen years bricklaying and then opens a P.I. agency in a city he's a stranger to–

and before he is fucking licensed even? Joe fucking Iocca, that's who."

"Ramona, stop, please."

"What kind of de-tec-tive," she said, a thousand accusations articulated with each syllable, "figures it out as he goes? Joe fucking Iocca. What kind of detective fucks over four out of five clients? Joe Iocca. And what kind of detective refuses all clues when colleagues impart a bit of sound advice or offer a little constructive goddamn criticism? You. Only you, Joe. Only detective Joe Iocca can't see his own bloody fingerprints all over the knife. Can't figure out what's best for him. What's good for him. What will make him what he claims to be and maybe, just maybe even make him happy."

"Enough already. Enough. This is *my* pain. *My* pain. I'm not the reason you're suffering. Just because I marched to the beat of–"

"A drunken child banging a broken drum."

"Because I went about things the way I did."

"The wrong way," she said with a jury foreman's sterile deliverance.

"My God, Ramona. What do you want from me? I tried. I always tried."

"No. You never actually tried. You tried the easy way. *Your* way. And when you couldn't see how truly fucked up your way was, you tried to ignore anyone and everyone who ever questioned your goddamn way. That *defines* ignorance. And that's the only thing you ever succeeded in doing."

"I couldn't do it," I screamed before I could stop myself.

I saw a break in the light, a shifting shadow, someone shuffling their feet up to our door, peering in and swiftly moving along, freeing the path for a few more tiny fragments of illumination. Ramona leaned in slightly and spoke softly.

"You're not a fucking invalid, Joe. You could have done anything you wanted. You could have done things right."

"Don't you see what I'm saying? I didn't have it in me. I couldn't do it. I physically couldn't do it."

"That's ridiculous."

"You know what I mean. It wasn't in me. Do you think it feels good to be the laughing stock of an industry? Don't you think I regret not going about things differently? Do you imagine I enjoy being a fraud? You think I don't know why I get stuck with shitty cases?"

"Shitty cases you couldn't even solve," she said. "Leaving me to demand your fees from justifiably angry and disappointed people. When I felt the same way they did."

"If it was so bad, why stick around?"

Ramona's eyes fixed on me, a nocturnal predator scanning the jugular. Brace yourself, old man.

"Because I'm one of those unfortunate assholes who thinks they can change someone. Thinks they can help a person in need. It was my job goddammit. You were my job. You fucking loser. You were born with that loveable loser charm—weren't you, Joe? Come out of your mother that way—lazy, trying to find a way around the work. Being single—that's lazy. The path of least fucking resistance. Well, look at you now, Joe. Look at what that got you. Look at us. Look at where we are."

"I don't know where we are," I yelled.

"We're in hell," she said.

"I don't believe in hell."

"Lazy again. Path of least fucking resistance."

"Stop calling me lazy. You've got no right. I just wanted to feel like I was making a difference. I got in my own goddamn way. People do that. You don't think I know that about myself? If you had any idea what I've been going through this past year, or however long it's been. Christ, I don't even know. And I've been here for you, through it all. You're here because of my help, Ro."

"We don't even know where here is," she said.

"I'll figure it out. I always figure it out."

"Well, Lord help us then. Because I've got news for you Joe, you *never* figure it out. And what kind of detective can't figure anything out? Say it with me now: Joe fucking Iocca."

CHAPTER FOURTEEN

A Very Blue Chair

I awoke in a very blue chair. It had a loose cushion on the seat and another tied to the back–both blue–and there were wide wooden arms, also blue. My back was killing me and my shoulder was throbbing.

A nurse had come into the room and, upon seeing that I had stirred, alerted me that she would now draw back the blinds.

"You shouldn't have slept there. At your age," she said.

Where is here?

The landscape outside seemed simple and new to me. Through the picture window I saw acres of lawn with only a hint of civilization lurking beyond what my blurry eyes were able to register.

"You'll make other arrangements today they tell me? For yourself that is," she said.

The nurse was a very dark-skinned black woman, hard for me to figure her age. I found her fullness sexy, even in the fog I was in. That part of me was unrelenting. Something stirred and I crossed my legs a moment too late. She looked down at me over her glasses and possibly smiled as slightly as you can smile. I couldn't be sure.

"That your wife?" she asked with a flip of her head, never releasing her judgmental gaze.

Ramona was asleep there. She looked lifeless and happy all at once: no longer angry. A doctor came in behind me. He was in his sixties, with yellow hair combed and cut like Shemp, a startling six foot nine inches and cadaverous – as unhealthy a man as I had ever seen in healthcare. He started talking to the man in the other bed. I then became aware that there was a man in another bed.

"How are you feeling this morning?" said the doctor to his patient.

"He seems his usual self, Doctor Tim," the nurse called out as she looked over Ramona's chart.

"I see we have a visitor already this morning," said the doctor.

"Someone made an exception last night. There's a note at the nurses station about this man. What's your name, honey?" she asked me.

"Joe," I said.

"Hi, Joe. I'm Doctor Tim," said Doctor Tim.

"Hello," I said.

The doctor shook my hand and looked over at Ramona.

"That your wife, Joe?" he said. I shook my head no as the doctor let go of my grip and joined the nurse at Ramona's bedside. "Her name?"

"Ramona," I said in unison with the nurse.

Ramona opened her eyes.

"Well, good morning, Ramona. I'm Doctor Tim."

"Well whoop de do, ghost," said Ramona.

Doctor Tim and the nurse laughed and Ramona looked at them like they were criminally insane.

"Joe, maybe you and I could speak for a moment outside," said the doctor. "You look like a man in need of a strong cup of coffee. Am I right?"

I stood up slowly, my back hurting like hell, and I gave Ramona a nod. Ramona looked back at me like I was the ringleader of the nut jobs. Doctor Tim and I walked out of the room, the doctor having to duck to clear the doorframe.

"What about these coons?" squawked Ramona.

"Jesus, Ro," I said as we left.

We took the hallway down to a small cafeteria. Some older people were seated at round tables in the salmon-colored room. No one looked up as we walked through and loaded up trays with coffee and donuts. There was a calendar behind the buffet table. It informed me that I was sixty-two-years old that day.

"How are you, Mrs. Field?" asked Doctor Tim as we passed a table.

Mrs. Field made a wonderful face and seemed like she was going to answer him for certain but only managed a charming series of noises: what I imagine a newborn pony sounds like. We took a seat at a table near the glass block wall at the front of the room.

"So, what's the story, Joe?" he asked as if we were old friends.

I pointed to my coffee and the doctor understood. I took some Sweet-n-Low off the table and poured two packets in, followed by two tiny containers of Coffee Mate. I took a short sip, acknowledged the coffee's ability to perform a function, and followed that with a much longer drink.

"This your outfit, Tim?" I asked, trying hard to pull my shit together.

"During the day, yep, you bet. At night there are only the nurses and a few other docs who share responsibilities for all of the wards. She'll be in good hands night or day, though. I can assure you of that."

"How long's this place been here?"

"We're in our second year out here. Have you ever been out this way before?"

"I don't believe so," I said.

"They've really developed the whole area quite a bit over the last decade. How did you find us anyway?" he asked.

I went in for the coffee.

"Most people say the internet," he said.

"Yeah," I said. "The internet."

"Well, you've done a good thing bringing her here, Joe. Any other facility charging less is going to offer less in terms of care. Real care, with a capital C. That's what we provide here. Alzheimer's, dementia: there's a lot we can do in the way of medicine and attention and environment to make these folk's quality of life as good as it can possibly be."

"But she has to share a room, Doc?"

"For now, yes. It's good for them to have as much companionship and interaction as they can get. May help bring that gentleman out of his shell, too, having someone nearby. If her situation were to worsen or require isolation we would address that, of course. But from everything we can see so far this is the way to go."

We finished breakfast and walked back to Ramona's room. It was just the big man in the other bed and Ramona, who was eating cookies and watching TV from one of the chairs in a corner of the room.

"There's a bathroom here," I said as I pointed behind her. "I guess you gotta share it. Maybe you can call someone with this intercom here if you feel like you need to go."

She looked at me like I was a sick, sick bastard.

"I'm gonna be gone for just a little while then I'll come back," I said. "You're gonna be fine here. They're good people."

I leaned in and kissed her on the top of her head. She reached up and touched it afterwards like she thought I had left something there. She chomped loudly on a cookie and the man in the other bed cleared his throat. I left the room, giving the man a cordial nod as I passed.

The nurse at the main station gave me directions out of the facility. I wanted to run from that place, wherever it was, if only for a minute. I needed to be alone with my thoughts. I needed to figure out what came next. From outside I could see that it was a series of buildings that were connected by long hallways, each of them made up of glass mostly, presumably for comfortable travel in cold weather. I apparently had parked in the visitor's area the night before, which was quite a hike from where I had left the building. The air was crisp and cool and I could faintly see my breath as I worked my way to the car. This was not California.

Just a few feet from the Camry, someone in the next vehicle over—a Lincoln Town Car with tinted windows: the kind that mobsters favor—opened the driver's side door and exited the car. He stood stiffly and removed his sunglasses, carefully stowing them in a hard-shell case, forcing the bulky container into his breast pocket with some effort.

"You're testing my patience, Mr. Iocca," said mister fucking mysterious from Ramona's driveway.

We drove east on the freeway. The sign said head east to St. Louis. So I drove east.

"You're an odd man, Mr. Iocca. I find you puzzling. Puzzling and troubling all at once."

"You're one to talk," I said.

"You've never encountered the diligent and the committed in your line of work?"

"That's putting it mildly, what you are."

"Care to share with me where we're heading?" he asked.

"That way," I said and pointed straight ahead.

We drove *that way* for some time, much of it looking unfamiliar. As we changed freeways, I began to feel things. At first they were just senses without any connection to speak of but they were gradually affecting me, until almost everything I saw was as it should be, just as I remembered it. I was fighting tears, trying hard not to break down.

"This is it, isn't it, Joe?" he said to me.

We pulled off the freeway and began to negotiate the city streets.

"That's one, isn't it?" he asked as he gestured to a restaurant with the name spelled out in big, green letters on a white background and underlined with a swirling red stripe. "Yes," he said. "It's all coming back to you now. How long has it been?"

It had been some time.

Yogi Berra was born and raised there, just across the street from Joe Garagiola on Elizabeth Avenue—two of the great Italian-American catchers of all time. In 1950, when the United States soccer team defeated England in the FIFA World Cup title match, four of the five St. Louisans on that team were from the Hill. For over a century this neighborhood of around 2,500 people has been overwhelmingly Italian. Homes rarely go on the open market. The community works hard to see to it that the majority of its residents can trace their origins to the north of Italy and Sicily.

This is a place that has a Bocce Ball League.

Driving on Kingshighway, as we neared my childhood home, I considered the great irony of my life. Thirty years prior I had moved 2,000 miles away from a place that had waged a successful campaign against change, only to come to realize that I, myself, was a man who deeply feared and detested progress.

"Do you feel like you may want to stop at St. Ambrose, maybe say confession first?" he asked me.

"How the hell do you know about St. Ambrose? Who are you?"

"I'm a man who sees prudence in thorough research, Joe. You of all people should appreciate that."

"Daryl. I'm naming you Daryl then, since you apparently aren't going to tell me your goddamn name."

"Why Daryl?" he asked.

"Cuz I've always hated that name."

"Interesting," said Daryl.

"And because the last thing you look like is a Daryl, so it will be an amusing thing to me, remembering to call you Daryl. That alright by you, Daryl?"

"Perfectly fine, Joe. I'm disappointed you so obviously haven't looked into me yet, but fine."

We drove by St. Ambrose, as it is impossible to drive through the Italian Hill and not soon come across the mammoth church.

"Not a goddamn peep out of you, Daryl."

We passed men who sat outside of cafés and restaurants, men who spoke and laughed easily with each other, their rapports having been forged over scores of years spent together in the same locales. Past the public hangouts, shotgun-style homes with immaculately manicured lawns came one after another, with hand-made lawn dressings and statues of the Virgin Mary in chaste multitudes.

Daryl took in the people.

"To a certain degree they really do all look alike, Joe," he said as he studied them.

"We all look alike to you? You know you look like you might have some Dago in you too, pal."

"Possibly," he said.

"We're just white people, Italians. White people only look alike to Asians, Daryl."

"Take me to that place where they have Toasted Raviolis, Joe," he said.

"That place? You realize that all these places, every restaurant you've seen out there, they all have Toasted Raviolis. We invented it here, Daryl."

"And the Spork. Well, not in this particular enclave but here, in St. Louis I mean."

I thought of how I was intimidated by this man's aura of obvious wealth and intellect when I met him that day in the driveway. Now I just wanted to nut-punch Daryl as he rambled on in the passenger's seat of my Toyota.

"So I'll dump you here at Milo's and you can have Toasted Raviolis and beers and whatever the hell else you want," I said.

"Excellent. And you'll come back for me within the hour. Or–"

"Or you'll find me. Yeah, I got it. Right here in one hour."

Two older women out for a morning walk said hello to us as the passenger door opened.

"Be nice to these people, Daryl," I instructed him.

The women smiled with discomfort and looked in at me oddly. I looked in the rearview mirror and attempted to pat down my hair, which had become a funny shape from sleeping on the hospital chair and Christ knows where else in the four or five days it must have taken to have driven to St. Louis from Pacifica.

Back in 1981 St. Louis was in the middle of what the papers dubbed "The Leisure Wars," named after a Syrian mobster who teamed up with a violent Irish labor racketeer nicknamed "The Fish" to take on the Italian Mafia in an effort to wrest control of the city's underworld. Car bombs maimed and killed Mafiosi around the city, paralyzing one of my cousins, offering me proof of the imprudence of that path, had I any thoughts of trading in my mortar trowel for a gun.

After the bomb partially detonated, some of my handier relatives built ramps for my suddenly paraplegic cousin. One ramp was installed over the stairs in front of his home. Others were made to fit everywhere my cousin would frequent. You could take a walking tour of my family, home-by-home, and the handicap ramps would inform like Mezuzahs.

I walked up the portion of the brick stairs that was left operational for the ambulatory. I grabbed the brass knocker, said, "Hello, Tony," to St. Anthony who was mounted just above it, and gave the bar a couple of taps.

"Holy Mackerel. Angie, come quick. It's Joe."

Mariano, or Motto as everyone calls him, looked up at me, his older cousin, and signaled for a hug. I bent down and greeted him warmly, patting him on the back and touching the crown of his head where a bald spot had appeared at some point in the two decades since we had last laid eyes on each other. It felt good to *feel* my family again.

"Oh, you almost smother me with that stomach," he said. "Angie, whaddya doin'? Joe's standing out here and he's got a boiler."

I heard Angie making her way to the front door, her heels pumping hard. I could also smell her coming. Her perfume hit me square as she came to the back of her husband's wheelchair.

"What? Which Joe?" she asked.

In my family there were—when I originally left for the west coast—three Joes, two Vinces, two Dominics, five Angies, three Maries, two Marys, three Johns, five Tonys and one Toni. With all the procreating and passing that had occurred in the past three decades there was no way for me to now tabulate.

"Oh-ohhh, big Joe. Motto, look at that boiler," she said.

I rubbed my stomach, pretending to laugh along with them, all the while considering the additional weight even a short visit to the old carbohydrate-based neighborhood would produce.

"Let's roll you out the way, Motto," said Angie as she backed him into the hallway and came around to give me an embrace. "Here he is. The one that got away."

Angie had been a part of the line of would-be wives for me, even though she was eight years younger. A walk down Bischoff Street at that moment would have produced at least three more of my jilted.

Angie was a woman who masked her natural beauty with department store harlequin make-up. She made Spaghetti and Eggs for the three of us in her bathrobe and heels, while Motto and I caught up in the living room.

"You here for Tony's wedding?" he asked.

I gestured with my hands that I was clueless. Whenever I return home my hands do much of the speaking for me.

"When is it? Next weekend I think," Motto said softly before yelling. "Ang, when is Tony's wedding?"

"Next weekend," she screamed.

"Next weekend, Joe," he said to me. "So you'll come."

"Of course," I answered, having no idea which Tony we were discussing.

"Of course," he said lowly before yelling behind him. "Joe's coming to Tony's weddin', Ang."

"Oh, goodie. I'll call Aunt Alvina right now."

"Like she can hear, that one. You oughtta listen to this conversation, Joe. Poor woman can't make out a word nobody says no more. She'd be better off walking over there," he said. "Angie, you'd be better off walking over there," he yelled.

"Who's gonna fix your breakfast then? Hmm? Who? You?" she asked as she walked into the living room. She leaned over and kissed my baby cousin, the smell of her having wafted room to room. "Joe, why don't you run over to aunt Alvina's with Motto here. Do him good to get some fresh air. You'd be doing me a personal favor, Joe, gettin' him out of here. He drives me pazzo, this one! The food will still be here when you get back. I'll add some sausage."

Motto pushed himself down the street with me at his side. It was important to Motto that he always rolled himself along. He wasn't a made guy when the bomb took his mobility. When the legs were done, he was done, gangster-wise. My dad's family came from Sicily and my mother was from the North. Of all the Sicilians in my family, Motto is the only one who ever did any mob work. Since the attempt on his life over thirty years ago Motto had worked in a local bakery. I'm sure Angie slept better at night.

We made our way for a few minutes and stopped near the end of the block. Alvina's was the house with the ramp.

"She's gonna flip when she sees you," said Motto. "Probably think you're the archangel, come to take her."

I slapped at his arm as we made our way to the door. Motto knocked loudly and for some time. We waited for nearly five minutes, grinning back and forth at each other, Motto reaching out to pat my stomach at one point.

"Aunt Alvina," said Motto as she opened the door. "Look who's here with me? It's Joe."

Alvina smiled and shook her head up and down as if she could hear a word Motto was saying. I put my arms around my father's only remaining sibling, hugged her gently, spoke to her ear in a Sicilian dialect, telling her it was good to see her again after so many years.

"It's a wonderful place, where you come from," said Daryl.

I would have preferred to drive in silence. I had it in my head to take this journey with the purpose of getting to the bottom of who the fuck Daryl was and to learn why and how he had followed me across the country. But that was the problem; I'd spent at least four days on the road, probably sleeping in contemptible hotel room beds with decrepit pillows, only to end up snoring away in a graceless hospital chair. My back was aching, my shoulder was barking, my mind was shot and, unless we're counting Daryl, there were no strange visitors, which was a welcome if not puzzling revelation. And, if that calendar was to be believed, it was my birthday dammit. I preferred to drive in silence.

"They're overwhelmingly democrats," he said, seemingly to no one. " I wouldn't have imagined that to be the case, what with the rest of the state being as red as it is. We talked politics, art, food; it was quite the enlightening hour. Did you know Yogi Berra was born here?"

I turned the radio on.

As we pulled into the parking lot of The Beacon Home in Wentzville, I asked Daryl if we could meet again in a day or so. Daryl expressed an interest in seeing The St. Louis Zoo, City Museum and going up in the Arch: a 603 foot monument that looms large over the Mississippi River downtown, known as The Gateway to the West. I informed Daryl that I would be looking for a place nearby to stay and Daryl informed me that he would find me.

"Begin your homework on me, Joe," he said. "I'm an interesting case."

It was late afternoon and a nap on the blue chair was beginning to hold some appeal.

The man in the other bed had a visitor stationed next to him in one of the seats. His guest filled every inch of the chair. Making my way through, I felt bad that the man had to scoot in closer until he was nearly on top of Ramona's roommate

"Pardon me," I said.

"No problem," he said.

Ramona was still watching television. I took a seat next to her.

"Are you comfortable, Ro? I'm gonna have to talk to the staff about maybe bringing in a recliner like you had at your place."

Ramona had no reaction. We sat together and watched a murder mystery show. It was near the end of the hour, the part where the detective was proving how a rich and powerful man had murdered someone and nearly gotten away with it. During the exposition, a comely young woman at the detective's side seemed to be getting aroused by his every confident word.

CHAPTER FIFTEEN

Torn Curtain

You've never killed anybody. People expect a version of grief, not for the deceased necessarily—this one was a serial rapist, a likely killer himself—but for yourself, for the little part of your soul that surely died with him. You've joined an exclusive club. How many murderers do you think you know, even if you live in Los Angeles?

Little Girl got up each morning and thought about the trucker. Some mornings it was, 'Fuck yes. I did that. I wish I could do that all of the time,' while others were plagued with the images and smells from inside the cab of the semi-truck, and the nagging questions that accompanied what the religious among us would call a mortal sin.

She made Henry promise he would speak to no one about what transpired on the road that day. Her friends would treat her differently, because she had murdered another human being and that *had* to affect her. She was equally uncomfortable being the recipient of both their sympathy and their judgments. She worried they would look upon her as a victim. Worse yet, she worried they'd learn the true nature of the peace the killing had brought her.

She headed toward Hollywood. With all the work she'd put in on the client's '74 Honda 550, it required a good, long test ride. She thought of Henry, and for the first time in doing so was able to connect a true sense of him, not merely a recollection of his physical characteristics or something clever he had said, but rather a feeling for who he was. That experience 37 miles outside of Bakersfield had been a reminder of the malevolence that lives inside of so many men, the thing that drives them to hurt another person with plenary disregard. That early afternoon on the freeway, in the wind, Henry felt like humanity and safety and grace, and she was drawn to see him.

"How did you get this job, Henry?" she asked with her hand on an electric ball that frizzed her hair.

"It's weird, right? I forget how weird it is sometimes," said Henry.

"No, it's cool. I think I get it now. The Bemusement Park. You've got a little science going on, the photos of circus freaks, and you in that super sexy dress, of course."

Henry was made up in drag. He was a very convincing woman, especially as the room's lights were a mixture of strobe, laser and constantly moving colors. It hadn't occurred to Little Girl that she was in fact attracted to his soft features, the ones that lent so well to the ruse. She hadn't thought of him as womanly before necessarily but he was surely a pretty boy and certainly a divergence from her usual rough and tumble type.

"Where's the strangest place for our first kiss, Henry?"

He took her hand and led her down a mirrored hallway that narrowed until their bodies were wedged together. Further along the corridor, just out of reach, she could see a well-lit wide space that contained a chocolate birthday cake with 16 burning candles. Projected on the wall was a video that looped images of men, women and children in states of euphoria. Puppies played with kittens on a plush rug that lay on the floor. The sound from a small waterfall was all she could hear. Henry struggled to free his arms enough to place his hands on the sides of her head. He slid them back across her ears and gently pulled her in.

Their second date was an art exhibition at a motorcycle shop. The store's owners rolled the used bikes out of the showroom once a year and replaced them with motorcycle-themed sculptures, paintings and photographs. Biker Billy was a welder by trade and had made the largest piece in the room. It consisted of worn out pistons, retired shocks, front ends and nearly every shunned metal part he had in his garage. Together they formed a seven-foot tall woman with huge headlights for breasts.

"Billy is a boob man," Little Girl said to Henry as Biker Billy walked up from behind them.

"We are all, each of us, boob men, ma lady," said Billy.

"Henry, this is Billy," she said.

"Nice meeting you, Billy," said Henry.

"You too, kid. What do you think of the piece?"

"Outstanding," said Henry.

"She's mostly Japanese. I wouldn't give up American parts for this thing. She'll end up at the dump anyhow."

"Aw, that's a shame. Isn't everything here for sale?" asked Henry.

"Who's gonna buy this rickety old chick? Who would even have the room for her?" said Billy.

"The furry-seat vagina is a nice touch," said Little Girl.

"Now that part's American. Pure Milwaukee 1970's bush."

A young Hawaiian woman walked straight up to them and hugged Little Girl, pulling her in tight against the woman's broad, pliable breasts. Billy elbowed Henry, smiled and nodded his head at her bosoms. Little Girl nearly pushed the woman away when she came in for the full frontal assault. She was the ex-girlfriend of a guy Little Girl briefly dated years prior, and Little Girl thought she was looking for a fight.

"How are you, honey?" asked the woman.

"Dude," said Little Girl as they disengaged from the embrace.

The girl looked at her with a motherly smile and went to pet her hair. Little Girl swiped at the woman's hand and the woman reacted as if she compassionately understood, holding Little Girl's hand momentarily.

"I'm here if you want to talk," said the woman before walking away.

"What the fuck was that?" Little Girl said to Biker Billy.

"That chick's weird. I think she's on ecstasy too. I should check," he said while patting Henry on the back. "Good meeting you, brother."

Henry and Little Girl pushed through the crowd and made their way to the makeshift bar. They asked for two pale ales, and the bartender who looked semi-familiar to Little Girl handed them the beers. Henry pulled out his wallet and gave him a twenty.

"Just five bucks for the one," said the barkeep. "I got yours, Little Girl."

They walked away and grabbed a spot in front of a series of black and white photographs that had been taken earlier in the year at a vintage flat track race up in Auburn.

"That was odd," Little Girl said as she looked back at the bartender who gave her a friendly nod and smile combo.

"I think he's sweet on you," said Henry.

"I think his wife waxes my...I don't know that guy at all. How's he even know my name?"

"Maybe he just guessed. You have so many," said Henry.

Indian Jim walked up with a sweet look on what could be seen of his bearded face, his eyes smiling and his nose retreating a bit.

"How you holding up, old girl?" he asked.

"What's going on here, Jim? Why are people suddenly concerned about me?" she said and turned toward Henry. "Henry," said Little Girl in an accusatory tone.

"What?"

"Billy told me what happened up in Bakersfield, Little Girl," said Indian Jim. "Filled him full of holes, I hear. Good on ya."

"Jesus fucking Christ. Billy? How the hell does he know?"

"You ok, sweetheart?" asked Indian Jim.

"Sweetheart? Don't call me sweetheart. Not like that. All fucking fatherly and sincere, man. Where the fuck is Billy?" she said as she looked around the room.

"He's sitting over there," said Henry, pointing toward a couch that was made from old tires.

Little Girl walked briskly toward Billy and the Hawaiian woman who was on the sofa with him.

"Billy, what the hell, man? You're telling people what went down up there?"

"I was worried about you," he said.

"We all are," said the woman.

"Worried? You fucking *all* are?" Little Girl said as she looked around the room and noticed a portion of the crowd looking at her. "How do you even know?"

"My sister heard," said Billy.

"I can't believe that happened to you, Little Girl," said the woman.

Little Girl pushed her palm into the girl's forehead and shoved her back a few inches.

"Man, fuck you. Nothing happened to me," said Little Girl.

"Hey, I'm on ecstasy," said the Hawaiian woman.

"What's wrong with you, Little Girl?" asked Billy. "Everybody cares here, man."

Little Girl flipped Billy and the woman off and walked back toward Henry, who was watching her as he chatted with Indian Jim. She barreled into a ten-year-old girl, knocking the kid's soda water to her feet.

"Watch where you're going, why don't you?" said the girl.

"Piss off, " said Little Girl as she walked away.

The girl lifted her leg and kicked Little Girl in the small of the back, sending her into a doughy biker who spilled his whiskey sour on Little Girl's face as she was falling off of him. Henry rushed over and helped Little Girl up from the floor. She jumped out to scare the kid but Henry quickly restrained her. The bartender came around the bar and grabbed at the young girl.

"What are you doing, Alice?" he asked his daughter. "I'm sorry, Little Girl. She didn't know."

Little Girl had turned her phone off the night before. She didn't want to hear from anyone but Henry, and he was sleeping next to her. They made out from midnight until four in the morning but stuck with an earlier vow to keep their clothes on.

The night may have gone differently if they had found themselves in her bed only weeks before. Little Girl hated that the trucker had a say in her decision not to express her feelings for Henry physically so soon after the attack. The experience had been a gruesome microcosm of everything that she had learned about life in one vivid example: there was always a price to be paid. The truck driver ponied up for his actions, and rightly so. But any honest cost analysis of the events that took place on a dirt road outside of Bakersfield would surely include the toll levied on her. Yes, the matter was in some ways simple. There was conflict and there was resolution. But was there a verdict in his death? Or would that trial continue on inside of her, never reaching a consensus, as she now knew she would always be the lone holdout. Should she have opened her door and ran? Could she have left after the first shot? Had he really leaned in? Would he have stopped? That is the power that doubt wields when it takes up residence in hindsight.

"Do you have to work?"

"Day off," he said with a groggy grin.

She hit the power button on her cell and it began to beep with text messages.

HE'S OUT.

HE'S BEEN TRANFERRED TO SOME PLACE. BUT HE'S FREE.

I'M GOING TO GO SEE HIM SOON.

When did my mother become a texter, she thought.

Henry and Little Girl made breakfast together and decided to take a bike ride up the coast to get away from it all. Henry suggested they spend the night in Santa Barbara. They rode along the coastline late that afternoon and when they arrived in town they found a room at a hotel on the beach. They drank Mexican lager and shared portions of their pasts well into the night. Henry spoke lovingly of his mother, a woman he characterized as having integrity to spare and being "whip-smart" and a "spitfire" who didn't take any guff from anyone. He said she was a champion for the marginalized, infamous for taking up causes, big and small, and always willing to fight for the underdog. Short of the tattoos, he could have been describing the woman Little Girl was becoming.

She admitted that the incident near Lebec had unlocked something in her, deepened her need to see justice served. She spoke passionately, at times maniacally about retribution. She became drunk and used the term bloodlust over and over. She slurred about her father's murderer, at one point standing up and screaming to the heavens that she would find the true killer and see him pay for what he did. Henry listened, remaining mostly silent. As she fell asleep it occurred to Little Girl that her honesty may have put him off, and she worried he would leave her under the cover of darkness.

The next morning Henry called his boss and said a family emergency back in Kansas was going to take him out of town for some time. He was told he'd have a job whenever he returned. They kick-started their Triumphs and made their way back home, stopping at Little Girl's to pack first, heading to Hollywood next to collect some of Henry's things before loading their motorbikes into the back of Henry's pick-up truck and heading east for St. Louis.

A rubber ball came hard off the road and hit the side of the car next to them, bouncing in through Little Girl's open window and clocking her on the side of the head before caroming off and finding the open air again.

"Jesus fucking Christ," she said as she rubbed her right ear. "What the hell was that?"

"Someone needs to see to it that you're not killed," said Henry. "That's my new job."

They drove for several hours, through Arizona and New Mexico, eating only gas station food and pausing for bathroom breaks at rest stops. Little Girl felt Henry attempt to inconspicuously scrutinize her every time they saw a parked semi-truck. This didn't bother her.

In Oklahoma they drove under the giant McDonald's restaurant freeway overpass and Little Girl asked if he'd mind her turning the truck around so they could witness the spectacle of people that had to be there. Henry was instantly excited at the prospect. It seemed like an odd place for these two vegetarians, and that was exactly the point.

"I've got a silly request," said Henry as they drank milkshakes amongst the largely obese.

"Shoot," she said.

"Can we go up in the Arch? When we get to St. Louis?"

"I like the way you approach life, man. It's refreshing. Most guys I know have mastered the 'whatever.' But when you're excited about something you don't try to hide it. It's like you're cool *because* you don't concern yourself with cool. Sure, we can do the touristy thing and see the Arch. I've actually never been," she said.

"But you're from there."

"My mother is afraid of heights. I've been to it, just not up it."

242

"What's she like? Is she afraid of a lot of things?"

"I don't know what my mother is really like. The second half of my life, we don't really communicate. We used to just communicate poorly. At some point we pretty much stopped altogether."

Keith and Steve the catcher had dropped Deborah off at the house, picked up another friend and went camping, as had always been their plan. Angel had to work late and met up with Wayne for dinner in downtown New Hope. Wayne and Angel came home around 8:30 that Friday evening, Angel flushed and giggling from too much wine as they walked through the door to find Deborah on the couch clutching her knees to her cheeks.

Angel made a beeline to the downstairs bathroom. Wayne said, "Hi, honey," to Deborah as he passed to grab a beer from the kitchen. He refused to drink and drive and clearly relished the Molson's he'd pop open whenever they came in from a night out. He walked into the living room and looked at the TV, which wasn't on. That was never the case.

"Debbie, you ok?" he asked while putting his hand on her shoulder.

She flinched.

"I need to speak to my mother," she said.

"Did I do something wrong, honey?" he asked.

"I want my mom."

Angel came out of the bathroom and entered the living room.

"Everything alright in here?" she asked.

"She wants to talk to you," he said to Angel.

Angel sat on the other side of Deborah. Deborah stared straight ahead at the dark TV and began to rock back and forth. Her eyes began to move rapidly between Wayne and her mother.

"I need him to go," said Deborah to Angel.

"Ok," Wayne said as he stood up. "I'll be in the garage. Let me know when I can come back in, eh."

Wayne walked to the door that was off the kitchen. Angel waited until she heard it shut behind him.

"What's wrong, Deb?" asked Angel with her hands stroking Deborah's shoulder and shin.

"They raped me," said Deborah, crying and screaming the moment she spoke the words.

"Oh, God," screamed Angel.

Wayne opened the door and hurried to the back of the couch.

"Get him out of here," yelled Deborah.

Angel waved at him with both arms and pushed at him when he didn't immediately go.

"What," said Wayne. "What's wrong with her?"

"Get out," yelled Angel.

Wayne left through the front door. He remained on the porch, pacing back and forth.

"Tell me what happened to you, baby."

Deborah looked up at her mother and stared. She was shaking still and her eyes and face were soaked. Angel grabbed a blanket and put it over her daughter. She took tissue from a box on the coffee table and tried to wipe at Deborah's face but Deborah pulled her head back, still staring directly at Angel, looking delirious.

"Keith," said Deborah.

Angel froze and looked at Deborah for a long moment, a moment that would later register fully with Deborah as one of doubt.

"What did you say, Deborah?" she asked in staccato.

"With his friend. In his truck," she said a little more calmly now.

"What friend? When? What are you saying?"

Deborah exploded off the couch and began to run between all of the rooms on the lower level—all the rooms but Keith's.

"We've got to get out of here. I need to go, Mom. He could come back. We need to go. We need to leave this house and never come back. Right now, Momma. Right now."

Angel sat on the couch in shock for a long moment. When she finally got up she chased her daughter down.

She grabbed her in the hallway. Deborah was cradling two pairs of shoes that she dropped when Angel shook her.

"Listen to me. We need to take you to the hospital."

"No," said Deborah with a crazed look in her eyes. "No. No. No."

"Sweetheart, just let me bring Wayne in."

"No," she screamed thunderously.

"I won't tell him anything. I swear. He can drive us to the hospital."

"No," she yelled again, releasing herself from her mother's grip and running to her room. She shut the door behind her and locked it. Angel tried to open it and shook the hollow-core door but could not get in.

"Sweetie, I'm just going to get Wayne," she said.

"I said no," screamed Deborah through the door.

Angel walked down the hallway and quietly opened the front door. Deborah could hear their muffled conversation through the double paned windows as they spoke on the front lawn. The security light went on just outside of her bedroom as they were walking back and forth on the lawn, having tripped the motion sensor. Deborah went to her window and began to bang on it.

"No," screamed Deborah over and over through the glass as she pounded away. Wayne looked at her in complete bewilderment. He ran back into the house and pulled at Deborah's door.

"Go away," yelled Deborah.

Wayne took a couple of steps back and leaned into the door with his full weight. He destroyed the privacy lock on the first attempt. Deborah ran for her closet. Wayne came into the room and grabbed at her from behind, pulling her out from the waist. She slapped at him and kicked her feet and he immediately released her. Angel came in and kneeled by her side as she lay there on the floor crying.

"Honey, you have to listen to me now. Wayne's going to drive us. "

"No. YOU drive me," said Deborah with her head buried in clothes.

"Honey, no, I can't. I've been drinking," said Angel.

"I don't care," yelled Deborah as she looked up at Angel.

"Fine, let's go," said Angel.

"What?" said Wayne. "You can't leave. I don't even know what's wrong with her. Is she having some kind of episode?"

"Wayne, please, we have to go. I'll call you from the hospital. Deborah come on, honey. Let's get in the car."

After settling in at the hospital a female police officer came in to take Deborah's statement. There wasn't much said beyond who the boys were and that they had raped her. She couldn't give details. Every time she began to recount anything specific she punched and screamed and cried. Finally, the officer said she had enough for the time being and that she'd follow up with them in the next forty-eight hours. They gave Deborah a sedative. Before the drugs fully knocked her out, she saw Wayne speaking to her mother outside of her hospital room. Angel touched his arms for a moment while speaking; he unfolded them and burst down the hallway.

Little Girl was nuzzled up next to Henry as he drove. They crossed into Missouri and Little Girl put her head in Henry's lap. Just as she started to doze off she felt a tear fall to her forehead.

CHAPTER SIXTEEN

Little Joe

The burial was at 9:00 AM. Lewis put on a suit and a tie. He would see his father after the service, during visiting hours. It would be a trying day and more than anything he wished his dad could be there.

Lewis held it together through all of the readings, just as he had made it through the wake the evening before without publicly breaking down. When they lowered the casket into the ground it was too irreversible a goodbye. He walked away from the cemetery plot, looked to the tall trees, wept and wailed.

"The funeral was this morning, Daddy," said Lewis.

Terrence looked at him with cold eyes, stoic and unwavering.

"It was tough," Lewis continued. "Lot of people there hurting."

Terrence had become harder to talk to. He rarely said a word, expressing himself through often-intense facial expressions, a communication skill a man develops when he has been locked away.

"I know you wanted to go. I know you did, Daddy. I'm sorry they say you can't leave here. Auntie would have understood," said Lewis.

Visiting his father in this place was far more difficult than he'd imagined it would be. Lewis found himself longing for how things used to be: those hours upon hours they had spent in the visitation rooms at the Missouri State Penitentiary and later the Jefferson City Correctional Center. He felt guilty for having thoughts like these. His father was a free man after thirty-four years in jail. And yet, all things considered, this was worse for Lewis. His father seemed like a stranger to him now.

"He isn't talking at all today?" asked the nurse.

"Nah," said Lewis. "He seem alright, though. He ain't been angry or nothing, has he?"

The nurse looked upon Lewis with kind and sympathetic eyes.

"You don't have to ask me that every time, Lewis. He's not a danger to anyone. You think they'd let him stay up in this room with her if he was? These doctors know. They know what kind of man your daddy is, Lewis. You'd be better off worrying less about all that."

Lewis adjusted himself in the chair and glanced hurriedly across the room before returning his eyes to his father's bed. He had been polite that morning, just as he had been the previous day, not wanting to stare back at Ramona when she locked her gaze as she was doing just then.

The nurse exited through the doorway just as I was coming in. We rubbed up against one another and I was sure the nurse was beginning to think of me as a dirty old white man. I caught Ramona mad-dogging Terrence and Terrence giving it right back to her. I nodded to Lewis and made certain to position myself in their sightlines.

"How are you, Ro?" I asked.

"Bobby, who are those people over there?"

Bobby? I guess Uncle Beer Belly hadn't made the trek east.

"Well, they're..." I turned around and addressed Lewis directly. "I'm sorry, we haven't actually met. Name's Joe. Not Bobby," I said quietly. "This lovely young woman here is Ramona."

Lewis stood up and reached to shake my outstretched hand.

"Hi, Ramona," he said with a wave. "My name's Lewis. This is my daddy. His name is Terrence."

"Nice to meet you, Lewis," I said. I raised my left hand and gave Terrence a peace sign for reasons I could not fathom, leading me to instant remorse. "Good to meet you as well, sir," I said sheepishly.

Terrence studied me. A large part of Terrence's process seemed to be a steady calculation and recalculation of exactly whom people were and whether or not he was supposed to already possess that information. This brought him to often murmur his frustration, but never any physical movement toward that end, or much at all. He was a statue of a man. Ramona, on the other hand, was either falsely certain of a person's identity and relationship to her or simply didn't give a shit. Her interest in Lewis and his father came from the part of her that had become suspicious and paranoid, something the staff had told me they would address with pills.

"Ramona, you wanna come on over and meet our new friends?" I said.

Ramona made wide eyes at me and turned over on her side to face the window.

A squirrel—just a pretty rat really—ate an apple from a branch of the only tree in Motto's backyard. The squirrel spit the skin out incrementally, so that it collected in a neat pile atop the plush Kentucky Bluegrass, and his jaw moved at a rate of six hundred bites per minute.

I held a soda can in one hand and a lawn dart in the other. I hadn't a clue what to do with the dart so I tried on a few approaches. One choice was to throw it overhand but that seemed entirely wrong and particularly dangerous. Another technique had me pretending to toss it sideways like a boomerang, and the third choice, underhand, was probably the closest to proper lawn dart procedure. Angie's older sister joined me in the yard, just as I thought I saw Jesse Owens hurdling the chain-link fences that separated the lots all the way down the block.

"How you doin' out here, Joey?" said Angie's sister.

"Did you see that?" I asked.

"What'd I miss?"

I was closer to truly asking than ever before, but this was neither the time nor the person to trust.

"Joey, eh? You call a sixty-two-year old man Joey, do ya?" I asked.

"I'm seventy-one-years old," she said to me. "I still remember you in short pants. To me you'll always be little Joey."

"Better than Little Joe I suppose," I said.

"Haw! Bonanza! I still love that program. I watch it on demand."

Motto rolled out onto the patio and Angie wasn't far behind. I could see Angie's brother-in-law, who remained in the den, watching football and dunking salty chips into an onion dip. His black head hair looked like beard hair to me.

"You wanna play a game of lawn darts do ya?" asked Motto.

Angie threw her hands up in mock disgust.

"Here were go," she said. "Don't let him take your money with that game. He'll clean you out, this one."

Motto became increasingly competitive after the accident, and by then he was operating at an elite level in excess of three dozen activities.

"He's ranked number one in the Bocce league, you know," Angie proudly stated.

I declined the invitation using only my hands and my cousin took my abstinence as victory.

"When's Lena gettin' here?" asked Angie.

"Oh. That reminds me. You're still a detective aren't ya, Joey?" asked Angie's sister, whose name I could not remember.

"Joey. She still calls him Joey," said Angie.

"Never mind her, Joey," the sister said. "I just wanna ask you a favor. You remember my youngest, Lena, don't ya, Joey?"

My answer would have been *vaguely*, if she had paused for an answer.

"You tell me if she's lesbian."

"Would you stop it with that already," said Angie.

"This man is a professional detective. Am I right? If anyone in this house is qualified to tell me if my little girl is lesbian it's Joey."

"God forbid she just asks her," said Angie.

Motto and I took to smirking like two teenage boys who were thinking about two girls kissing.

"You can't ask her. She lies, that one. That's what they teach them in law schools. Am I right, Joey? Did I mention she's a lawyer? It's all big words, them, and how to argue with your mother and make her feel like she's wrong to even worry in silence about your life, much less ask."

"But she's had boyfriends," said Motto.

"Yeah, those. Don't even get me started with that bunch. She could do both! You just tell me, Joey. Give me a sign maybe. Some sort of hand signal would suffice."

"What are you talking about?" said Angie. "Even if he could know, why's he gonna give you a hand signal? She leaves—early like she always does—last one here and first one out the door, that one. She leaves and he tells you."

I wanted no part of this case. I would just tell her that her daughter was straight no matter what. It's what she wanted to hear. I liked the hand signal idea, though.

"What should it be?" I asked. "Maybe like this?"

I put my pinky and index finger out, curling my other fingers in, like a horn.

"Not that one," yelled Motto. "That's the cuckold sign."

I watched as Lena walked through the front door and spotted her father squinting at the television. She was forty-four, had straightened black hair that reached her shoulders, her skin was alabaster, her eyes dark and almond-shaped, framed by slim, red, rectangular spectacles. Her body articulated a sensible diet and a gym membership. I found her beauty to be unrelenting, the kind that finds its stride with every passing moment. She was also, in my immediate and professional opinion, not a lesbian.

"Hi, Pop," she said, kissing him on the cheek.

Her father looked up and gave her a smile that she likely invented within him upon their very first meeting.

"Ma's out back, is she?" she asked as she walked away and strained to see us through the sun at the end of the long hallway. She called out as she headed down the corridor, shifting a backpack higher up on her shoulder and walking like a woman who cared very little for walking like a woman.

"There she is. Lena, you remember Joe Iocca? Joey, this is my daughter Lena."

Angie rolled her eyes as Lena reached out to shake my hand. Motto pushed his closed fist into the back of my knee.

"San Francisco Joe. Sure, I remember you," said Lena.

"I'm getting a lot of names being back here," I said.

"Oh now, Joe. You know that's what we do here," she said.

"Listen to this one," said Angie's sister. "What we do here. She left the first chance she got. Soulard. Who leaves the Hill for Soulard?"

Soulard lies just south of downtown St. Louis. It's a mixed community. It went through a period of deterioration in the 1970's. The once-thriving neighborhood achieved slum status shortly after that. The 1980's saw a renaissance—appropriate for a part of the city that was once known as Frenchtown—when people like Lena moved in and rehabbed many a brick building.

The party moved back inside the house, and Lena now hovered over her father, who hadn't changed his position. The rest of the family milled about in the kitchen and I took my leave of the antipasti-lined countertops and found myself standing in the big open space near Lena's father, where Motto normally parked his wheelchair.

"So what brings you home, Joe?" she asked me.

"I've got a friend, she's in a bit of a bad way with Alzheimer's, so I brought her here to one of those facilities, this one out in Wentzville."

"Wow," she said. "You came all the way here for that? Must be true what they say about the cost of living out there, hmm?"

That was a perfectly plausible explanation.

"Yes. Yes, it is," I said.

"And what about your agency? You're still a detective? I imagine you must have other detectives that cover for you then. Probably a fair amount of satellite work you can do while you're here as well."

"What is he, an astronaut?" said Lena's dad.

I had been thinking of the exact same joke. Neither of us knew what she meant.

"Oh, you keep to your football game, Pop. It's *very* important you don't miss anything."

Lena's father waved above his head and she dodged his hands. They both laughed in a very similar manner.

"It matters, Lena. I got this receiver in my fantasy league," said Lena's father. "You in any fantasy leagues, mister?" he asked me.

"I'm not really comfortable with anything that has the word fantasy in it," I said.

"You know what's funny, Joe?" Lena said. "I'd say the ratio of conversations I've overheard in my life about this silly sport compared to, say, something political, something of value, of depth, something that actually affects everyone's life, everyone, each and every one of us. It must be a thousand to one. Probably more. Isn't that odd? Doesn't that just make your blood boil? I mean, think about it."

"Here she goes again," said Motto as he rolled into the room. "She's a hell of a lawyer, Joe. If the cops ever showed up here looking for you, not that they'd get a word out of me...but I'm telling you, she's your girl."

CHAPTER SEVENTEEN

Little Debbie

It felt like I knew them well, as if I'd known them for many years of my life, or their young lives anyway. They had obviously shared so much with me in what I had deduced to be several long days and evenings—possibly weeks— spent at The Beacon Home in Wentzville. But I'll be completely honest: I don't remember the hours specifically or how they all added up to make up a series of days.

It was unnerving, the memory loss, the lapses—more disconcerting than my past clients showing up again, or the sightings. Knowing I'd spent this time around doctors who specialize in dementia and Alzheimer's disease worried me. How could they not have known? I wondered if one day they might have entire facilities dedicated to Iocca's Syndrome. Your mother has Iocca's, ma'am. You may know it as a kind of manageable, self-aware madness. Probably seen the Lifetime movie on the subject.

Debbie and Henry walked in and Ramona lit up like the northern sky. Debbie said nothing, kissed my cheek, took her usual place next to Ramona, and Ramona began stroking her arm, petting her tattooed skin. I knew this happened every day. I also knew that Terrence had taken a speedy turn for the worse, unable to speak, unwilling to eat. I knew that Henry had dressed as Magnum PI for his tenth birthday and that the other kids had no idea who he was supposed to be, that only the adults at the doors understood, his mother's attention to detail reaching all the way down to the fold of the Detroit Tigers cap. I knew that Lewis had gone from a stuttering child to a comfortable speaker, and as such he really missed the bustle of his normal day shifts at the airport rental car company, the shifts he traded for the quieter graveyard hours so he could be with his father. I knew I was the only one who could call her Debbie. I knew she felt like a daughter to me. I knew my heart broke for her and I knew exactly why. I just couldn't remember precisely when it all came to be that I knew.

Debbie had told me of the day she came home. I remember that conversation clearly. We had talked about it one day when we were alone in the breakfast room, as Henry had stayed behind and consoled Lewis after Doctor Tim's gloomy prognosis. Henry and Lewis were made of the same stuff. I believe that some people are largely bad and may occasionally manage to do a good thing, while most of us are generally good but slip in a shitty thing here and there, mostly just to keep it interesting. These were simply two good men who always did the good thing, the right thing, the moral thing, never wavering, and I had little choice but to admire that in them, even as it made me feel worse about myself.

Debbie recounted how they had surprised her mother that recent morning.

"Are you ready for this, Lil?" asked Henry as they stood at Angel's door.

"Fuck it," said Debbie just before she rang the bell.

Angel answered in her bathrobe, wearing no make-up.

"Jesus, Deborah, what are you doing here?" she said.

"This is Henry, Mom," said Debbie.

"Hello. I'm sorry I look a mess. I was just about to get ready for work. Please, come in, Henry," said Angel.

"Me too, Mother?" said Debbie.

"Oh, hush," said Angel as they entered the home.

Debbie moved cautiously as the foyer transitioned into the kitchen, dining room and living room in the open concept home. Sixteen years prior, Debbie had found Bill watching TV from his pleather recliner nearly every time she returned home from high school in St. Charles, Bill rarely putting in a full day's work. The town had grown fast and large, and it now surpassed the city of St. Louis in population. In the years since Weebie had come there for open space, it had been completely overtaken by the new construction of infinite suburban neighborhoods, strip malls, big box stores, car dealerships, medical centers, a riverboat casino and tall buildings that were home to corporate headquarters. Growth pushed past St. Charles and into the former cow town of Wentzville and beyond.

"Is Bill sleeping?" asked Debbie in a quiet tone.

"Can I get you a little cup of coffee, Henry? There isn't much," said Angel as she turned to the kitchen counter where a partial pot was nearing the end of its brewing cycle.

"That'd be great, ma'am," said Henry.

"Call me Angel," she said.

Henry was taught to address new acquaintances by their last names, but Debbie hadn't told him Bill's surname.

"Will do," said Henry.

"I can't believe you're standing here, Deborah," said Angel as she placed a hand on the counter, her robe opening enough to expose the upper portion of her left breast.

Debbie walked up to her mother and adjusted her garment as Henry politely turned to tour the photos on the living room wall.

"I'll take a cup, too, Mom," Debbie said.

"I was going to offer," said Angel as she placed her hands on Debbie's wrists.

"Yes, I have tattoos," said Debbie as her mother studied her sleeves.

"I know. I'm on Facebook. It's just a little shocking in person. Give me a minute," she said.

Debbie looked down at her mother's narrow arms and noticed Angel's bare hands.

"Where is your gaudy wedding ring? And where the hell is Bill?"

Angel turned to remove three coffee mugs from a cabinet and took two deep breaths. She began to pour the coffee into the cups as she spoke.

"I can't look at you when I say this," she said with her head down. "Please promise me that you'll wipe the grin off your face by the time I turn around. I can wait as long as you think you may need."

"You left him?" asked Debbie as Henry made his way further into the living room.

"Other way around," she said, spinning her index finger in a circle but keeping her back to Debbie.

"That ugly fucker walked out on *you*?" said Debbie.

Angel turned to face her daughter who, by the tone of her voice, was not grinning.

"Believe it or not that actually helps to hear," she said.

"When?"

"I don't know. Over a year now," said Angel.

"Why didn't you tell me?"

"You don't answer my calls, Deborah. How was I supposed to let you know if you never call me back?"

"You have Facebook. Update your relationship status," said Debbie.

Henry returned to the kitchen. Angel asked if they took cream and sugar and both of them answered that they preferred it black. They sat at bar stools around a worn butcher block island in the middle of the kitchen, the wood full of cuts, stains and grooves—an island that Bill had built years before, just after Angel's parents had loaned them the bulk of the down payment on the brand-new home in the brand-new subdivision for their brand-new life together as a family.

"So why are you here, Deborah? Not that I'm not happy to see you. I'm sorry if this is awkward for you, Henry."

"Not at all, " he said.

"I'm not sure exactly," said Debbie. "I was worried after all of your calls and then those texts. Have you gone to see him yet?"

"No. I've tried. I'll take a morning off work, get myself ready. He's only a few miles down the road. And then I just drive to my job instead."

"Why do you want to see him anyway? Where is he exactly?"

"He's in a place called The Beacon Home in Wentzville," said Angel.

"Is that a halfway house?"

"No, it's an Alzheimer's facility. It's how he got out in the end. They say he can't remember the crime or why he was incarcerated."

"He's sick?" asked Debbie.

"I don't know. Maybe he faked it for all I know. They didn't give me any notice. Apparently he went in front of the parole board and they released him. The lawyer said they could do that, without even letting me speak this time."

"Well, if he's suffering from Alzheimer's—" said Henry.

"He doesn't know suffering, Henry," said Angel.

"I think he does, Mother. I think he knows suffering better than most. Better than you and I even," said Debbie.

"This man killed my daughter's father, Henry," said Angel. "I held his dead body in my arms. This son of a bitch took away any chance we ever had at being a family. And—"

"And he probably didn't even do it goddammit," said Debbie as she got off the stool and walked briskly up the stairs to her old bedroom.

Angel put her hand on Henry's arm and spoke softer.

"I'm sure she's filled your head with her theories, Henry. She acts like she knows better than the police, better than the prosecutor or the judge or the jury that found him guilty. Not that it matters any more. He's free now."

"Please don't be offended, ma'am. But I think the way Lil sees it, he's either served his time for the crime he committed or he's lost those years for nothing. And even the slightest possibility of that kind of injustice...well,

I haven't known Lil for long but I do know how much fairness and right and wrong matters to her," said Henry.

"Who's Lil?" asked Angel.

Debbie told her mother that she and Henry were checking into a nearby motel. Angel asked that they reconsider and stay with her. Debbie didn't like herself in that home. After only a few minutes in her old room she began to feel like an angry, confused little girl again.

They unloaded their motorcycles off the pick-up truck and got on the road. Debbie's mom said it pleased her to know that they would be returning, if only for the truck. It was the beginning of winter but the air still intimated a hint of Midwestern fall. Riding next to Henry placated Debbie, made her feel like herself again.

Debbie had punched in The Beacon Home on her map app to gather directions. They rode a few miles down the freeway and followed the service road into the facility. Henry admitted to being as nervous as he'd ever been but Debbie wouldn't say as much. That was the difference between their states of mind at that moment: Henry secretly thought he was about to meet a murderer while Debbie was convinced she was going to shake the hand of an innocent man.

"So what do we do now?" said Henry as they stood in the parking lot with their helmets at their sides.

"What do you think security is like here?" asked Debbie.

"We planning on breaking in?"

They walked up to the first building and entered the lobby. It was, in fact, the main building and there was a large information desk where a young man sat. He had a spiky Mohawk of sorts—there was shorter hair on the sides—and a very busy looking, garish tee that said *Ed Hardy* on it. Next to Mr. Hardy's name on the man's shirt was a nametag with his own name, which was also Ed.

"Hey, Ed," said Debbie as she read it from his chest. "We've got a friend here and we'd like to visit him."

"What's wrong with him?" asked Ed.

"Alzheimer's. Don't you just type his name into your computer?"

"Yeah, but this isn't Alzheimer's. This place is for people who are dying and shit."

"People die from Alzheimer's, Ed," said Henry.

"Yeah? I thought you just, like, forgot things."

"So where do they keep them?" asked Debbie.

"Just go back out this door and follow the yellow sidewalk to your right. Left. Right."

"So just follow the yellow brick road then?" said Debbie.

"I think it's concrete," said Ed.

"How's security over there?" asked Henry. Debbie bumped him with her shoulder and he looked at her and laughed.

Henry and Debbie walked out of the lobby and onto the yellow sidewalk, which was actually yellow on half and red on the other. All of the sidewalks had two colors that corresponded with a building. Alzheimer's was yellow, dying people and shit was red.

They entered the building into a hallway, helmets in hand, and began reading the signs on the walls that didn't tell them where to go. They were looking for residents, who were all housed at the end of hallways that opened up into a circle of rooms, like a cul de sac. I was stepping out for a bit of fresh air when Henry said, "Excuse me, sir."

"We're looking for someone. A friend. He's supposed to be staying here now," said Henry.

"What's his name?" I asked.

"His name?" he said to me and then looked at Debbie.

"Terrence," she said.

"Big fella?" I said to Henry who looked at Debbie.

"Yeah," she said.

"He's my friend's roommate actually," I said.

"Oh, wow," said Henry.

"Where is their room?" asked Debbie.

"How do you know him?" I asked Debbie directly.

"Through my family," she told me.

I watched Henry's reaction and could tell something was a little off with their story.

"My name's Joe," I said.

"Nice to meet you, Joe. I'm Henry."

"Little Girl," said Debbie.

"How's that now?" I asked.

"Everyone calls me Little Girl," she said.

"Well, now, not everyone I bet," I said. "What does the mean woman down at the DMV call you?"

"Deborah," she said.

"I'll call you Debbie then," I said.

"I'd really rather you didn't," she said.

"I'm twice your age, Debbie, so I make the rules. Now what do you say you two show me the motorbikes you rode up on while I take in the air?"

I escorted them out of the building and we walked over to their old bikes. I didn't know the first thing about these machines but I love history and these things reeked of the stuff. When Debbie told me that hers was about my age I felt a mixture of sadness and self-satisfaction. It was nice to hear that something that old appealed to her and still ran like a top, as she put it, but it was an oily mess and not the shiniest or prettiest thing I had laid eyes on.

"California plates," I said as I took a closer look at the back of them. I pointed toward my Toyota which was parked a few spots away. "Me, too."

"Weird," said Henry. "What the heck are you doing way out here?"

"Hell if I know, kid," I said.

"We live in LA," said Debbie. "You?"

"Bay area," I answered. "I grew up here, though. On the Hill."

"Always loved the Hill," said Debbie. "Bet it hasn't changed a bit."

"Not that I could tell," I said.

"I gotta take you there, Henry," said Debbie. "Toasted fucking Ravioli."

"So you're visiting?" I asked.

"My mom lives here," said Debbie.

"And what's your connection to Terrence?" I asked.

"They say he killed my father," she said plainly.

"Jesus," said Henry as he pushed Debbie's shoulder a bit.

"Have we met before?" I asked.

"I don't think so," said Debbie while the kid said, "No."

"So this isn't about you hiring me for some case then?"

"Case?" asked Debbie.

"What do you do, Joe?" said Henry.

"I'm a private detective," I said.

"And not a very good one, it would seem," said Daryl who came walking up behind me.

"Jesus fucking Christ," I exclaimed.

"Again, a good detective would have known I was there. Would have…detected it, you might say," said Daryl.

I grabbed Daryl by the arm and took him to his car. He turned his head back and called out to the kids.

"My name is Michael," said Daryl. "I'm Joe's son."

CHAPTER EIGHTEEN

Little Kids

Here's a test.

You're able to go back in time, dropped off at some perfect stage of your youth. Let's say the perimeters are ages twelve through eighteen, because those years are a fertile breeding ground for the kind of decisions and mistakes that can stick with you for the rest of your existence. You'll retain the memory of the life you lived prior to hitting the rewind button. All of those moments, those lessons you supposedly learned, the things you swear you'd do differently if given the chance, the regrets we all have—the opportunity to correct them all would lay there before you. Forget about investing in Microsoft, playing some lottery number or killing Hitler. That's not the point of the test.

There is a catch though—a rub if you will. You give up everyone you currently have in your life. If you're married you'll never meet your spouse. If you made your closest friends in college they will never make your acquaintance. If you've got a loyal golden retriever you'll never toss a tennis ball to him again. You're stuck with your family, though. It's cruel that way.

You will pave a new path, make other friends, try a different career, find a man or woman to replace the loved one you lost, or maybe decide to go it alone. And if you were single before maybe you'd try not to be this time.

We'd trade it all for youth. We'd give up everything just to do it again. To do it right, to be further from death's door, to spare someone you love the hearty little messy confection that is you. Some of us would make the same errors in judgment and some would be dead inside of a week. We'd prosper, we'd fail; we'd take chances and speak our minds earlier in life. We would try harder to become the person we always knew we were capable of, finally living up to our full potential. We'd eat healthier, travel more, learning new cultures and languages. We'd exercise, take piano lessons, avoid those friendships with poison personalities, and know exactly who we are and how to become the best version of ourselves that we can be. Our skin would be tight again. Our bodies wouldn't hurt for every waking moment. We'd appreciate time in a way that no young person has ever appreciated time in human history. We would love our lives. We would love life.

Most over the age of forty would say, "Hell yes, sign me up." We'd be joined by a good amount of thirty-somethings as well. There would be a number of fuck-ups in their twenties too. We'd all hit the reset button and make instant peace with our decision to give up every person we had ever met, excited by the prospect of the new. We'd come from different walks of life and have various and plentiful reasons to want to relive it all, or rewrite it all, or simply escape where we are in this moment, this phase of living. I can imagine them. I see them when I wait in line at the grocery store. I watch them in the waiting rooms of doctor's offices. I could roam the earth, tapping them on the shoulder to indicate which ones I believe would make willing candidates for this voyage through time. I'd be right more often than not, I can tell you that. Anyone who would tell you they'd stay put is either a liar or a parent. From what I've seen most people believe a child is worth suffering all of the relentless and unspeakable little hells life has in store for us all.

Michael had grown tired of his game. I'm still not exactly sure why he chose to play it in the first place. Michael's mother had kept my identity a secret for many years. She told him I was no one worth knowing—a sperm donor in the end—and that God wanted her to have and raise her beautiful child on her own. Teresa, Michael's mother, had made a fast friend when she moved from St. Louis to Stamford, Connecticut. This woman sympathized with a young mother–to-be who was staring down a lifetime of single-mother struggles. The woman had a husband who worked on Wall Street and she ordered him to take Teresa under his wing. He prepared her with books to study by day and "evening classes" held at their very impressive home throughout her pregnancy. A few months after Michael was born, Teresa began a routine in which she left him with the couple's nanny during the day and went to work for her friend's husband in New York City. Without so much as a day of college in her lifetime, she eventually became a full partner at a brokerage firm, and provided Michael with the best education and opportunities this country could offer.

I would have guessed Michael was in his late forties. He had salt and pepper hair and the kind of skin that had seen ample sun specifically from tennis courts and golf courses. He was 39 when we met that day on Ramona's property. He had hired an agency to find me and showed up in person to see what kind of man his father was. It is in his nature to go about things in roundabout ways. I know this about him now. It could be that he wanted me to like him for who he was, before letting me know exactly who he was to me. I'm not sure that's even possible with Michael. He is odd and off-putting. As I looked at him deeply from the passenger seat of his parked Lincoln, I could now see the slight physical resemblance between us.

"Who are these people, Joe?" asked Michael.

"The kids? I just met them. Never mind them," I said.

"Why are they waiting for us?"

"I said I'd take them to see someone inside," I said. "Why would you blurt that out, about you being my son, Daryl?" I asked.

"Michael," he said.

"Yeah. Okay. So it's Michael now, is it?"

"You're the one who insisted on calling me Daryl."

"You wouldn't give me a name. So I gave you one. Mister fucking mysterious."

"I did want to give you a mystery to solve. Clearly you had no interest in me or my case."

"You didn't present a case. You said something about me doing something illegal for a lot of dough."

"I wanted you to know that I'd done well in life. And I wanted to see your relationship to money firsthand. I know you don't have any. Was this the absence of greed or just a lack of opportunity, a lack of vision or moxie? Maybe you were just lazy. I imagined one of those fathers that crawl out of the woodwork when his abandoned son becomes a rich and famous athlete. I wanted to protect my assets."

"That's the stupidest thing I've ever heard, Daryl," I said.

"Michael. Please."

"When you say something stupid you'll get a Daryl. *Capisce?*"

"*Mi parla bene l'italiano. Sei?*"

"I still speak some, kid. So what was all that back on the Hill? Like you didn't know Italian culture already?"

"I lived in Italy for three years. No offense, but that is *not* Italian culture. That's Italian-American culture. There is a world of difference between the two," he said while laughing in a self-amused sort of way.

"Did Teresa die?" I said.

"Why would you ask that?"

"I'm trying to figure out why you're here."

"The time had come for me. Mother fought me on this for many years."

"Aw, geez. You're not the kind of man that calls his mother 'Mother,' are you?"

"I imagine she was quite a different woman when you knew her. It was fascinating to finally see where she came from. Where both of my parents were raised, that is."

"I barely remember her, kid. And now I'm thinking she's an asshole for taking off and not letting me know I was gonna be a dad."

"Would you have wanted to? Be a father, that is."

"Geez, I don't know. I mean, you seem alright I guess but to be honest I keep thinking about how much better you might have been had she given me a chance to help bring you up. Maybe not better off. But better."

Debbie tapped on the passenger's side window.

"Should we come back?" she asked. "Or just go in without you, Joe? Maybe it's a bad time?"

"Nonsense," I said.

I opened the door to get out of the car.

"You'll find me again, of course," I whispered to Michael.

"Si, ma certo," he said. "Pleasure meeting you both."

277

My head was nothing if not fucked. I've got Daryl being Michael, who's supposed to be my boy now, and then there's this pretty little tattooed lady and her, "Terrence may or may not have murdered my dad" bit, and as if I didn't have enough on my plate they were carrying Cleopatra into the building before us on one of those, what do you call them, those carts the slaves carried people around on. Well, it wasn't the actual historical Cleopatra. It was Elizabeth Taylor playing Cleopatra. I don't know what the real life Cleopatra even looked like. I've heard she was black but I don't know if that's true.

No sooner did I think about that then she turned around to look at me through the curtain and she looked like Pam Grier.

"I'd like to go in first," I told Debbie and Henry. "Terrence has a son."

"Lewis," said Debbie.

"Yeah, that's him," I said.

"He was a friend of my dad's actually. And my mom— before my father died."

"He's usually there by now, and out of respect for him I'd like to have you wait outside, make sure he's ok with you coming in."

I opened the door and there was Lewis watching his father sleep. I closed it softly behind me and Lewis nodded hello to me. Ramona was asleep as well. The room seemed tranquil and I knew that was just an illusion itself, and that

278

the illusion was about to be tested. I tapped Lewis on the shoulder and quietly asked if he could step outside with me.

"Debbie, Henry—this is Lewis," I said.

"Nice to meet you," said Lewis as he shook their hands.

"This is awkward, Lewis, but I just met them outside and it seems they were wanting to pay your father a visit," I said.

"You know my daddy?" he asked.

"I do," said Debbie. "Well, no, not really. I saw you both at a parole board meeting when I was a kid."

"What you doin' there?" asked Lewis.

"Marco was my father."

Lewis scrunched his face and looked back and forth between Debbie and I. He looked disgusted and surprised, and seemed to be taking a moment to react in a different way.

"My daddy free now. He don't need to see you," said Lewis.

"Lil," said Henry to Lewis. "Debbie, I mean. She doesn't want to—"

"I don't think your father killed my father, Lewis," Debbie said.

"So what? You come to say you sorry he went to jail?" said Lewis.

"No. Well, yes," said Henry. "She just wanted to speak with him I think."

"He ain't gonna talk to you," said Lewis.

"Maybe he can decide whether—" said Henry.

"He don't talk no more. Can't," said Lewis. "I don't know why you come here. I know your mama, girl. You need to go now. I'm going inside. Joe you get these young people out of here. Please."

He opened the door and Debbie craned her neck to see around Lewis, trying to catch a glimpse of Terrence. When Lewis passed over the threshold we could see that Terrence's eyes were open and that he was looking right at us.

"My God," whispered Henry.

Ramona woke us all from our late afternoon naps—Terrence, Lewis and myself. She was screaming for Lindsay. It was the first time she had asked about her daughter or said her name. She was thrashing around in the bed and yelling so loudly that the nurse came in before any of us could properly react. Terrence looked back and forth between Lewis and Ramona and he clutched at the sides of the bed. Lewis comforted him as the nurse and I tried to do the same for Ramona.

"Where's my daughter?" Ramona screamed.

The nurse looked to me for an answer. The staff wasn't made aware of Lindsay's recent passing. I had meant to take it up with Doctor Tim at some point, preparing them for the possibility that Ramona may regain some temporary clarity again and wonder where her only child had gone. I had somehow forgotten to do that.

"She's not here right now, Ro. It's ok. Let's just calm down and we can talk—"

"Don't you tell me to fucking calm down. I don't listen to you. I know you're in on it. We don't have any money. Just give me my daughter."

She was grabbing at me and yelling louder and louder, her words becoming a jumbled slobber of syllables.

"I'm getting the doctor," said the nurse as she hurried out of the room.

Lewis came over and stood behind me while Ramona was going on about kidnappers, ransom and her poor Lindsay.

"Anything I can do to help?" asked Lewis softly.

"Get the fuck away from me, black boy," screamed Ramona.

Lewis backed away immediately and gave me sympathetic eyes.

"What the fuck was that look? He's in on it too? You're all in on it? Give me back my daughter goddammit," she said.

The doctor—not Tim but another—came in and they quickly moved to sedate Ramona. Within moments she was silent, and then she was asleep.

"Has this happened before?" asked the doctor.

"She's never upset," said the nurse. "She's grumpy and rude but never angry or frightened. Who's Lindsay? Is that a real person?"

"Her daughter," I muttered as I sat.

"She has a daughter?" asked the nurse. "I thought the niece we spoke to in Wisconsin—I thought she was the closest living relative."

I stared at Ramona as she rested.

"Her daughter killed herself a while back. A few months now—I can't remember when exactly. She left a note asking that no one tell her mother. She wanted the police to call me specifically. I'm a private detective so they gave me the courtesy. Ramona's doctor agreed it was probably best. Lindsay struggled with depression. She just wasn't happy, not like she should have been, never for long enough anyway. And then this...with her mom... it got to her. Ramona couldn't even recognize her any longer. That was it. She could go."

CHAPTER NINETEEN

Pleased To Meet Me

Henry had explored the greenhouse in awe, borrowing the look of the seven-year old girl that now stood next to him. The young girl had separated from her mother and her older sister who were calling her name from just outside the building. The girl touched a carnivorous plant on its tip, rapidly, as if holding her finger there for a nanosecond longer would be the swift death of her. Henry was bent at the knees and he gave the kid a look that confirmed she had just defied the grim reaper. The mother entered the spacious glass structure and retrieved her child. Henry continued his studies alone, as Debbie and her mother had taken a seat on a bench near the entrance.

"I can't believe I haven't been here since you were little," said Angel.

"This place is fucking rad. I'd come here all the time if I lived so close," said Debbie.

"Would you?" said Angel. "Ever live close again that is."

"Absolutely not."

"Do you hate me that much?"

"I don't hate you. I was never particularly fond of St. Louis. But I've made my peace with things as far as you're concerned."

"Oh, bullshit, Deborah. The last thing you are is at peace. Anyone can see that."

Henry came up with a smile on his face and asked if they could find the Japanese garden section. They consulted a map near a fountain outside and followed a path to that area.

"Why don't we have botanical gardens like this in LA?" he asked.

"We do," said Debbie. "There's a place called The Arboretum."

"Really? We've got to go there when we get back."

"I hope you're not heading home soon," said Angel.

"Not sure," said Debbie. "Depends."

"On what?" asked Angel.

"You maybe," said Debbie.

Henry spotted the lake up ahead and waved for the women to quickly join him. They walked along sections of weathered wooden planks that bridged the mossy water below, overlapping at ninety degree turns, stepping up and then down again.

"What kind of plant is this?" said Henry as he touched a grassy growth that emanated from the water next to the deck boards. He stood and briskly walked ahead before getting an answer.

"I like Henry," said Angel. "Is it serious?"

"We saw Terrence yesterday," said Debbie.

"What? Without me?"

"His son wouldn't let us in the room but I could see him. He looked spooky."

"Well, yes, he's a murderer," said Angel.

"No, I don't mean that. He looked lost in his own skin. Like an animal that thought it was paralyzed but wasn't at all."

"Why would you go there and not let me know you were going?"

"There's a detective. A private investigator from California. He's there with them. He has a friend who is Terrence's roommate. He's odd, the detective—a little off I think. But he's likeable. I want to hire him."

"Please don't start this."

"I don't have any money. Not enough anyway. I'm sure he's not too expensive. I'll do what I can but I need you to help."

"You think I'm giving you money to waste like that?"

"What if the person who took my father from you were out there, getting away with it all these years? If the man who stole that from me, who changed my life, who changed *our* lives the way he did, if he still walks this fucking earth, free and happy, knowing he got away with what he did to us, I want to see him suffer. I need to see him suffer."

We got out of our cars and walked together to the front door, Lewis and I. Wanting to apologize for springing the kids on him the day before, I had offered to take him out to dinner once his father was resting. We had driven to a BBQ joint near the home at my suggestion, which immediately felt like a prejudiced proposition. But St. Louis barbecue was something I missed now and again.

It was a cozy place. This worried me. When a small business is that small I tend to assume it's that way for good reason. They weren't spending whatever profit there was on the décor either. Maybe I'd just gotten used to the on-the-snout decorations that the barbecue restaurants of the West Coast always favored: pig-themed tin signs with references to the great American South covering every millimeter of paneled walls. Truth was I'd forgotten that less means more where this particular dining fare was concerned.

There was a thin man eating alone at a table in the middle of the room and a rotund couple dwarfing the bench seats of a nearby booth. I eyeballed their meal, which gave me a good idea of the menu, as the entire lineup seemed to be laid out before them.

We slid into the next booth over, our stomachs fighting the table the whole way. A young man brought our orders and we dug into ribs, chicken and link sausage. The following conversation was covered in red sauce.

"About that girl yesterday," I said.

"Don't wanna talk about that," he stated without looking up from his plate.

"I understand. Must have been quite a shock. I just wanted to say sorry for escorting them to the room. I'm not advocating for them or anything."

"I hear you say you a detective?" he asked.

"Recently retired. I'm no longer seeing clients," I said.

"You tired of working?" asked Lewis as he waved a rib in a quick circular motion.

"No," I said.

"So you happy retiring?" he said.

"Well, it just set in. Not sure I have much of a choice in the matter to be honest."

"Your company make you leave then."

"No, it's my own little business. Out in San Francisco."

"Oh," he said.

"But I'm here now and the customers are there so…"

"You can't work here?"

"Well, I don't know. I mean I'm not licensed in Missouri but I hadn't even considered it really," I said.

"How much you charge?"

"It depends on the case. How many hours something looked to take and how much extra cost there may be."

"Hmm," he said as he chewed on a rib.

"What do you do, Lewis?"

"I work at a rental car company. Out at the airport."

"You like it?"

"Yeah. Good people there. Friend of my daddy got me the job just out of high school."

"I'm sorry to hear about your dad. That girl seems to think he may have been wrongly convicted."

"She does, huh? Well, she right about that. You wanna help me prove that the case?" he said.

"I don't understand. Does he have to go back to jail?"

"Nah. Just ain't right, people thinking what they think about him. Ain't fair what they did. We didn't have no money to fight. When he went to parole, Angel, that's that girl's momma, she show up and say how he took her little girl's daddy."

"That's terrible. I'm not sure what I could do, though. I'm not a lawyer and I've never handled this kind of case as a PI. To tell you the truth I don't even know what kind of a PI I am anymore."

288

"Sure you'd do better than I would alone. It's important to me. Something I'd like to do for him. Something I like to give him 'fore it too late."

I felt the shared wall of the booth begin to shake behind me. Lewis grabbed the table to stabilize it as I was shoved closer to my bowl of baked beans. I heard a woman shriek. She called out, "Oh my God, Leonard."

As I stuck my neck out and struggled to free myself from the seating, my entire view of the restaurant was briefly eclipsed by the sight of the male half of the couple who had been parked in the next booth over. He had lifted himself out of his seat and spun toward us. He grabbed at his throat and lost his footing, landing on the solo diner who hadn't reacted at all to the commotion behind him, continuing to chew his steak instead, a serrated knife in his right hand and his fork in his left. Three hundred pounds of choking man collapsed on his spine, obscuring the wiry man from our view upon impact. The screaming wife had moved like a cat and was blanketing her husband as he was gasping for air and turning bluer with every attempt. I looked to Lewis to confirm that he was seeing this as well. Lewis looked to me as if I were the kind of man that knew how to save a person's life.

The woman cried out for help as she added her substantial weight to the spasming dog pile. Lewis and I stood as the counterman ran up and ducked underneath the choking man, grabbing at his chubby cheeks and opening his mouth. The woman let out a terrifying, shrill howl and raised her right hand to the air. It was covered in blood. Lewis and I grabbed at the large man's shoulders and pulled too hard. We yanked him into our bodies and fell to the floor. The wife smeared her bloody fingers around the panicked eyes of her soon-to-be-dead husband. Looking up, I saw the knife lodged in the throat of the lifeless thin man.

By the time Debbie approached me with the idea of hiring me I had already agreed to help Lewis for the same purpose. I had sent Debbie and Henry home for the day and told them I'd speak to Lewis about a meeting between everyone. I told him they'd like Angel to join us. Debbie was trying to open her mother's mind to the possibility that it wasn't Terrence who had killed Marco. Lewis picked a spot for us to gather together and we agreed on 8:00 P.M. the next evening.

I pulled into the parking lot and saw Lewis waiting, leaning on the hood of his car. In the distance there was a football field and a game was in progress. One of the players had left the gridiron and was walking up behind Lewis. He stopped when he got to Lewis's Ford Fiesta and began looking it over. He put his leather helmet on the roof and climbed underneath it for a moment. I don't need this kind of distraction today, I thought. As the footballer grabbed his lid from the car, silent shots came in and blasted him full of holes. I turned to look over my shoulder and saw the Thompson gun in the hands of a mobster. He winked at me, tipped his fedora, climbed into his 1928 Cadillac and sped away.

These moments had become like a radio playing in my mind, with the dial caught between two stations and giving off overlapping, competing signals. Lewis was the soothing classical chamber music, the visitors were Mexican drinking songs.

"You alright, Joe?" said Lewis.

"Sure. Thought I heard someone coming. Maybe the kids."

"I'm the first one here. Been here a little while now. Used to live right up the street over there," he said while pointing. "We went here, me and Angel. Marco, too, before us. "

"You get back here often?"

"High school reunions? Nah, guess I ain't much for that kind of thing. Only went here a little whiles anyway."

"So is it how you remember it being?" I asked as I leaned on the hood next to him.

"Seem smaller. Kind of figured that be the case. Even drove by my old house. Seem smaller, too."

"Yeah, my old neighborhood felt the same way to me recently. It's funny you picked this place though."

"Me and Angel got history between us. I'm thinking maybe I'll do better seeing her here again, like when we was kids, maybe help me forgive how she showed up to keep Daddy in jail those times. Forgive her like the Lord expect me to."

"I know that can't be easy," I said.

"Ain't never known life to be," he said.

"You sleep alright? Past couple of nights?" I asked.

"Nah. You?"

"I keep seeing it, over and over, every time I close my eyes," I said.

"Same," he said. "Just keep thinking about it—those poor men. Taken like that, the two of them together. Didn't have to be neither. Maybe that skinny one eats somewhere else that night or has that knife pointing down—maybe that other man don't order all that meat. Lord got a plan for us all though. This I know. Just hard to figure, hard to watch sometimes is all, hard to bear that witness. I figure maybe you're more used to that—maybe not that exactly—but death. You being a detective and all."

"I'm starting to think maybe people have the wrong idea about my work. Truth is, I'm just a guy who used to look for bad behavior. And when I managed to actually find it, I guess I thought I was helping…but what kind of help is that really?"

"You helping me."

I gave him a look of appreciation that was riddled with dejection. It was a moment in which I became suddenly and keenly aware that melancholy was winning the war between my bullshit charm and enormous sadness, and that it wasn't even a battle anymore.

We got hit with the headlights from Angel's car. Henry had stayed behind at the hotel. Debbie was quick to get out and say hello. Angel took a little time opening her door.

"It's nice to see you again, Lewis," said Debbie as they shook hands.

Angel got out of the car and walked up to us with a hesitation in her stride.

"Hello, Lewis," she said.

"Hello," he said.

"I'm Angel," she said, waving slightly to me.

"Nice meeting you, Angel," I said. "My name's Joe Iocca."

"Yes, my daughter's told me about you. You're a PI from California?"

"Here, originally. But yes, I live in San Francisco."

"Joe gonna help prove my daddy didn't kill Marco," stated Lewis.

"I've never blamed you personally for what happened, Lewis. I would have liked for us to have stayed friends," Angel said.

Lewis made a face and looked down at the paved parking lot for a few moments.

"This used to be gravel, didn't it?" he said.

"I don't know. I guess," said Angel.

"I remember that time your boyfriend have that fight here. And all those times he come around raisin' Cain about you."

"Why did you have us meet you here, Lewis?" asked Angel.

"You ever think maybe it was him? Maybe your boyfriend found out about you and Marco?"

"What? No. I mean... No. I honestly can't even remember his name," she said.

"Well you need to try," said Debbie. "Right, Joe?"

"We'll want to look at anyone who may have had a beef with Marco. From what Lewis has told me this old boyfriend is just one of many suspects we'll need to track down."

CHAPTER TWENTY

Casual Interrogations

An interview with Skinny

How did I end up living on the streets in fucktown Arizona? My boy being a faggot for one. His mother protected him. Tried to hide it from me. You can't tell me it wasn't my right as his father to beat the tar out of him when I caught him using butter to jerk his little faggot friend off. MY butter. MY son. MY house.

Well, he's dead now. AIDS got him. His mother called just to spite me. Her being there with him in the end, holding his fucking hand. The spic-sucking whore that she is. I'm supposed to feel bad about it? I don't give two shits if it's God's plan or whatever you want to call it. He did it to his own damn self. He deserved it.

I got a cousin lived out here. He's dead now too. Fuck work. I get mine any way I can, but I will answer to no fucking man. You've seen my sheet. I ain't confessing nothing new. Taking copper pipe from construction sites, breaking into homes, stealing that laptop computer at that faggoty café...it's all better than pretending to be happy with a cunt-face wife, a faggot son and a shit job. I'm above all that. Fuck the whole damn thing. Society. Fuck you. They rigged the game against people like me. I gotta have an address to qualify for this handout or that fucking thing to which I am owed. I'm white. Jews run the damn planet. Always have. I got no friends out here. To hell with 'em. Whores, thieves, lazy fucking Mexicans or Indians or whatever they are. I take a newspaper, everyday, I take it from the diner. That ain't stealing, it's fucking used already. I go right to the obituaries and read about all the people who fucking died before me.

I win.

An interview with Phil

After high school I joined the Marines. I hadn't planned on being in the armed services but my father let me know it was either college or enlistment. No school would take me, so when I graduated Hazelwood High I spent the summer partying, knowing it was my last hurrah before boot camp in the fall.

I never saw live combat. The boys and I would have done anything to go into Iran and whoop some towelhead butt, after what happened with the American hostages, but they never gave us a chance. I spent six years being moved around the world. I was stationed in Guam, Germany and Saudi Arabia. We rode Harleys in the desert and I even hooked up with this Sheik's daughter for a little while.

It wasn't until after I discharged that I found Jesus. I was living in a mobile home parked on a buddy's place down in North Carolina. His uncle was a Pentecostal minister who had done three tours in Vietnam, and he taught me how to reconcile the violence of our nature and to live in the light of God's love. He met Oral Roberts back in '72 and Mr. Roberts set him on the path to righteousness. He always said there wasn't nothing that could happen to a man in wartime that a good faith healer couldn't fix.

I didn't always know that God had tasked me with helping the suffering. I figured that kind of thing went to God's chosen ones, men who had natural discipline, practiced abstinence and self-control. With my background I seemed more like a candidate to be saved and then go on preaching the good word to all ye sinners. It was my friend's uncle who saw the healer in me and helped coax it out.

By 1987 I had my own tent revival and was travelling the southern parts of the country, making a real difference in people's lives. When I think about how many Americans got sucked into watching MTV or playing the stock market or snorting cocaine, when all the while they could have been saved if they had just called His name, just come out and saw what I could do as a humble servant of the Lord. It breaks my heart.

It's been a quarter century of good living for me. We spend about half the year on the road now and the other half at home here in Mexico, Missouri, where my mother was raised. The Baptists in town don't appreciate snake handling or speaking in tongues because they're just ignorant and afraid. Jesus Christ has taught me many a valuable lesson in my fifty years on this earth. I no longer raise a hand to any man. And it is not my place to judge or forgive. God will cast the final judgment on us all. God's forgiveness is the only forgiveness man requires.

An interview with Go Way

I feel good. Feel like I'm finally getting my act together. My daughter and her husband are letting me stay in their basement for now. There's a pool table and some old video games to keep me occupied. I'm checking in with my PO, looking for work like they want me to. I been sober since the last few months in the penitentiary. So that gives me nearly seven months clean this time. I really want to be the kind of man my grandkid can look up to, be proud of.

I can't change my past. I'd like to meet the man who could. A prison cell is nothing more than concrete walls filled with regret. I think it's supposed to be remorse. But that ain't always the case; almost never from what I've seen. An inmate feels sorry for himself, not for what he's done. The Chaplain taught me that.

I got a deal in place with my girl. She says if I can stay out and stay clean, my grandson will never have to know what kind of a fuck-up I've been. But one more time and she's cutting me out for good. I know how easy it is to screw up a kid with just one bad example, just someone they can point to that didn't walk the line. All the positive role models in the world can lose out when just one blood relative gives them reason enough to see another path. He doesn't want to go my way. My way never has been any damn good.

CHAPTER TWENTY-ONE

Detective Work

Lena being a lawyer came in handy. She rang a friend in the public defender's office out in Phoenix. Within two days I got a call from this woman, letting me know she'd tracked down Mr. Wiener, the neighbor they all called Skinny.

"He's a mess, Mr. Iocca," she said. "He shouldn't be on the streets at his age. I'm surprised he's survived as long as he has out there."

"If I wanted to locate him again, how hard would that be?" I asked.

"He doesn't roam. It only took me the morning to find him once I got the call from Lena. Everything on his record is within a few downtown blocks pretty much. Did his family hire you to find him? I know you can't say but he really does require treatment. He needs to be in psych."

"I appreciate you taking the time out of your day for us, ma'am," I said.

We could have looked at DNA evidence if the cops had done a better job. You hear about that kind of thing exonerating the falsely accused all of the time. What you don't hear about is how they didn't see the science coming, or simply didn't care. In 1978 things got lost and tossed. Lewis said the lawyers brought this up in one of Terrence's appeals but the judge wasn't persuaded.

The good news was that this was exactly the kind of thing that really steamed Lena. She went on and on about a miscarriage of justice, the disproportionate incarceration rate vis-a-vis minorities to whites in this country (her words, not mine), and the way the system favors the wealthy and punishes the poor.

The staff at the Beacon Home wasn't sure what to make of us. Some days you could barely move in that little room. There was Ramona, Lena, Angel, Debbie, Henry, Lewis, Terrence and myself—all of us poring over records and trial notes with the exception of the two permanent residents. Terrence slept much of the day and Ramona had entered a phase of near-constant joy. Between the progression of the disease and the mix of meds she had lost her anger and frustration, and now seemed to genuinely enjoy and benefit from our company.

"Don't none of you people have jobs?" cracked the nurse as she pushed through the bodies to reach Ramona's bed.

"I do," said Angel as she raised her hand from a seated position in the back of the room.

"Doc says we'll be moving Terrence to his own room soon," said the nurse. "Can't imagine what your new roommate's gonna think of all this, Ramona."

Ramona smiled at her. For all of the times I was able to make her laugh or feel a little loved years before, it seemed like this was the first I had seen her truly content. The constant worry she carried for her daughter had always tempered her own happiness.

"Maybe it's best for my daddy, him getting to be alone," Lewis said.

"We're always gonna do what's best for him, Lewis," said the nurse. "You remember not to worry, hear me?"

Angel looked at me and it was clear that we both understood that the nurse had feelings for Lewis. It was equally obvious that Lewis was unaware of her interest.

Hours after Angel had discovered Marco's body, the police pulled Terrence off the baggage line and briefly interrogated him inside of an office at the airport, before bringing him in. Skinny had received a call that morning from his wife and Skinny thought it best to phone the police immediately and let them know that he had recently overheard Terrence threatening Marco. The police report shows that Mr. Wiener recounted hearing Terrence telling

Marco to, "Stay away from my boy or I'll kill you." He also noted seeing Lewis enter the house multiple times after this threat was made. He gave details about the kind of men that came to see Marco and speculated on the purposes for their visits. This helped to confirm the picture the police were piecing together of Marco as a drug dealer who had enlisted the help of the naïve fifteen-year old Lewis, and how this enraged their prime suspect.

Lewis's aunt picked him up that night and, after visiting Terrence in jail, they drove back to East St. Louis, where Lewis would soon enroll at a new high school and finish his studies there. Having a parent in prison was relatively commonplace in his new school. It became an icebreaker, an awful thing to bond over, and within time he began to make a few new friends. He recalled his junior and senior year with some warmth, in spite of the difficult weekend trips to Joliet, and the constant longing he felt for his parents' presence and embrace.

Lewis graduated and took the position at the rental car agency. It was his first and only job. Commuting from Illinois to Missouri everyday, he said he often thought of Marco, and how he had once taught him to drive. He moved past the heartbreak and resentment he felt for his friends. More than anything he just missed spending his days with them. But there was no getting around the negative association he felt for his relationship with Marco and how his father was set to spend the rest of his life incarcerated. What if Weebie hadn't offered them the house? What if his mother had worked at any other restaurant? What choices would

Lewis make in his life that may, in some unforeseeable way, lead to personal disaster and heartache? He chose a simple life. He became a church-going man at the behest of his aunt and grandmother. He took the exact same route into work every morning, at the exact same time, brought his lunch, ate in the break room, and retraced his path home every evening. Saturdays he drove to see his father. Sunday mornings were dedicated to the artlessly-named Church of God near his home. Afterwards, the whole family would go out to lunch together. This was the only meal he ever had that was not prepared by either his grandmother or his aunt. He never went on a date. He never married.

I drove Debbie and Lewis to Ferguson. We wanted to search old microfiche related to the case. We were gathering a list of suspects based on the trial notes and what Angel and Lewis could provide. Before we confronted the men who had already popped up on our radar, I needed to be sure there weren't other players.

"Half of the files burned up years ago in a fire we had at the building next door," said the county clerk. "Anything you can find will be on those machines in the back there. Good luck."

We spent a fruitless day searching. Occasionally one of us would hit on something and it turned out the clerk was exactly right: the other half of the information was missing.

"Jesus fucking Christ," said Debbie as she slammed her palm onto the table. "How can they have been so irresponsible with records?"

"Can't control fire, kid," I said.

"Wish you wouldn't say that, Deborah," said Lewis.

"What?" she asked.

"That thing you say, taking the Lord's name in vain like you do."

I chuckled lightly as I stared at the poorly lit screen of my machine.

"You say it, too, Joe," said Lewis. "You know it ain't right."

"Sorry, Lewis," I said.

"We don't mean to offend you," said Debbie.

"You offending God," said Lewis.

Debbie wanted to see where her father had lived. Lewis directed me on how to get to Barto Street. As we drove up the initial hill and along the flat stretch of road, we saw a lot of people spending time outside of their homes. Everyone there was African-American. We reached Marco's old place and stopped out front. Debbie got out of the car and went to knock on the door.

"I don't think that's a good idea, Deborah," said Lewis as he got out of the passenger's side.

"Lewis is right," I said.

She knocked, of course. A woman in her forties came to the door in her robe, her maroon hair in curlers.

"What you want?" said the woman.

"Sorry to bother you, ma'am," said Debbie, "but my father used to live here."

"So?" said the woman.

"Well, I was hoping to maybe come inside and see where he grew up."

"Black man," she said to Lewis, "get over here and take this crazy white girl off my stoop."

"Sorry, ma'am. C'mon now, Deborah," said Lewis.

"Hey," said Debbie. "There's no reason to be so damn rude."

"Bitch, fuck you," said the woman as she pushed her screen door open wider and came face to face with Debbie.

I moved as spryly as I could and came up behind Debbie, grabbing at her shoulders.

"Let's go, Debbie," I said.

"For fuck's sake I just wanted to see the place where my father was fucking killed," said Debbie as she tugged away from my pull.

"Don't nobody give a shit 'bout your daddy getting hisself killed, bitch. Motherfuckers be killed all the time. Best watch yourself, be damn sure you ain't end up just like him—hear me?" she said with her face now inches away from Debbie's.

Lewis walked up behind Debbie and we both took an arm. We yanked her off the porch and walked her back to the car. She was yelling at the woman the whole way. I saw that a few neighbors had gathered on the lawn across the street. From Angel's description and the geography I knew this was the old Wiener home.

"Take that bitch on out of here," said a teenage girl who stood at the edge of the lawn.

"What the fuck did you say?" said Debbie as she began to get out of the back of the car, prompting Lewis and I to stop from opening our own doors.

"Fuck you, cray-cray," said the girl.

She reached down and picked up a rock from her yard. She threw like Don fucking Drysdale, hitting Debbie on her left breast, dead square on the nipple if I had to guess.

"Motherfucker," said Debbie as Lewis and I pushed her back into the car.

Lewis climbed in next to Debbie and all but sat on her. I got back in the front seat. We pulled into a driveway just down the road and I turned the car back. The girl had grabbed another rock, this one a little bigger, and she chucked it our way, hitting the front quarter panel of the Camry.

"Jesus fucking Christ," I said as we sped down the road.

I had apparently switched hotels on Debbie and Henry's recommendation. Theirs was cheaper and a little less depressing than where I had been lodging for God knows how long. I got the room next to them. One morning I woke up in a bed that smelled less like Lysol, as I stared up at a whirling ceiling fan. I walked outside in my jockeys and a tank top undershirt and was shocked to find I was on the second floor. Henry came out from the next door over and said good morning. I pretended to know how I got there and where exactly "there" was. Henry asked if I slept okay adjusting to the new bed and I surmised that it was my first day at the Roadside Motel, seeing the tall sign out near the frontage road as I did at that moment.

My clients stayed away. It wouldn't make any sense, them travelling two thousand miles to rehire me for the same old San Francisco cases. So there was sense to be made of it all. That helped me hold it together. I had adjusted to what I now considered to be the background noise of the sightings. If someone seemed out of place and didn't make any sound, the odds were good I was just imagining them there. I figured all of this out on my own. It didn't take a doctor or a psychiatrist or any mixture of pills to help me get a handle on what was happening to me. I felt good about that. I felt proud.

Waking to being expertly fellated by Marie Antoinette that next morning did catch me off guard.

At first I thought I was having one of my better dreams. But those moments of confusing your waking life and slumber only last for a few seconds at most. I felt the warmth of her mouth on me and I reached down to grab her by the powdered wig. It felt stiff, like my grandmother's hair fresh from a visit to Lucia's Salon, which was not the image I cared to have at that moment. Marie Antoinette gazed up at me without breaking her stride, so to speak. I was just getting comfortable when Angel knocked on my door.

"Joe, are you in there?" she said.

Marie Antoinette winked at me and stood up. She took elegant steps across the room and pulled back the curtain that partially covered the closet near the front door. Her ball gown stuck out through the bottom and the sides of the drape, and I could see the top of her light blue hair.

"Just a second," I said as I searched the room for my shirt and pants.

I put my clothes on, patted down my hair in the mirror and opened the front door toward the closet. Marie giggled and kicked me softly with her now bare foot through the bottom of the curtain.

"I'm sorry, Joe, I didn't mean to wake you," said Angel.

"Please, don't apologize. I'm up. I'd invite you in but the place is a mess. Real uneven performance from the maid service around here."

I caught Angel shooting a couple of quick glances toward my crotch and I realized I was building a reputation as an uncommonly virile older man.

"Sorry, Angel," I said.

"Joe, please. I shouldn't have come by so early. I was on my way to work and wanted to speak with you before saying hello to the kids. Really, I don't mind the mess."

"Fair enough," I said as I motioned for her to enter the room.

Marie Antoinette opened the curtain and walked to the bathroom. Angel didn't notice her and I hadn't really expected she would. With the former clients I could always feel them when they touched me, hear them when they spoke. After that day in the café with the pink woman I spent the evening wondering what I must have looked like to the patrons, talking to this imagined person from my past, if she was indeed merely a figment of my imagination. During our conversation I remember scanning the room to see if any of the customers were looking at me like I was a crazy person who was talking to himself. That's a common occurrence in San Francisco, though, and most folks will just ignore the wacko as they seemed to be doing with me. Half the city seemed filled with people losing their minds from living on the streets too long, while the moneyed half walked around talking in to their phones with some kind of earpiece, so it looked like practically everyone was having a conversation with an imaginary friend.

But Marie wasn't some client from my past. She was an 18th century royal and there she was, buck-naked on the bathroom counter, in full view of the room. I worked hard not to notice as she began to play with herself, squealing from the first touch.

"I'm worried about my daughter's involvement with all of this," said Angel.

I pointed to the chair that was next to the bed. She sat down, her back to Marie, and continued as I took a seat on the bed.

"Debbie likes to pretend she's tough. Maybe she truly is now. Unfortunately I can't say. I just don't want anything bad to happen to her."

"I'm being very careful not to put anyone in harm's way," I said.

"Yes, but so far you've just been looking at files and asking Lewis and I questions. What happens when you think you've got a lead? What happens when you confront one of these guys? Is that the plan? Or will you take what you find to the police?"

"Lena and I agree, the cops won't want to get involved until we have something substantial. I'm bouncing everything off of her. The hope is that we can make a good argument that one of these other players had motive and opportunity. At least cast the doubt in some official manner. Maybe the papers will write a story. Something to help clear Terrence's name. I'm not deluding myself into thinking that we're going to find much in the way of physical evidence. This was a real botch-job on the police's part. Short of a confession my guess is we may never see actual justice served. That's why I couldn't take Lewis's money. Or your daughter's."

"I don't think that's the reason," said Angel as she stood. "You're a good man, Joe Iocca. And I know you won't put Deborah in a position where she could be hurt."

She gave me an unexpected hug and walked to the front of the room.

"Can I ask you something, Angel?"

"Of course."

"All those years convinced it was Terrence—why the sudden change of heart?"

She looked at me with a small smile and tilted her head slightly.

"I wouldn't say I've had a change of heart. But there's a part of me that now hopes you're right. I like Lewis and can understand why he'd want to see his ailing father found innocent, of course. Do you have any children, Joe?"

I nodded and my stomach felt tight as I did, as if I had told a lie, because Michael felt a little like a lie.

"After twenty years of battling her," she continued, "feeling like I had lost her. If this is what it takes to get my daughter back, letting go of what I've believed for so long, well, it's not even a contest. But I won't risk her safety. You have to promise me that. Whoever did this—if it wasn't Terrence—he's obviously dangerous. Some scumbag drug connection of Marco's maybe. If it wasn't Lewis's dad it's someone like that I'm sure. Those dealers—I met some of them briefly. They were all very sketchy, scary people. I always hated that Marco did what he did and I was proud of him for walking away. To be honest it makes me feel guilty now, knowing that he quit for me and thinking that may have gotten him killed. But Terrence was always the obvious choice, and that's what the police believed, so that's what I believed."

"I grew up here, too, of course. And I can tell you one thing for certain, the police liked their suspects to be black back then. I left here long ago but it wouldn't surprise me to learn they still do."

We said goodbye and I closed the door behind her. I heard her knock on Debbie and Henry's room. I turned to face Marie Antoinette. She said something to me in French but I don't speak French. I made my way across the room and went down on the former Queen of France.

We took a look into Mr. Wiener's alibi for that night. Separate officers had spoken to the Wieners: one talked to Mrs. Wiener in person, and one spoke to Mr. Wiener later that day by phone. There was a discrepancy in their statements. Mr. Wiener had claimed they were both sleeping together at the time of the murder, which the coroner's office had placed between midnight and 6:00 A.M. Wiener had initially told the police that he retired to his marital bed somewhere between 10:00 and 10:30 that evening. He stated that his wife had gone to sleep some time after 9:00 and that he did not wake her when he entered the room. Looking at the wife's version, there was different information given. Mrs. Wiener had indeed said goodnight to her son, Jerry, just after a favorite television program had ended at 9:00 P.M. But according to the record, her husband had gone down to their finished basement shortly after dinner at 6:00 P.M. and, from what she could tell, remained there until she heard the shower running at 5:30 A.M. She said that neither her husband spending the night alone downstairs nor the hour that he prepared for work was a departure from his ordinary routine.

There was a follow-up visit to the Wiener home many weeks after the homicide, and an interview was performed that had attempted to resolve the conflicting statements. They were likely done at the insistence of the prosecutor, preparing for the defense. A police report detailed an officer confirming Mrs. Wiener's version. It was at this time that she described a sexual encounter she had instigated with the deceased, oral in nature. She asked that, if possible, this could remain confidential. The policeman noted in the file that Mrs. Wiener gave this new information in what the officer speculated was an attempt to provide motive for her husband. She suggested that he might have known about the incident, noting her husband's behavior had become erratic afterwards. She stopped short of accusing her husband of spousal abuse but described his violent nature, his temper and a hatred for other races, especially mixed race people like Marco.

An officer was dispatched to Mr. Wiener's place of employment shortly thereafter. When presented with his wife's account of the evening, Mr. Wiener confessed to falling asleep on a couch in the basement. He disclosed that he had been watching stag movies well into the night and said he was too embarrassed to admit that at the time of his original statement. He communicates in the report that he thought the information was inconsequential, as he had little to no contact with the victim and no reason to wish him any harm. The court-appointed defense attorney submitted this into evidence and called both Wieners to the stand during the trial, but obviously the jury did not view either of them as potential killers, as the defense intended to show. Mrs. Wiener filed for a divorce and was granted full custody of their child just prior to being called to testify in the case.

Marco had recounted to Angel the story of the day he confronted "Skinny." She and Lewis also told me of the tension they both witnessed at times between Marco and the neighbors. I didn't figure Marco for a braggart. If anything, his willingness to tell tales like the day he chased Mr. Wiener on his lawn or how he had cut ties with the man everyone knew simply as Go Way, provided a clear picture of the closeness of the relationship Marco had forged with Angel.

I consulted with Lena regarding what we had on Mr. Wiener, which clearly showed motive and opportunity. She agreed, but thought that since a jury had already been made aware of these facts, it wouldn't be any more convincing on its own this time around. She also warned that even a full confession in his current state of mind would be difficult to bring to trial. He was a seventy-five year old man who had lived on the streets for at least a decade, and the psychiatric evaluations given at various points of incarceration in his life determined him to be a delusional paranoid. Between the travel required to speak to him in person and the odds of convincing the state of Missouri to extradite him, we decided to explore the other suspects first and leave open a possible stop in Phoenix for Henry, Debbie and I on our way back to California.

I was more interested in what we had discovered when Lena did some rather impressive detective work. Lewis and Angel had both painted a picture of Denny, Marco's stepfather, as a violent, hateful man who would have been their first thought had he not been in jail at the time of Marco's murder. Lena figured the connection between Marco and the drug dealers went directly through Denny, and hoped to gather some info, like the true name of Go Way, for instance—something Lewis could not recall. While looking at Denny Whitehead's tome of a rap sheet, she noted a prison escape on his record that occurred several weeks before Marco's death. Denny had run off with a fellow prisoner while clearing a field in southern Missouri. He was eventually picked up in The Lake of The Ozarks but had been on the lam for nearly ten months. He was in and out of jail until the late 1990's, and that's where his relationship with the penal system dropped off. In fact, no other traceable sign of him appeared after that date: no bills in his name, no parking tickets or even a driver's license renewed. Given that he would be eighty-two years old at present time, we assumed he had passed away, knowing what we did about the kind of a life he had led. But Lena couldn't find a death record on Denny Whitehead, only his last known residence in Wentzville, the one he gave to the parole officer after his final release from prison. With Angel at work that day, Debbie convinced me to let her and Henry accompany Lewis and I to the address Lena provided.

"This is exciting," Henry said from the backseat.

"Dork," said Debbie as she pushed at him like they were a couple of eight year olds.

"Some of this place still look like I remember," said Lewis as we drove on a rural road.

"I imagine they'll develop this far from the freeway someday," I said.

"I swear this look just like the place Denny take me," said Lewis.

We pulled onto a long driveway and I slowed the car as we approached a dilapidated single family home. There was an old truck on blocks in front of the house and indications that the structure was uninhabitable in its current condition, like broken windows and missing sections of roofing material. There was a shoddy ramp leading up to the front door where stairs had once been. The screen door opened and closed a matter of inches as the wind blew and the front door itself was partially ajar.

"This is it. This the house he took me to," said Lewis as we exited the car.

"Lena said the owner of record was named Whitehead too," I said. "He died years ago, though. Seems like Denny used to stay here."

Debbie wasted no time climbing the plywood ramp and Henry quickly followed her. Lewis and I each looked around a separate side of the house before walking back to meet them at the door. Debbie was peering through the partial opening as Lewis made it halfway up the ramp and reached back to grab my hand. I took three steps and the thing caved.

"Oh God," said Henry as he kneeled on the porch and reached out to grab for Lewis and I as if we were in quicksand.

"You guys alright?" asked Debbie as she hopped off the porch and came to my side. "What are you even doing, Henry? Get down here."

I tried to pull myself out of the hole but we were wedged tightly together, Lewis and I. Lewis squirmed and squeezed until he faced me and we were belly to belly. Debbie got up on what remained of the side of the ramp and began to stomp out a board.

"Shift that way if you can," she said as we moved away from her.

She kicked again and pulled the board back and began to enlarge the opening. Lewis and I remained still and watched as she worked. Henry came around to the back of me and put his arms on my shoulders. He pushed his face up against my back and looked up from behind my head.

"Guys," he said as he pointed to the doorway.

An old man in a wheelchair who was missing a front tooth and both of his legs pushed the screen door open and rolled onto the porch. There was filthy duct tape holding a sawed-off shotgun on each arm of the chair, and the man placed his shaking hands near the triggers.

"Who the fuck are all you?" he screeched.

"That's Denny," said Lewis.

"How you know my name, fat boy?" said Denny.

"I'm Lewis. I was a friend of Marco. You remember?"

"Fuck you, porch monkey," said Denny.

"Sir, my name is Joe Iocca and I'm a private investigator—"

"Well, fuck you too, wop," said Denny. "Git the fuck off my property 'fore I blast you all."

"They're stuck," said Debbie.

"Well now, you can stay," said Denny to Debbie as he looked down at his crotch. "Everything still works."

Lewis put his hands on my shoulders and managed to free his legs. As soon as he stood on what was left of the edge of the ramp he tumbled backwards and took a hard fall onto the gravel and spotty grass below.

"Heh, heh, heh," cackled Denny.

Debbie and Henry helped Lewis up and I extricated myself.

"Which one of you gonna pay for that ramp?" asked Denny as he moved his chair from side to side, pointing his guns back and forth.

He took his hands off the wheels and put his fingers directly on the triggers. His arms were shaking hard and

I realized he must have been suffering from Parkinson's disease. The last thing you want is a gun trained on you by a man who's fighting the tremors.

"You three homos git now. Leave the girl. She'll pay for it," said Denny.

"Fine," said Debbie as she climbed up the edge of the ramp and extended her arms.

Denny smiled and reached out to grab her hands in an effort to pull her up. Debbie yanked him out of his wheelchair and he landed on his chest at the top of the ramp, his stubby legs and ass dangling just before the broken section. Debbie held him there as he screamed.

"Did you kill my father, you nasty-ass motherfucker?!"

"Let me go," he cried.

"Lil, what are you doing?" said Henry.

"Marco Whitehead. Did you kill Marco Whitehead?" she said.

Denny was shaking hard and flopping around so Lewis and I pinned him to the ramp from the sides as Debbie continued her interrogation of the suspect.

"Did you kill your stepson, you piece of shit?" she said.

"We kin?" said Denny as he looked up at her.

"Fuck no, you legless fuck. Answer the fucking question or we'll throw you in that hole and take turns shitting in it," said Debbie.

"Jesus," said Henry as he paced.

"Did you kill my father?" she said.

"I can't…" said Denny just before he clutched at his heart.

The paramedics were nice fellas. Debbie did a swell job explaining how she had come to meet her step-grandfather, and had the terrible luck of seeing him die of a heart attack. She really nailed seeming traumatized, too, and the police were quick to console her. One of the cops pulled me aside and said, "Just between you, me and the corpse, the girl is better off having not known stumpy here."

We weren't doing a very good job of ruling anyone out. On the drive home from Denny Whitehead's, Lewis said he thought Go Way had a girl's name. I called Lena as soon as I got back to the hotel to tell her to keep an eye out for something feminine. Before I could let her know she told me about a police report that mentioned Marco Whitehead, taken in nearby Florissant just before his murder. It was dated the day before his slaying. Lewis had told us about the altercation and it was why Go Way was on our list. That incident report would be the kind of thing you would have thought the Ferguson police department might have spotted immediately. Lena said when the cops approach a case with such a limited scope and are focused on one suspect in particular, especially a black suspect, these are the kinds of things that get missed. When she was calm enough she told me that Go Way's real name was Leslie Belcher and that she had a current address on him.

"You don't look like a junkie or an alcoholic," said Debbie to Henry.

"I'm in recovery. For the role, I mean," said Henry.

We sat by an empty pool at the Roadside Motel. The wind was picking up. The dark afternoon skies and the smell of the air told me there was a storm on the way. There would be thunder and lightning, rarities in the Bay Area, and I missed that part of nature's immense repertoire.

"Joe, I'm the obvious choice for this recon work, aren't I?" said Debbie.

"Recon? What is this, Vietnam, babe? We're talking about an A.A. meeting," said Henry.

"I say we let Henry take a crack at this," I said.

"Dammit. Really?" said Debbie.

"Seems like it'll make him happy. The kid comes all this way to help, I say it's only fair we let him have a little fun."

"Okay," said Debbie. "Point taken."

She brought him in for a quick kiss. I could see their relationship was progressing nicely. I could also see the munchkin Mayor from the Wizard of Oz entering the pool area from the gate.

"Got a second, Joe?" asked the Mayor.

322

Henry and Debbie waved goodbye as they walked arm in arm out of the recreational portion of the motel and toward the stairs.

I gave the mustachioed dwarf a slight wave to follow me and I headed to the public restroom. The door was locked so we walked around the back of the small building. I looked around and decided it was safe to talk.

"You gotta be careful here, Joe," said the Mayor. "You're taking chances with people's lives. That could have gone a lot of other ways back there at Denny's."

"Yeah, I hear ya. But Leslie's not going to hurt the kid at an A.A. meeting," I said.

"If you got any shot at that doll Angel you're gonna screw it up nice if anything happens to her girl or the kid," he said.

"I was leaning toward Lena."

"Lena? The lesbian? She's practically related to you, Joe."

"Why does everyone think she's a lesbian?"

"She's too young for you anyway, man. They both are. What's wrong with you, man? Heck, if Little Girl didn't show up with a steady beau I bet you'd be drooling over that sweet little hiney, too."

"Little Girl?" I said.

"That's what they call Debbie. You gotta keep these things straight in your noggin, Joe. How do you expect to solve this murder if you can't even remember that?"

"I'm going through a rough time here, Mr. Mayor. I never caught a murder before. This seems bigger than me, above my pay-grade. I got a lotta self-doubt right now."

"This is what you've been waiting for, old boy," he said as he poked me in the boiler. "This one will put you on the map. Think what happens when the papers get ahold of this. You'll be a hero in your hometown. Just keep it together and watch out for these kids. Lewis too. Anybody gets hurt while you're the ringleader and they're gonna put you under the microscope, boy. And don't look for me to help you then. Nuh-uh, no, sir. Those white coats with their butterfly nets come around, well, I'm an easy target now ain't I?"

The rain came fast and hard, and I heartily enjoyed watching the munchkin run for cover.

Henry entered the church basement through a door on the side of the building. Debbie and I watched as he waved back at us and she made a funny snorting noise when she laughed about him and smiled long after the laughter had stopped.

"You like him a lot," I said.

"I do," said Debbie with no hesitation and no less a smile.

"Well I, for one, approve," I said.

"Thanks, Joe. That means so much," she said.

I'd characterize her delivery as a sarcastic offering but I'm not sure that would be an accurate depiction. A couple of hours of listening to heavy raindrops falling, and a half a box of donuts later Henry opened the back door of my car and slid in.

"Was he there?" asked Debbie.

"Yep," said Henry.

"Are you sure it was him?" she said.

"Yep," he said again.

"How can you be sure?" she asked.

"Because he said his name. They do that, you know. Like, 'Hi, I'm Leslie and I'm…' "

"I told you he'd go there again," I said. "Just like the other day. Now *that's* recon work. Did you speak with him?"

"I did."

"And?" asked Debbie.

"And he agreed to join us for bowling tomorrow night."

"What?" Debbie said.

"I never mentioned anything about bowling with him," I said.

"He said he wanted to meet my girlfriend. And her Uncle Joe."

"So we're going bowling with the man who possibly killed my father? That's what you're telling me?"

"He said he likes to bowl," said Henry.

Lena insisted on joining us. She picked us up at the motel and drove to Lucky Strike Lanes in Florissant. We exchanged our shoes and Lena bought a pair of socks from a dispenser, the way you would a chocolate bar or bag of pretzels. She caught me staring at her delicate feet just as Leslie strolled up.

"Hey, Henry," said Leslie.

"Leslie, nice to see you again. This is Deborah, my girl, and this is her Uncle Joe and his friend Lena."

"Good to meet you all," he said with a shy wave.

"Grab some shoes, Leslie," said Lena. "We were just about to get started."

Leslie walked up to the counter and spoke to the woman there with his back to us.

"This is so fucking weird," said Debbie.

"Right?" said Lena.

"Everybody just calm down," I said. "Act natural and let me do the subtle work."

They all grinned at each other. I could tell I had a ways to go if I was going to impress Lena that night. Leslie came back with a pair of clown shoes. He was probably a shade under six feet tall and roundish but boy did he have some feet on him.

"It's been a while since I rolled," he said.

"Why's that?" asked Debbie.

Leslie looked at Lena and then took a glance at me.

"It's ok, Leslie," said Henry. "There are no secrets here. These guys know about my problem. They support me. They don't judge. And you said it would be fine for me to tell them how we met, correct?"

"Yeah, sorry. I hate to make a bad first impression is all," said Leslie.

"So I'm guessing you were in jail then. Why were you in jail?" asked Debbie.

"It was nothing. I'm going to find a ball now," he said as he walked away.

"Pushing a little hard, aren't you, babe?" said Henry.

"Bowling with convicts. Is there some etiquette I'm unaware of?" said Debbie.

"Let's just get to know him and see what we all think at the end of the evening," said Lena as she finished typing in our names on the screen. "Leslie," she called out as he walked back up, "you're first on the board."

"Oh. Okay," he said as he made his way to the boards.

"Careful with the toe foul," I said loudly. "Tough not to go over the line with those big boys."

Leslie looked down at his feet and then back at me with an innocence about him.

"Any chance the cops took note of footprints in the yard?" I said quietly to Lena as Leslie laid down a seven ten split.

"Of course not," she whispered.

"Too bad. Those things are a crime scene's wet dream."

We bowled three games each. My back was killing me, and the fact that Lena scored higher than me every time wasn't doing much for my ego. St. Louis is home to the Bowling Hall of Fame, though, so I couldn't be too upset. Everyone there can roll. We walked Leslie to his car, which turned out to be a bicycle that was meant for a teenage boy. Watching him pedal with those size sixteens was comical and sad at the same time, particularly with the rain hitting him in the eyes. We loaded into Lena's SUV and began to give our assessments of the suspect.

"I like him," said Henry. "I know I'm not supposed to but he seems like just a sweet guy in a way."

"Yeah," said Lena. "I have to say, he just doesn't give off that killer vibe, you know?"

"I enjoyed his prison stories, too," I said. "Seemed like he had some good friends in there, helping him get clean and all."

"What do you think, Lil?" asked Henry.

"I think it's a pretty shitty way to find out if someone killed your dad. Take him bowling. Pretty shitty. That's what I think."

"We were just trying to figure out what kind of a man we were dealing with face to face," I said. "What did you expect us to do? Tie him up in some old building and whip him with a hose until he confesses?"

"Works for me," she said.

"So you still think he could have done it then?" said Lena.

"Fuck if I know. People walk around knowing the shit they've done in their lives all day long, every damn day, with no one being any the wiser. The guy's been in and out of jail for years."

"Yes, but mostly for petty, drug-related stuff," said Lena.

"We don't know what else he could have done and never got busted for," said Debbie.

"Well," I said, "this may sound a bit silly, but when you bowl with a man like that, you get a good idea of his character."

"Jesus Christ. I'm sorry, Joe, but I am so glad I'm not paying you for this right now," said Debbie.

I came walking out of Motto's house and Michael exited his Lincoln.

"You shouldn't wait in a Town Car outside of an Italian's house, Mike," I said.

"This is your cousin's home?" he said, looking it over.

"Like you don't already know that," I said. "Where have you been anyway? It's been a couple of days since I've seen you."

"It's been over a week. How are you feeling?"

"I'm fine."

"Are you sure? You can confide in me."

"So am I supposed to follow you somewhere or get in your car and we'll circle back later? How's this work, Mike?"

"Have you eaten? I was hoping we might grab an early dinner. I've a hankering for some of those toasted raviolis we spoke of."

We sat at Joey B's on the Hill and dunked the meat-filled pasta into marinara sauce. Michael made noises each time he put a piece in his mouth. After a short while his pleasure was making me uncomfortable.

"So where'd you disappear to?" I asked.

"I had some business to attend to in New York. You've been a busy man in my absence."

"How do you mean?"

"Tell me about this thing you're working on? With these kids and that large African-American man from the home?"

"How do you know about—you put a tail on me, didn't you?"

"I never removed them," he said as he went in for more sauce.

"Them? Jesus, you got guys following me all over town? Why?"

"They're on retainer. They came here to find you. Don't worry about that. Are you sure you're alright?"

"Michael," I said as I leaned across the table. "You cannot have me followed. Do we understand each other on this?"

"You never even asked for my email address or phone number," he said.

"Well don't look so damn sad, kid. I don't even know how to email anyone."

"Do you have any interest in maintaining a relationship with me?"

"Geez, I don't know, Mike. I've got a lot on my plate these days with Ramona and these kids."

"Believe me, I know," he said.

"Well what the fuck is that supposed to mean?

"It just means that you seem to be behaving erratically lately," he said.

"Lately? How long have you had these tails on me goddammit?"

"Anyone can see you're showing signs of stress and fatigue. I've watched some surveillance videos on you and they bring up a lot of questions."

"Who the hell are you to violate my privacy like that?" I said.

"Well, excuse me for saying so, but you of all people should understand. You of all people should realize there's no such thing as privacy in this world any more."

I stood up and tossed my napkin onto the table. I leaned in close and locked eyes with him. He looked amused.

"Listen to me, pal," I said slowly. "I don't know what you think you're up to but I'm here to tell you it ends today. You hear me?"

"Please sit down," he said.

"We're through, kid," I said and began to walk away from the table.

"Fine. Suit yourself. But then you'll never know who really killed Marco Whitehead."

CHAPTER TWENTY-TWO

Revival

We didn't need Michael and his national agency—they could have been the damn Pinkertons for all I cared. We were making headway. Everyone seemed to be enjoying themselves for the most part, too, which is important. It's the journey, not the destination, as they say. This smug little shit thinks he's going to just swoop in and solve the thing for us? We were this close. I could feel it. All we needed was to catch a little break. We hadn't looked at Angel's ex boyfriend yet and there was still Skinny out in Arizona. Or finding proof that Denny had done it. I just wasn't going to let someone take my work from me again. Even if it was my son. Even if I wasn't being paid.

"So this man said he knew who killed Marco and you just kept walking?" asked J. Edgar on the drive home.

"Don't act like you weren't in the other room listening, Hoover. I've had enough games played on me for one day."

"You've got a professional responsibility here, son," he said.

"It's pro bono," I said.

"You're still operating under the capacity of a private detective."

"I'm unlicensed in the state."

"You can keep hitting me with technicalities from here to Siam, son, but we both know there's an imperative in play here."

"The guy's been free and getting away with this for over thirty years for Christ's sake. What's a few more days going to mean in the grand scheme?"

"Oh, I see, you think you are just days away from cracking this thing wide open, do you?" asked Mr. Hoover.

"I'm asking for forty-eight hours. Just give me two more days and if we don't figure it out we can track Michael down and ask him to share what he has."

"I think you're making a colossal mistake here, Joe."

"Yeah, well, you may be right," I said.

We drove in silence for a while and the former head of the FBI observed the scenery with a studious and conscientious comportment. I took note of this and told myself to try something like that out the next time Lena was around. You could practically see the wheels turning in his head. He was clearly a man who didn't miss a thing. I'd put good money down that he could describe everything he saw out there on highway 70 many years later, with pictorial detail, expressed eloquently and with natural prose. No sir, there were no flies on him.

"Who killed Kennedy?" I asked.

Hoover gave me a look and we returned to our quiet time.

The first settlers in the region had found a wooden sign. The sign pointed in a southwesterly direction. It read "Mexico." Legend had it that it was easier to name the town Mexico than it was to change the sign.

Mexico, Missouri, is a couple of hours west of St. Louis. I had never been there and wondered if the local people referred to themselves as Mexicans. On the drive to Mexico it was Lena who filled us in on the town's historical points of note. She told us it was home to about twelve thousand folks, most of them being white, with less than one percent Latino. According to Lena, the town is known for breeding and selling riding horses. The Miss Missouri pageant is proudly held there every year. Mexico once claimed to be the firebrick capital of the world, too. I probably laid some Mexican bricks in my day, I murmured to no one in particular, possibly not even out loud at all. I was in the passenger's seat and Lena was in the back of the rented mini van, so I was unaware that she was simply reading all of this from the Internet.

Angel drove, with me by her side, while Lena, Lewis, Henry and Debbie sat in the two rows of back seats. I had sensed some extra tension in the air from the moment

Angel, Henry and Debbie arrived at the Beacon Home to pick us up. I would later learn the details of the dinner conversation that had occurred the evening before.

"I was on Facebook today and noticed that you are friends with Wayne," said Debbie.

Henry stopped chewing his garden burger and looked up at the women.

"He contacted me awhile back," said Angel. "I wouldn't say we're friends."

"Facebook clearly disagrees," said Debbie.

"He's back in Canada. After Keith died—"

"He's fucking dead?" said Debbie before a laugh.

"Deborah. Please," said Angel.

"Oh, I'm sorry, Mom. You'll have to forgive me for wanting to high five someone after being told the guy who raped me is dead."

"Molested, Deborah. He molested you. Henry, I'm sorry you have to hear this," said Angel.

"I can step outside if you prefer," said Henry.

"No," said Debbie. "You stay right there. I told Henry exactly what happened to me. I don't have anything to be ashamed of."

"Of course you don't," said Angel. "Nobody ever said you did, Deborah. But there's still a difference between being molested by two stoned, drunk teenagers and having, forgive me Henry, but having your virginity stolen."

"Let's explain to Henry, shall we?" said Debbie. "You see, Henry, when those fun-loving teenage boys forced me to drink and got me high, they thought it would be a gas to fondle me, to strip me, to expose themselves to me. And somehow my mother has never understood how having someone force you to kiss them, to kiss…oh, fuck this," said Debbie as she stood up. "Come on, Henry. Let's go."

Henry stood and Angel put her hand on his arm. Henry looked at Debbie, imploring her to stay. Surprisingly it worked. They sat down and Angel composed herself before speaking.

"No one has ever said you weren't abused by those boys, Debbie. And that was a terrible thing that happened to you. It still enrages me more than you can ever know. But I think my actions after that day speak loudly as far as my support and trust in you."

"But the courts didn't see it that way, Henry," said Debbie. "I was fucking traumatized and apparently the fact that I called it a rape wasn't accurate, was somehow misleading for those fucking squareheads up there. So they basically got off and—"

"And we left Minnesota and came back home. End of story," said Angel. "Except that it really wasn't. Because Deborah here could never seem to comprehend what I gave up for her. How in love with Wayne that I was. How much I was supporting her as a mother. And still she's resented me ever since."

"What, Mom?" yelled Debbie. "We could have just stayed there with him? Maybe Keith could have moved in when he got out of his measly three months in juvie. We could have worked it out and been a happy little family."

"I don't think that's what your mom means," said Henry.

"Please don't do that," said Debbie. "You're a sweetheart of a guy and you always mean well, but don't do the thing where you take my mom's side or try to make us see eye to eye or whatever. You weren't there, okay? You didn't see the look on her face when they pressed me on what had happened. You don't know how humiliating it was."

"I'm sorry, Deborah, but you technically lied. I know you didn't mean to but you lied at first. And that's all they needed. You can understand how Wayne didn't want to have this ruin Keith's life."

"Well, he's dead now, so fuck him. How did he die? Someone shot him I bet. They did, didn't they? Some lucky fucker got to blow his fucking head off."

Angel shook her head and looked down for a moment. Henry put his hand on her upper back. Angel raised her head, gave Henry a look of gratitude, broke a small smile and spoke.

"He asphyxiated…during…" she said before pausing and making a very slight masturbation gesture.

"Well that's just fucking perfect, isn't it?" said Debbie in disgust.

We arrived at the address Lena had pulled from the website. The Northern and Southern Church of the Most Holy Redeemer had a small building next to a clearing in a field where people parked their cars come Sunday. Well behind the brick structure was a large, tattered tent. It had red and white stripes across the top of it, reminding me of a circus, of course. I stared at the sign that was mounted near the one-story and wondered what The Most Holy Redeemer had against the East and West.

"Please grab the camera from the back, Lewis," said Lena. "Henry, you can set up the boom microphone now as well."

We all grabbed our props as Lena instructed us to do. Debbie and Angel were to portray a mother and daughter who were considering a visit to the revival for the purposes of ridding Debbie of her lustful ways. Considering what Debbie and Angel had been through, this was probably not a very good choice for a cover story.

Angel seemed nervous to be there. I worried she might slip up and blow our cover. Lewis shouldered the heavy camera while Henry walked, tethered to him with the audio equipment. I mentally prepared myself to be a documentarian and tried hard to ignore the hundreds of snakes that slithered behind us as we headed toward the building.

"What you want?" asked a sickly looking man as he came from around the back of the red brick office.

"We're looking for Reverend Phillip," said Lena.

"Reverend Phillip? Ain't nobody call him Phillip. No reverend neither. He's Minister Phil, man in charge," said the stranger.

"Are you a part of this congregation?" I asked.

"No, sir. I am many things but Pentecostal I am not. Baptist."

"Where can we find the Minister, mister...?" asked Lena.

"Name's John," he said.

"John. The Baptist," said Debbie.

"That's right. Think I ain't heard that one before, Tattoo?" said John.

"What do you do here, John?" asked Henry.

"You recordin' me, boy?" said John to Henry and Lewis.

"Who the hell are you calling boy?" said Debbie.

"That one. The white one with the mic. The damn boy," he said.

Henry shook his head no.

"Again, sir, where might we find the Minister?" asked Lena. "Is he inside?"

"You can knock, can't you?" said John.

"Then why the fuck did you ask what we wanted?" said Debbie.

"Deborah," said Angel.

"You taking her to church for that mouth, ain't you? Maybe Phil get them snakes out and take that ink up off you, too," said John.

I looked back and saw the herd (do you call it a herd?) of snakes holding their ground in the parking lot behind us.

"Why we wasting time sitting out here talking to this man?" asked Lewis.

"Well, I dunno," said John before staring at everyone for an uncomfortable moment and then walking past us and into the snake pit where he had parked his car.

When John drove off we walked up to the door and gave it a rap. No one answered. We decided to head out into the field. The serpents followed along. The sky was a fair blue overhead but to the west I could see that more rain was on its way. The whole town, and state for that matter, is so flat that when the winds pick up like they had been for days it could take you off your feet if you weren't careful. Debbie wasn't careful as she ran to the tent and the wind knocked her flat on her ass.

Henry and Angel helped her up and she looked as though she were angry with them for doing so. We sallied forth, fighting the wind in our faces, until we reached the huge canopy. It flapped around and seemed ready to come off its stakes. The noise was loud and frightening. As we walked into the large opening in the linen walls, a foldout chair flew by and nearly hit Lewis and Henry, splitting right between them.

"Grab a sandbag," instructed the man inside.

He was hustling to place small plastic bags of sand on every seat. He must have already done about a dozen and with our help they were secured in minutes.

"Hopefully they hold until tomorrow, God willing," he said. "You have my gratitude. I'm Minister Phil."

"Phil," said Angel in a soft voice.

"Yes," he said as he reached out to shake her hand. "What can I do for you good people?"

"Phil, it's me. Angel."

Phil took a moment and his face turned from a polite smile to that of wonderment as he looked at Angel and then at us. Lena put her hand on Lewis and looked at him and then the camera, instructing him to begin recording.

"I don't understand. Angel?" said Phil.

"From high school," said Angel.

"Why are you here?" he said as his face and tone changed.

"You seem annoyed, Phil," said Debbie as she stepped in closer to him.

"Phil, this is my daughter. Deborah."

"Call me Little Girl," she said as she stared up at him.

"What?" Phil asked.

"Little Girl. I want you to call me Little Girl," said Debbie.

"What are you all doing here? And why are you filming? I have to get ready for tomorrow," said Phil as he looked behind him for a moment, no doubt searching for a viable excuse to relieve him of the conversation.

"My name's Lena and this is Joe. We're documentary filmmakers, sir. I hope you'll excuse us but we needed to capture that moment where you two see each other again for the first time in over thirty years?"

"Yeah, I'm thirty-four now. So a little over thirty four years—right Mom and Phil?" said Debbie.

"Why are you here?" he asked again.

"Lena and I are documentary filmmakers," I said.

"You said that," said Phil, still staring at Debbie.

"Yes," said Lena, "I'm sorry this is obviously so awkward but Angel and Debbie wanted to speak with you about something."

"Are you my child?" asked Phil with a bit of wonder in his voice.

"What?" Debbie said as she let out a huge laugh. "Fuck no."

"Do not speak to me that way, girl," said Phil.

"Little Girl," said Debbie. "Stupid fuck. Little Girl."

Angel pulled Debbie away from Phil and stepped in closer herself. She spoke softly, seemingly trying to avoid being recorded.

"Phil we'd like to talk to you about what you do here. Helping people with their problems. Just share with us how you heal folks, that's all. I'd heard—"

"You want me to fix your daughter?" he said.

"Yeah, Phil. I got problems," said Debbie in a deadpan.

"I'm not sure that's a good idea," said Phil.

"Pussy," said Debbie, taunting him.

"Deborah," screamed Angel, so loudly that it startled us all. "I don't have anywhere else to turn, Phil. I've heard you do good work here. People back home talk. We're just here for your help and then we'll be gone and you'll never have to see us again. I swear."

"They talk about what I do?"

"Yes, Phil. They speak very highly. We've come all this way and we'd appreciate it if you could make us a part of your event tomorrow. Then we'll leave you be," said Angel.

"It'd mean a lot to us, Phil," said Debbie, sarcastic for sure this time.

We walked out together, none of us looking behind. The snakes led the way and no one spoke. The gusts of wind had increased and I'm sure none of us expected to see the tent still tied to the ground the next afternoon, when Phil had agreed to attempt to remove the demons that plagued Angel's daughter.

"He's really big and scary," said Henry just before we got to the mini van.

We decided it would be best to stay off the roads and hole up in Mexico for the night. We stopped at a restaurant and near the end of the meal Lewis rang the nurse at the Beacon Home to check in on his father and Ramona. Terrence was nearing the end of his life and Ramona would not be far behind. Angel knew Lewis was afraid to be left so alone in the world.

"She likes you. You know that, don't you, Lewis?" said Angel as he ended the call.

"Who? That nurse?" he said.

"Yes. What's her name?" said Angel.

"Bonita," he said.

"That's a pretty name," said Angel.

"It actually means pretty in Spanish," said Henry with gusto.

"Do you like her?" asked Angel.

"She alright," said Lewis.

"You're making him uncomfortable," said Debbie.

We finished eating and Lena paid the check. I probably appreciated that gesture the most. The hotel bills were adding up and I needed to make some money soon. The kids would be fine. Debbie would return home to a waiting list of needy classic motorcycles. Henry would continue to make his wage at The Bemusement Park. I couldn't remember if I had paid that month's rent back in San Francisco, or the last time that I did.

I expected a bigger crowd. Minister Phil said the weather was keeping people away but no one was buying it. Not that the winds weren't a factor, but ultimately this was a pathetic excuse for an operation. A fella at the hotel told us that Baptists ran the town, and that everyone thought the Northern and Southern Church of the Holy Redeemer was something of a joke. There were nine people seated in the chairs as the proceedings got underway. They were old, every single one of them, close to death and afraid of it, hoping that something like this little carnival of faith would bring them peace and quell their fears as they negotiated their final days on earth.

Minister Phil was dressed in a dated suit, the width of both his lapel and tie broadcasting that his best days were two decades in the rearview. An androgynous person followed him around with a microphone that was hooked up to a P.A. system. It seemed to me that Phil could have held the mic himself. I suppose it freed him to gesticulate as he did when he spoke endlessly about the Holy Ghost. He really liked talking about that ghost. There were some incidental moments when he would mention the spirit and a group of chairs would tumble from the wind. He would follow those with a wide-eyed look and a hand gesture that was intended to corroborate the validity of his words.

Lewis moved in and out with the camera. At times Phil physically pushed him away. Henry grew angry each time Phil put his hands on Lewis. At one point in the long-winded build-up to the exorcism (or whatever you want to call it) Henry relaxed his left arm and the wind stopper bumped the top of the minister's head.

Phil stopped talking and kneeled on the grass. He put his head down and closed his eyes. His helper moved in and positioned the unnecessary microphone near his lips.

"Now," he said softly. "I can feel the presence of evil, right here in this holiest of places."

Debbie rolled her eyes and we shared a smile.

"I sense a young woman struggling with her virtue," he said.

Never mind the fact that Debbie fought hard that morning to wear something "super slutty" to church, or that we had actually told the man of the cloth that we would be there to address Debbie's uncontrollable libido.

Minister Phil rose and walked over to the front row, where Angel and Debbie were seated.

"Ma'am," he said to Debbie as he reached out to take her hand. "Are you willing and able to stand with me now, to humble yourself in the eyes of the Lord, our God and Savior, and to offer yourself to the healing hands of the Holy Spirit?"

"The ghost has hands?" said Debbie.

Minister Phil grabbed Debbie by the shoulders and pulled her up. Angel instinctively came out of her chair to protect her daughter but reticently sat back down. Phil spun Debbie around to face the back of the tent. He kept his hands on her shoulders.

"There is wickedness in the hearts of men," he said. "Yours is filled with a carnal desire. It shames your mother. It shames you. It has no place in the Kingdom of God, and therefore we must remove it so that you may one day take your intended place next to the Lord, with all of God's children."

He reached across Debbie's body and placed his hand at the top of her left breast as he spoke of her heart.

"Fucking creep," she yelled as she slid to escape his grasp.

"There's that demon," yelled a woman from the 'crowd.'

"Amen," said another.

"You leave me with no choice but to call upon the Holy Ghost, young lady," said Phil.

"Call whoever you like, you fuckin' perv," said Debbie.

"Holy Spirit," yelled Phil, "I ask that you enter this sacred place of worship and help our troubled, disrespectful daughter."

"Totally," said Debbie.

Phil walked up to Debbie who flinched. He put his hands on the tops of her shoulders again and spoke.

"I can feel you here with us now. I can..." he said before closing his eyes.

And just like that he began to speak in tongues. It sounded like a white guy making fun of an Arab. He rolled his R's a lot and repeated many of the sounds. At times it was closer to Hebrew, and at others it seemed like he was ordering from a French menu. He kept his hold on Debbie. In the beginning she looked back and forth at us all with a what-the-fuck look as she openly mocked him. As it moved along she locked a steady stare. She looked upon him as a liar, as an idiot, as a con man. He continued to babble on, shaking her and throwing back his own head. His assistant struggled to keep the microphone on him and his jumbled jargon went in and out of the P.A. He pushed his aide back and the person stumbled and fell, dropping the microphone and causing horrible feedback to echo throughout the field. The helper got up and pulled the cord on the microphone. He or she hit play on a recording of gospel music. It was clear to me that this was all on the day's docket as part of the show.

Minister Phil shook Debbie and continued to speak in tongues, although it was hard to hear him now with the music so loud. He dipped her as if in a dance and spoke directly into her ear. Lewis brought the camera in and Henry followed with the boom mic. The winds were heavy outside and the sky had turned so dark that it felt like nighttime. The walls of the tent waved in and out and made a slapping sound each time. They would hold for a few seconds and then either get sucked out or blown back in.

Debbie kicked at his shins. She screamed for help and I jumped in to pull her from his clutches. Henry dropped his microphone and stood in between the Minister and Debbie. Debbie began to yell.

"What the fuck did you say?" she screamed.

Phil 'came to' and looked at her perplexed.

"Did you hear what he said to me?" she asked all of us.

Phil went into the aisle and began instructing his parishioners to leave the tent.

"You have to go now. It's not safe for you here," he said as he lifted an elderly man up from his seat and escorted him toward the tent's opening.

"I fucking heard you. Tell them what you said," yelled Debbie as Henry, Lena and Angel restrained her from running toward Phil.

Phil waved his arms in the air and screamed at the top of his lungs to the three people who remained, including his helper.

"Go. Get out. The devil is here. Get out of this place."

They ran for the exit, slowed by the increasing gales and the merciless rancor of geriatric bones and enervated muscles. Within moments we were alone with the mad preacher.

"Tell them," said Debbie. "Tell them what you said."

"The spirit spoke through me," he bellowed.

"You said you killed my father. You asked for my forgiveness. I heard you," she said.

"What?" he said. "You crazy little harlot. I said no such thing."

"Are you sure?" asked Lena as she looked into Debbie's eyes.

"Yeah, I'm fucking sure. I heard you admit it," yelled Debbie.

"Deborah, are you *sure*?" said Angel.

"You think I'm lying? He said it in my goddamn ear."

Phil charged from the entrance. Lewis put the camera on the grass and the two of us moved to shield Debbie. He came into us and we stood our ground. We each grabbed a part of him and dug in.

"Get this Babylonian whore out of my sight," he said. "I will not stand here and let her speak that way in the house of the Lord. All of you. Leave this place. Now."

"Fuck you, murderer. I'm calling the cops and getting you locked up, you piece of shit," said Debbie as she tried to reach her phone in spite of Henry and Angel's grasp.

Phil pushed and sent Lewis and I to the hard ground. My back locked up as I tried to stand. Phil stomped his way toward the four of them. He easily outweighed the heaviest of them by one hundred pounds. I couldn't move. I couldn't do anything but watch, as he got closer to them. Lena cowered next to them. Angel came out to the front to take the brunt. Henry bear-hugged Debbie. Fiery red devils flew through the opening and every hole in the tent.

Within seconds the place was full of them. They began to taunt me. They spoke in every language I had ever heard. The noise was loud and grating. I checked my ears to see if they were bleeding from the drums, but everywhere I looked was blood red so I couldn't be sure. They poked at me, grabbed at me, pulled at my hair, my arms, and my legs. They stretched me flat on my back and tugged at each limb. There were brief moments when I could see through them. In one flash I saw Phil slap Angel to the ground as though she were nothing more than a department store mannequin. I saw Lena gather herself enough to stand and cover Debbie and Henry. I saw Phil reach over to grab Debbie's throat. In another flash I could see Debbie's feet as her legs kicked in the air. I saw Henry crying but I couldn't hear him over the noise of the demons and the din of the gospel music. He was mouthing for Phil to let her go, grabbing onto his massive arm. I saw Lewis flat on the ground. I saw Lena claw at Phil's eyes with perfectly manicured nails. I saw Phil use Debbie's slight body to shake Lena and Henry off of him. I saw Angel jump onto Phil's back, only to be swept off with ease.

A devil leaned in and obscured my view entirely. He seemed calm and curious as he studied me. He looked back over his shoulder at the violence behind him. His tail moved above his head and he turned back to me. He came in close and spoke to me in the soft voice of my father.

"Don't worry, Joe. This is where the good things happen."

He reached his arms to the sky and bent his neck until his head touched his back. He closed his eyes and grinned. The devils began to chant in unison, but in a language I had never heard. It became so loud that my ears were ringing, and then there was complete silence. I could hear nothing.

My devil moved his palms ever so slightly, cueing the pack to exit with him. They ascended and blew out the top of the tent as they made their way through the gloomy sky. I was still unable to move. I looked to my friends and saw Lewis holding the boom stick over Phil's twitching body.

CHAPTER TWENTY-THREE

Gone with the Mexican Wind

"Are you okay, Joe?" asked Lena.

Could I move, was there anything broken, was I *okay*?

I cannot tell you how she got me from that tent to the brick building where we now took shelter. It must have been one hundred and fifty yards. I remember staring at Lewis as he hyperventilated and then this: a sweet face worrying about me.

"Joe?" said Lena.

I got up from the seat she had plopped me into and gingerly walked toward her. She stood looking nervously out the window.

"I'm telling you, they'll give him the gas chamber for this," said a suddenly manic Lena. "So she's got marks on her neck? So what? Those people watched him put his hands all over her. You don't think they'll say it was part of the—whatever the fuck that was? Say we came here to get him? I mean, we kind of did, didn't we?"

I stared at Lena.

"We need to be air-tight with our stories," she continued. "He was saving her. He was absolutely saving her life. Jesus, he's a black man who killed a white man in America. They'll fry him if we aren't all on the same exact page. Clear. Perfectly clear. Joe, are you perfectly clear on what you saw?"

"I don't think you should count on me, Lena," I said in a defeated tone.

The roof of the building came clean off before I could even comprehend what the savage sound was. Shingles and lumber flew out in every direction. Lena grabbed ahold of me as we were knocked to the floor. I heard loud cracks against the building, as things were slamming into the walls. We remained there curled up tight on the ground together for a long while until the fierce noises finally died down a bit. We incrementally raised our heads and bodies up the nearest wall, clutching at the windowsill just before the glass and frame were completely sucked out. I looked out the hole where the window had been and saw that our friends had finally fled the tent and taken to the ground. They held onto each other as objects flew through the air. I saw the tent behind them. It was whipping around in circles, turning itself into a smaller and smaller thing. It rose higher in the air until a funnel sucked it in and sent it promptly out of view.

I was back in the chair again. Not sure how I got there. Everyone else was seated on the floor: Debbie and Henry to my right, Angel and Lewis to my left, and Lena straight ahead, just under the window. Lewis was rocking back and forth. His eyes read scared with a touch of crazed. Angel reached out to comfort him and he jerked away, looking at her like she was Satan's favorite call girl.

Henry had his arm across Debbie's lap. At first I thought he was holding her hand but I soon realized he was preparing to hold her back.

Lena gave me a look that I probably should have understood.

"Are you fucking kidding me?" screamed Debbie across the room.

"Deborah," said Angel as she started to rise.

"FUCK. YOUUUUUUUUU," yelled Debbie, leaning forward and hosing the words out like lit kerosene.

"Okay, so maybe this isn't the best time for this," said Lena. "We should probably go. Like now."

Debbie mad-dogged her mother, rabid, probably foaming at the mouth if my eyes were good enough to have said.

"Should we drive in this weather?" said Henry. "I mean, that was a tornado."

"Debbie, please," said Angel.

"Why?" Debbie screamed. Angel looked around the room, clearly afraid but also embarrassed. "Why, you fucking bitch?"

"Jesus," I said softly, causing Lewis to look up as if his Lord and Savior was actually entering the building.

Debbie skidded her feet on the dusty concrete floor to stand. Henry forced her down and her legs went parallel to the ground. She swatted at Henry but he didn't budge.

"So... should we maybe head out then?" asked Lena as she stood.

"I'd prefer we talk in private back at the—" said Angel.

"Fuck what you want. Whore," said Debbie.

"Deborah," said Angel.

"Well?" Henry asked Angel sheepishly.

Angel began to speak but produced only a few heavy breaths and the popping sound of the letter P before sighing and covering her eyes with her hand.

"Of course it is," said Debbie to Henry.

"Maybe she just said it to get him to stop," said Henry as Debbie and Angel both shook their heads.

"So he's really her father?" asked Henry in shock.

"Was," said Debbie with her head down before glancing up at Lewis.

"Wait," I said.

"How could you lie to me, man?" said Debbie.

"Because he basically raped me," Angel screeched.

"Oh, my God," said Lena, slowly sitting down again.

"What?" said Henry.

"Who are we talking about?" I asked.

Angel looked at me annoyed and angry, a look that said she wondered why I was there.

"What the fuck does, 'He basically raped me' mean?" said Debbie through a disgusted laugh.

"In his car. One day after school. You remember that day, Lewis. You were there," Angel said, trying to gather herself to tell the story.

"Did you report it?" asked Lena.

"No. I didn't. Because it…it wasn't like that, exactly. He harassed me for months. You remember, Lewis?"

Lewis looked at her as if she was attempting to incriminate him.

"He was always trying to win me back," she continued. "And one day I just… I agreed to take a drive after class, to make him stop. He wouldn't shut up about it. 'I love you, Angel. Let's get back together, Angel.' He never stopped," she paused and looked to the dark sky above. "So I finally just had to. I had to tell him to make him understand."

"Tell him what?" said Lena.

"About Marco," she said softly. "I told him I was in love with Marco."

Lewis stood up. He looked down at her with big hate in his eyes.

"He knew who Marco was?" he yelled.

Angel put her head down and shook yes. She had been crying for a while but now it came harder.

"You knew he knew?" said Lewis. "And you don't think maybe he killed him? You don't think that then?" he screamed, his voice breaking like a pubescent boy.

"I don't know, I don't know. No. No, I'm sure I…It's just that…I'm not the one who decides. And your father threatened him, Lewis. He didn't have an alibi."

"He was sleeping!" said Lewis.

"You know what I mean, Lewis," said Angel with forgive-me eyes. "I was just a confused kid. I wasn't a cop or a judge or a—"

"Fuck you, Angel," screamed Lewis.

"I'm sorry," cried Angel.

"Fuck your sorry. My daddy lose his life. *I* lost him. And you help keep him in jail. Why you wanna keep him there, Angel? Why?"

"I didn't know. I swear, Lewis."

Debbie laughed.

"Deborah, please. I didn't know. This happened months before, with Phil. Months before. I didn't think he cared. Not really. He knew about Marco for months. After he—"

Debbie made air quotations and said, "Basically raped you?"

"Yes. After he forced himself on me. He kept saying, 'One last time. One last time, baby.' I finally just…let him."

"Let him?" screamed Debbie.

"Yes. He said he'd leave me alone if I did."

"You're a fucking idiot," said Debbie.

Lewis came across the room and sat next to Debbie. Lena looked out the window and then scoured our faces. She sat back down, almost pouting. There was a long silence. All I could hear was Angel sniffling.

"Why did you lie?" asked Debbie in a hushed tone.

"If I tell Marco, he kills Phil, and then I lose Marco," said Angel.

"I'm not talking about your fucking drug dealer boyfriend."

"My plan was to tell Marco you were his. He would have been a good dad. I know he would have." She paused for a moment. "Maybe I was going to tell him the truth once we got to Boulder. And then he was just…gone. Phil stayed away like he said he would. When I heard he joined the Marines I just figured, well, I'll never hear from that piece of shit again."

"That piece of shit was my father," said Debbie. "And now he's dead. Dad's dead, Mom. Again."

"Are you sure it was him. Not Marco's?" asked Henry.

Angel shook her head yes.

"Well, a fucking paternity test is off the table now anyhow," said Debbie as she stood.

Henry stood quickly and got in front of her. Debbie paced on her side of the room. Henry went toe to toe with her.

"Tell me why you lied to me, Angel," said Debbie.

Angel looked shocked.

"Tell me why you lied to your daughter," Debbie continued.

Angel stood and walked toward her. Debbie raised her hand and pointed her finger. She said, "uh-uh" and directed her mother back. Angel remained on her side of the imaginary line that was drawn between my chair and Lena at the window.

"I didn't want you to–" said Angel before crying.

"Oh, just spit it out," said Debbie.

"You couldn't be born that way," said Angel. "Not like that. I know I said yes to him but... I just wanted you to be Marco's. I didn't want you to know how you came to me. I loved Marco. I loved the idea that you were ours. I couldn't let that...I couldn't let him have you. You were mine, honey. You were mine."

Debbie got up and walked toward the door, passing her mother along the way. She stared at Angel and no one could be sure what her plan was. Henry trailed Debbie and seemed at the ready. Lewis had fallen into the slouch of a total malaise and seemed to hardly notice their movement. Lena looked heartbroken for everyone in the room.

And me? I felt like a jackass just for being there. Why the fuck was I there? Who was I? What place did I have in their lives? What business did I have in their stories?

"We're taking the car," said Debbie as she stopped and looked down. "Henry will drop me off at the hotel. He'll come back for you all. Even you." She locked eyes with her mother. "*Do not* bother me again. Understand? Never again."

Angel wailed.

Debbie walked out of the door and into the wind, which had calmed, in an eerie sort of way, feeling completely disconnected from the violent nature it had so recently been.

CHAPTER TWENTY-FOUR

Unreasonable Doubt

Terrence had died peacefully. The last two weeks of his life were spent in a room of his own, and that was something Terrence had not had in nearly thirty-five years. Lewis had taken a leave of absence from his work at the rental car company and spent every moment he could with his father. He quietly told his daddy that justice had been served, and that God would forgive him for it—for how could he not—and that they would be together with Momma and Grandmamma and Auntie one day soon in Heaven. When Terrence drew his final breath, Lewis was there to hold his hand.

The staff at the Beacon had opted not to fill the vacancy when Terrence was transferred. Ramona had gone silent and our visits had become nothing more than two people staring at a television screen. My favorite show, a reality program about a tattooed female motorcycle builder out in California, did much to remind me of Debbie, long after she had left Missouri.

Henry and Debbie had stopped in to say goodbye one afternoon. They had spent that morning with Lewis at his father's bedside, and after one last peck on Ramona's cheek they would return to Southern California.

Debbie and Henry expressed their concern for me. I knew my behavior in the tent might have thrown them for a loop. I couldn't be sure how much, if any, they had heard me say or what they may have seen me do that was out of the ordinary. I gave them my number in San Francisco. Henry said they'd call and leave me a message when they arrived safely in Los Angeles.

"How did you leave things with your mother, Debbie?" I asked.

"Fuck my mother. Fuck this place. And Joe, seriously, enough with the Debbie. Please."

She managed a smile, and with that they were gone.

Lena asked if I could meet her on The Hill. We ate lunch and she told me what she had learned in the two weeks since we had watched Phil's murdered body, wrapped up like a big burrito, flying through the Mexican air.

"We were right to leave town so quickly," she said. "I was worried Phil's assistant may have said something to the police, or possibly one of the attendees. Maybe they did, I don't know. It doesn't matter anyway. They've already ruled his death accidental. He was the only fatality from the storm, according to reports."

364 .

"What a stroke of luck that little twister turned out to be," I said.

"Well, I'm sure a lot of property owners in the area would disagree but, yes, for our purposes, fortune was basically smiling on us that day."

"You really think a jury would have called it a murder?"

"I was there and I'm not sure what else to call it. Was he attacking Deborah? Yes? Was he going to kill her? He was frightening, definitely, but he…"

"What?" I said.

She looked around the restaurant and lowered her voice even more as she leaned in to speak.

"He had let her go, Joe."

"How do you mean?"

"Phil. He dropped her when Angel blurted out that Deborah was his kid. Deborah was struggling to breathe but she was okay."

"So Lewis just—" I said.

"Went flippin' apeshit. It was horrible. He hit him over and over. How could you not have seen that? Were you in shock?"

"I got jarred pretty good there myself."

Lena looked at me with an attorney's suspicion. I fought the urge to look up at the ceiling and whistle like a dope.

"How's he doing?" she asked.

"He's hanging in. I've been staying with him since we got back. He's got a nice place out in St. Charles. The nurse keeps calling him to check in. Eventually I'll get him to act on it I'm sure. It's a little soon for him I suppose. Doesn't think it's the right time for happiness."

"You planning on staying, Joe?" said Lena.

"Not sure. Maybe that depends on you a little," I said with a grin.

"On me? How do you mean?"

"Well, I was kind of hoping we could make these lunches a regular thing. Maybe throw in some dinners, take some walks."

"Oh, Joe. Sweetie, I'm flattered but–"

"You're not interested in an old man. Say no more. I was confused, that's all. I completely understand."

"Joe, I'm gay."

"How's that?"

"Honestly, I thought you could tell. I'm sorry," she said.

"Please, no need to apologize."

"Well, I'm not. But I am in a way I suppose. I live with my girlfriend. Please don't tell anyone in the family, though."

"Of course," I said.

"It would kill my mother," she said.

"You really deserve to be who you are."

"I am exactly who I am, Joe. I'm also a girl who loves her mama, even if she is from the seventeenth century. Who needs that kind of drama in their lives anyway?"

"*Capisco,*" I said.

Michael walked through the front door with two men in suits right behind him. I watched as he spoke to the men before sending them to the bar to wait as he walked to our table.

"Joe, madam, I'm sorry to disturb your meal, but could we speak outside for a moment," he said to me.

"Will you excuse me for a moment?" I said to Lena.

"Of course," she said.

We walked out to the parking lot and the two men followed us. They kept their distance, leaning on his Lincoln as we spoke a few spots away near my Camry.

"What are you doing here, Mike?" I asked.

"I was wondering if you were ready to take me up on my offer? It's been weeks," he said.

"What offer is that?" I asked.

"The identity of Marco Whitehead's killer. Your case, Joe."

"Oh, that. Yeah, don't worry about that. I'm through working cases. We're all good here, sonny boy."

"I see," he said. "So my friends here were correct in their assumption then."

I looked at him without a care in the world, hoping he'd get my drift and just drop the whole damn thing and let me get back to my now-cold cannelloni.

"You believe the man who died in Mexico, the man you all killed in that tent, you believe he was Marco's killer?"

I grabbed Michael's arm and pulled him in between the cars. His men jumped to attention and locked eyes with him. Michael called them off with a look.

"Listen here, pal," I said, "whatever you think you know and whoever knows what, well, you need to squash this thing. Pronto. Do you hear me, son?"

"Should I call you Dad now, Joe?" he said with a fucking face on him.

"I'm serious. This ends today. Got it? I don't want to see you. I don't want to hear from you. I don't want to get Christmas cards from you. And above all else, I don't want your fucking henchmen following me around anymore. Do we understand each other?"

"Phillip Donald Tressmeyer was in Chicago, Illinois, the night that Marco Whitehead was brutally murdered in his home. Mr. Tressmeyer was in Chicago that entire week, in fact. He had 'run away' if you will, trying to escape an overbearing father. I wonder what that's like, having an overbearing father. Or having a father at all for that matter?"

"Joe," said Lena as she came out of the restaurant and walked my way. "Is everything alright here?"

"Yes, Lena, thanks."

"Is something wrong?" she asked.

"Hey, no, don't worry, kiddo. We're all good. Let's get back in there."

Lewis made coffee, just as he did every morning before heading into work. It was a good, simple cup, the way I liked it. We had much in common, Lewis and I. It wasn't so much the specifics like taste in music or movies or what have you, but the way we liked to live our lives. I missed the job, but the part of me that liked everything to be in its place, just as I expected it to be, the kind of man I was—a man that ordered the same thing from a menu every time he went to a diner because he knew it was good and didn't want to take a chance with his happiness at that moment in life—well, that man had found a partner in Lewis.

We never once talked about what happened in the tent. Evening would come and we'd watch the History Channel or a sitcom and some nights we'd hardly speak to one another. But I looked forward to his return every day and I was still enough of a detective to say the same was true for him. I'd push him to call that nurse when the time felt right. But I was happy just doing crossword puzzles, helping around the house, making dinner even; just waiting for my friend to come home.

Michael knocked on the door and I answered it before looking through the window. I should have looked. I could have pretended I wasn't home.

"Either you view these files or I will take what I have about that Sunday in Mexico to the authorities," he said.

We sat at the kitchen table and I got my first look at what big detective agency reports look like. There was more detail in there about the case than I had ever imagined possible, given what little evidence there was to go on. It mentioned suspects that we had never heard of: Marco's drug dealers by name, an ex-girlfriend, one of Denny's cousins who had some beef with Marco.

"What lays before you is all the information necessary to disqualify all parties mentioned in the murder of your roommate's best friend, including the recently deceased Phillip Donald Tressmeyer," said Michael. "You will, however, note the absence of one name."

"Skinny Wiener," I said.

"Correct. Mr. Wiener had been informed of Mrs. Wiener's indiscretion by his brother-in-law on a family vacation together. Apparently Mrs. Wiener had confided in her brother's wife, who shared this information with her husband. As far as we can tell from interviews with the family, Mrs. Wiener's brother told Mr. Wiener during an argument—something about the way he treated his son—and then threatened to castrate Mr. Wiener if he ever admitted to his wife that he knew about the brief affair."

"So Skinny murders Marco over a blow job? Doesn't add up," I said.

"There is plenty of evidence to support the idea that Mr. Wiener has never been sound of mind."

"Why the fuck would you go to all of this trouble?" I said to Michael. "None of this makes any sense to me."

"I was trying to give you the thing that you wanted most in life, Joe. With everything that you've gone through over these recent years, seeing former clients, the dead among them in some cases, visions of people, the sightings—it was important to me that my father got to be the one thing he had always wanted to be. Before life changed, before it stole what you loved, this fuck fuck fucking life."

I looked at Michael and I knew I was in deep trouble.

He said he could fly us to Phoenix that night. He told me there was enough there to get Skinny off the streets. I stopped listening after awhile. I asked him to leave but he kept talking. I looked at the clock that hung on Lewis's wall, next to the macramé owl, and I watched the hand move, ticking at me like small kicks to the groin. I knew Lewis would be home soon. I again asked Michael to leave. He kept talking, showing me things in files, photos of Skinny, of Marco's dead body, of the bean bag chair, close ups of Angel's face as that boy made her orgasm with his fingers, my Chrysler K car with the curb feelers, Debbie's bloody shirt, the Pacific ocean at sunrise, Ramona's face lit only by the moon, Roger Croon in the street, the bleeding hobo on the floor, the pink woman and her fucking poodle, the Huns and the Mayans and Gary Butto's shorter fucking arm, the Mexican gardener and his happy fucking teeth, J. Edgar and his disappointed countenance, Denny grasping and clutching at his feeble heart, the dying men in the restaurant, Lindsay dancing, Nana's candy bowl, Lewis's dusty Mongoose, Phil's quaking body, Lindsay hanging, swaying, choking, gasping, dying, terrified, screaming for help, dying, begging me, dying, dying, dying all the time.

He wouldn't leave; I asked him to leave, but he wouldn't go.

CHAPTER TWENTY-FIVE

Killers of the Community

I am told that I imagined many things. But this I already knew. I am told that I imagined things that I didn't know I had imagined—if that makes any sense. You'll have to forgive me.

I live here now, with Lewis and his wife Bonita. They are lovely people, so kind and warm. It feels like I've known them for many years, but I cannot tell you of more than the hours I can be sure of. I do remember meeting them both. Bonita was Ramona's nurse. When Ramona passed away I could tell that it affected Bonita on an uncommon level. She knows death all too well. Ramona had been just awful to her in the beginning, too, calling her names, saying things that I would never had dreamed were kicking around up there in her sweet, sweet head. Eventually they bonded, more so than Bonita was able to with Terrence. They freed Terrence too late, and as a result he was never really free. He was gone by the time we all had the honor of making his acquaintance. What they did to him, putting him in a cell like that. I can only begin to imagine his frustration, knowing he was an innocent man, knowing that something beyond his control altered the course of his life that way.

My own son was taken from me. Not in the way that Ramona lost Lindsay, or Terrence lost Lewis for all those years, but in a way that I did not expect and still cannot fully fathom. One day I found myself on the steps of a brownstone building in Soulard. A woman answered the door. She took me in and waited with me—stroking my hand and saying, "there, there" as people often do. When Lena came home to find me on her couch being comforted by her partner, she carefully explained some things to me, things that to this day I trust as true, because I know she is worthy of that kind of faith.

She told me how I had excused myself that day at lunch. She said she had seen my face go blank that way before. It had been cause enough for concern that she had searched the internet for examples of my behavior; however one does such a thing. When she found me between the two cars as I was, she approached me and told me that I "came back" when I heard her voice.

I didn't want to believe that Michael existed only in my imagination. I didn't like him but he was my boy. Lena suggested that I call Debbie in LA and ask her about the day that Michael told me he was my son. Debbie and Henry recounted how we had been speaking in the parking lot before I went to sit in my car. After some time, Debbie knocked on the window and I walked with them into the Beacon Home. She said I had been alone, that Michael was never there.

Michael is gone now. I don't see him anymore.

She would want me to call her Little Girl when I speak of her. Knowing everything she has been through and how tough she remains—there are days when I do little more than sit under the Missouri sun and think of Little Girl.

Once, in my apartment back in San Francisco, I killed a man with a golf club. I'm not sure if I ever told you this. He had followed me into my home and it was there, in front of so many witnesses, that he tried to rob and assault me. It was a wedge—the club—an old thing—and I admired the craftsmanship and enjoyed the patina. I hit him in the head and he died on the hardwood floor. I don't remember much about it. Al came to find me in St. Louis, and he told me what I had done. He took me back home. We saw the sea again before I turned myself in. There were proceedings. They declared me unfit to stand trial. Al says that they believed I acted in self-defense, but said that I shouldn't have run.

I spent some time in a hospital. Al says I'm confused, and that I am there now, not with Lewis and his wife at all. He says that Little Girl plans to visit me soon, that she will ride her motorcycle up from LA. I have good days and bad. I hope she comes on a good one. Things aren't always clear. Bonita may be medicating me; it's hard to say. I overheard her talking about the *lesions in my brain*.

It's possible that she said *legions in my brain*. I'll have to look into that.

Bonita put Velcro on the bottom of the remote control and another strip on the wide wooden arm of the blue chair. It kept slipping to the cold floor, and it's sometimes hard for me to get up. I feel guilty for controlling what we watch as often as I do, but I like a routine, and Lewis and his bride never seem to mind. We can always agree on *The Rockford Files*. It reminds of us of a better era.

I need to rest. Little Girl shouldn't see me like this. I'll get out of this bed. I'll go through the door and follow the yellow sidewalk. She will be there, waiting for me, like a daughter, and we will walk the brick roads of old St. Charles.

Tailpiece

I was nearing the bottom of my stairs when the box hit me square in the forehead. The impact plopped me right on my ass. I had been looking down at the keys in my hand, positioning the Camry fob between my fingers. I hadn't seen it coming. From a seated position on the third to last stair, I called out to the kid.

"Okay," I said. "Okay."

The box sat unopened in my foyer for days. I had signed with my finger and he had effortlessly carried it up the stairs and into the house. Before leaving that day he turned and said some words that I cannot shake. He spoke evenly but with some compassion in his voice, and his demeanor had completely changed yet again, as it always did. He seemed like a regular person now, in spite of the cartoonish muscles with their veins exploding from every surface, his neck now as thick as his head, his legs now so massive and defined that he had made the switch to short pants.

"You've made the right decision, Joe," he said as though we were boon companions. "It wasn't an easy one. But it was inevitable. It's best we don't take up the fights we cannot win. Better to just accept our fates, to sign for our deliveries. In all my years doing this no one has ever held out as long as you. I've lost count of how many times you turned me away. I'm saying this so you can feel a sense of pride. Everything in life is an accomplishment.

Every success, every failure: a triumph. Success, failure, they're relative, subjective. Who's to say? You did the best that you could. You did the best that *you* could."

I've never opened the box. I will never open the box. I signed for it, it's true, but no one can make me open it. It will remain in my living room, pushed up against the wall next to my chair. I don't need to open the box. I know it's a casket.

97761218R00215

Made in the USA
San Bernardino, CA
26 November 2018